FALLING IN LOVE WAS DANGEROUSLY TEMPTING . . .

"You make it easy to say yes to things I have not considered for many years." Justin smoothed a strand of Angela's hair back beneath her bonnet.

"We should not be talking like this. Without a chaperon, we—"

He laughed as the door opened, and his daughter rushed out to embrace his legs just as Seth had the duke's. Setting one hand on Delicia's hair, Justin put his other under Angela's chin. He tipped her face closer to his. "We have a chaperon now."

"A little girl."

"But a little girl who reminds me that I should not put into action the thoughts I had when I saw you here amid my overgrown garden."

"Thoughts?" Angela knew she should not let the conversation continue, but she could not bear to bring it to an end when she was able to look into his emerald eyes.

"Do you really wish to know how I could not decide if I would rather admire your pretty lips or your prettier curves? Do you want me to say how I cannot wait for the next time your eyes snap at me with fury because your fiery spirit enthralls me? Do you want me to say anything?" He bent toward her as his fingers trailed up her cheek. "Or do you want to be done with talk altogether?"

Also look for these books by Jo Ann Ferguson

A GUARDIAN'S ANGEL

Jo Ann Ferguson

ZEBRA BOOKS
Kensington Publishing Corp.
http://www.kensingtonbooks.com

For Debbie Hall

Hope you find this "spiffy"

One

Certainly nothing else could go amiss today.

Angela Needham brushed away a nagging bee that seemed to believe the flowers on the brim of her straw bonnet were real. Frustration narrowed her eyes as she looked back at her carriage, tilting at an odd angle in the middle of the road. Although she knew well the dangers of wandering alone down an unfamiliar country lane, she had to get away from the carriage, which had hit a chuckhole and broken a wheel. She could not blame the driver. This road was rife with holes. They were only a few miles from her destination of Oslington Court, but too far to walk unless she wished to meet the duke looking as dusty as the coachee, who was trying to fix the carriage.

She let her exasperation sift away as she recalled how startled and excited she had been when she received the note from His Grace, the Duke of Oslington, with a request that she act as a companion for his ward. As her mother had been a companion to His Grace's mother before the duchess's marriage, it seemed somehow meet to be coming to Oslington Court three decades later.

Tears burned in her eyes as she thought of how impossible it would have been for her to accept the duke's offer if Mama had still been alive. Dear Mama, whose most obvious legacy to Angela had been her pale blond hair and dark-blue eyes. Since her mother's death during the winter, Angela had been living with her older brother and his wife in London. That uncomfortable existence—where her sister-in-law made Angela feel like an unworthy and unwanted petitioner—had been put to a blissful end with the duke's letter. Her brother had entreated her not to accept the offer, because he appreciated her deflecting his wife's fierce temper.

But that life was over, and a new one was about to begin.

Putting her hand on the brim of her poke bonnet, Angela shaded her eyes as she looked across a lushly green meadow. The scene was picture perfect. The rolling hills of Northumberland needed nothing more than a fine mahogany frame to hold the scene like a favored memory. She smiled as she imagined how luscious it would be to have the hot sunshine now dripping through the trees and the scent of freshly cut hay captured and hung over a mantel for a wintry eve. The birds were hushed with the afternoon heat, but insects buzzed eagerly along the stone wall by the road.

Touching her reticule, which hung from her wrist by a green cord, Angela listened for the crinkle of the duke's letter. Rodney Abernathy, Duke of Oslington, had recently returned from his service with the East India Company. With him, he had brought the obligation of being the guardian for a fellow officer's daughter.

The details in the letter were sketchy, but he had written that the girl had lost her mother years ago and that her father had died in India just before the duke's return to England. Miss Leonia Sutton, at nearly 18 years, was ready to leave the schoolroom, and she needed a companion to prepare her to enter the Polite World.

When she paused to examine some brightly colored flowers by the wall, Angela was careful not to let any twigs or briars catch on her gown of light green muslin. It was her best traveling dress and was decorated with a trio of flounces at the hem. Matching rows edged her short sleeves, but they were barely visible beneath the lacy shawl she had thrown over her shoulders to protect her from the summer sun.

Carefully, she tipped a pink blossom toward her. She

loved flowers. She hoped Oslington Court still had the luxu-
rious gardens her mother had spoken of.

A voice drifted toward her on the slight breeze. Angela
started to straighten at the excitement in the boyish voice.
Something struck her—hard—and she choked back a gasp
of pain and shock. Rocking backward, she feared a sudden
fog had enfolded her, for her eyes blurred. She almost stran-
gled on the scream battering her throat.

Her panic lasted but a moment. It was replaced by vexation. Catching sight of a redheaded, gangly form running
away at top speed, she sighed. She was not the victim of
some knight of the road unless one of them had taken to
capturing their victims in a net, for that was what surrounded her.

She fought the fine netting, but it was caught on the stiff
brim of her bonnet. Hearing a muffled laugh, Angela
whirled. Wood clunked against wood, and the netting tangled more tightly about her.

Her eyes widened as, through the mesh, she saw a dark-
haired man standing on the other side of the stone wall. He
wore a red riding coat over a waistcoat as black as his hat.
The cravat tying the white collar of his shirt shook when he
laughed, his eyes crinkling closed.

"This is hardly amusing," Angela said with what compo-
sure she could scavenge. She batted at the netting, which
was clinging to her face. "Is it too much to ask that you
help me get free?"

The man leapt over the low wall and pushed through the
briars, not pausing when sharp twigs caught at his dark
breeches. "Do stand still," he ordered in a voice as deep as
his laugh. "You are making a complete muddle of this."

"Me? I was taking a walk along the road, enjoying the
flowers, when—"

The man laughed again.

What a boorish cad! As he walked around her while he
carefully dislodged her bonnet from the mesh, she stared
straight ahead. He laughed again, but she clamped her teeth
together to restrain her tongue from forming a retort. Speak-

ing harshly would do no good, for she needed his assistance. She did not wish to return to the carriage with the net's handle dragging behind her like a well-whipped cur's tail.

"There, miss," the man said, the humor still in his voice as he lifted the last of the netting from over her head. "You are quite free of our inadvertent trap. Are you all right?"

"As well as can be expected," she said as she settled her bonnet back on her hair. A sharp pain throbbed across her head. "I vow you scared nearly a year off my life."

"You look young enough to be able to afford it."

Angela faced him. She must have moved too quickly, because the world twirled around her. She forced her eyes to focus. As she looked past her bonnet's brim, she discovered the man was quite tall. He rolled the netting around the long handle, and she noted his broad hands ended in tapered fingers that should belong to an artist or a musician.

"You had no idea of my age before you swept that horrible thing—" She pointed at the net he propped against the wall "—over my head."

He shaded his green eyes as he peered along the road. "I believe your shrieks frightened my young friend out of a year of *his* life. The poor lad is nowhere to be seen. I can assure you that he had no idea you were lurking behind this wall. You should be more considerate, miss."

"Me?"

"Yes, you should think twice before squealing like a banshee. The lad must be quite distressed at the thought of having hurt you."

"He could have stayed to ascertain that I was unhurt."

"He would have." The man's eyes twinkled brighter. "I sent him on his way, for I suspected, from watching you thrash about with the net, that you would be in an infernal mood upon your release."

Tucking strands of her hair back beneath her bonnet, she winced as her head pulsed with the bone-deep ache. "Then I must prove you mistaken. As you can see, I am quite composed."

"Admirably so."

"It would be admirable as well for you to teach your son to take responsibility for his mistakes."

"Thomas is my friend, not my son. I find him a boy of unusually keen mind and wit, so I suspect he has learned his manners well."

With her throbbing head and her nerves strung tightly as she anticipated her first meeting with the Duke of Oslington, Angela was anxious to put an end to this aimless conversation. "I thank you for your assistance, sir. Now if you would be so kind as to excuse me, I am in a hurry. I must—"

He leaned his hand against a tree at the edge of the lane. "You need be in no hurry if that is your carriage back there. Your coachee and his helper are still struggling to get it repaired."

Angela sighed and looked at the sun, which was heading toward the horizon. She would be late in arriving at Oslington Court. Being tardy would not make a positive impression on the duke. He might send her back to London. She prayed he would not, for she had no wish to return where she was as wanted as yesterday's garbage.

"Your coachman looks as if he is making slow progress," the man went on. "You need have no fear of being left on this road overnight. I suspect you shall be on your way within the hour, Miss . . ."

"Needham." With her head feeling disconnected, she did not want to share pleasantries with this abruptly sympathetic stranger.

"Do you have far to go?"

Not only was he discourteous, Angela decided, but unbelievably presumptuous to ask her such a personal question. Reminding herself that he might be trying to engage her in conversation in an effort to redeem himself, she struggled to think. Her brain seemed to take an eternally long time to form the simplest thought. "Not far. Our journey was to have come to an end before nightfall."

"That should be no trouble if your coachee is competent."

"I was assured he was when we left the Black Dove."

The man's dark brows arched almost to the ebony hair

falling across his forehead. "The Black Dove? Then you must have come from London." His smile returned. "Well, well, you have put me quite to the stare. I must say we seldom have ladies coming to visit the shire during the whirl of the Season's end, Miss Needham. This quiet life here in the north of England offers little in comparison with Town."

Angela was about to retort when another painful pulse scored her head from temple to temple. The green meadow contracted into darkness, and her knees wobbled. Hearing a soft gasp, she realized it had come from her lips. She did not want to succumb to vapors, but her head was as light as dandelion fluff.

A hand beneath her elbow kept her from collapsing. She was guided to her right and pushed gently to sit. The firmness of a stile stair welcomed her.

She leaned back against it and closed her eyes. Softly she said, "Forgive me for being—"

"Forgive you?" He held her trembling hand between his as he sat beside her as she waited for the world to right itself. "*You* have nothing to apologize for," he said softly so his words did not resonate in her tender skull. "We gave you quite a scare and, I fear, a blow against the head. How are you faring?"

"I shall be fine," Angela answered, hoping she was speaking the truth. When she blinked her eyes, the pain began to diminish. Looking up at the man, she saw his smile return. "Why do you have that net with you?"

"Isn't it quite obvious, Miss Needham? We were hoping to catch something."

"What?" she asked, although she was being brazen.

"Butterflies."

"Butterflies?" In spite of her aching head, she laughed. He did not join her, and she halted, realizing that *this* was not a joke. Looking from the long-handled net to his intense gaze, she bit back her questions about what a grown man, who was dressed in high kick, was doing chasing butterflies across a field.

"Yes, Miss Needham," he replied, his voice as frigid as

hers had been, while he set himself on his feet, "I was hoping to catch butterflies."

"Oh." Angela was unsure what else to say. Deciding the best thing would be to end this conversation, she stood and clasped her hands in front of her. She waited for the man to speak, but he said nothing as he retrieved his butterfly net. She thought he might walk away, but he faced her. The stern lines of his face seemed to belong to someone other than the man who had been laughing minutes ago.

He tipped his hat. "It seems that you are quite yourself again, Miss Needham. I trust you will accept my apology for any discomfort our outing might have caused you. Please take my advice and return to your coach."

"I was not planning on walking much farther."

"Miss Needham, I must insist you return to your coach."

She was now certain this man must be the most irritating she had ever met. Even her brother, when he behaved like a henpecked husband, was less vexing.

As she began walking back toward the carriage, he fell into step beside her. She was surprised anew when he said nothing. Before, he had been a prattle-box. What a peculiar man! When she stumbled, he put his hands out to steady her. She waved them aside. She could not lurch into Oslington Court for her first meeting with the duke, so she must get her feet firmly beneath her. If only this man and the want-witted lad had opened their eyes and seen her standing by the wall, this whole episode could have been avoided.

Relief raced through Angela when she saw the carriage was on all four wheels. Her delight was muted when her foot caught in a chuckhole, and the man took her arm. His boots awoke the dust on the road on every step, and it cleaved to the flounces on her skirt. The good impression she had hoped to make upon her arrival at Oslington Court was doomed by this man's misguided determination to see that she was safe.

From behind the carriage, the coachee popped out like a puppet pulled by its string. The thin man's clothes were covered with dirt. As he wiped his hand against his filthy cheek, his eyes widened. He tilted his cap and started to speak.

The man beside her cut him off by saying, "You have repaired the carriage, I trust. Miss Needham is anxious to be on her way." Not giving the coachman a chance to answer, he added, "I bid you a good afternoon, Miss Needham, and offer my hopes that the rest of your journey is uneventful."

"Thank you."

When she said no more, he nodded politely and, setting the net's handle on his shoulder like a laborer carrying a scythe, walked in the same direction the carriage was headed.

A twinge of dismay cramped her center. Did this strange man live close to Oslington Court? Or worse, did he live within its walls? Mayhap he was a member of the duke's household. His voice suggested he was educated, so he might be an upper servant. Although she knew she was revealing a complete lack of manners to speak so of a stranger, she needed to know more about him before she made an utter cabbage-head of herself again.

"Who was that?" she asked, trying, without much success, to sound nonchalant.

The coachee took off his cap and slapped it against his dusty coat. "That be Lord Harrington, Miss Needham."

"Lord Harrington?" She clamped her lips closed when the coachman's grin became as wide as his eyes had been.

"A viscount, so I hear." Glancing at the repaired wheel, he gave it a tentative poke with his toe. "That's not all they say about him. I hear his lordship's got an odd kick in his gallop. Avoids London." He gave Angela a broken-toothed grin. "Guess he can't go 'bout chasing butterflies in Covent Garden now, can he? That's why he lives here in Harrington Grange."

"Is the carriage set to travel?" she asked. Her questions had been as ill-mannered, so the best thing to do would be to put an end to this.

But that man was *Lord* Harrington?

The coachman grumbled something, and Angela knew he

had hoped to regale her with more stories about the eccentric lord. Although she wished to learn more, she must not listen to gossip. At least, she reminded herself, Lord Harrington did not live within walls of Oslington Court. What was Harrington Grange, and where was it? It could not be far, so she might encounter Lord Harrington again.

When Angela let the coachee hand her up into the carriage, she could not halt from glancing in the direction Lord Harrington had walked. This was not a good beginning. The viscount might be a welcome guest at the duke's home. But which Lord Harrington would call at Oslington Court? The jester? The fiery man who defended his young friend? The gentleman who had worried about her well-being?

Whichever one it might be, she must be ready to deal with him and his loose-screw ways. She wondered if she could be.

TWO

Angela stared at the grand house as the hired carriage came to a stop beneath a stone porte-cochere. Like an aging queen, Oslington Court sat amid her emerald gardens and waited to be admired. Age and salt from the not-distant sea had stained the brick walls, but the windows marching along its front elevation sparkled back the last rays of the day's sunshine.

No two windows were identical. Unlike the symmetrical façades on London squares, long expanses of glass were set side-by-side with small, stained-glass windows that looked as if they had been taken from a monastery. Flat glass and bay windows marked a tower rising next to the double doors.

Beyond the house, as the hill dropped back toward the road, Angela could see clumps of trees. Rosebushes were green shadows against the brighter grass. Other flowers had burst from their beds in a barrage of color. She hoped she would find time to explore those gardens soon.

Angela stepped from the carriage as the tiger held the door. Climbing the half dozen steps to the double doors of Oslington Court, she was glad the trip from Town was over. Her head still hurt, and every muscle recalled the hours of rough travel from London.

Beneath her shoes, the risers were worn with the tread of uncountable other feet. One of the black walnut doors, which were decorated only with the thick heads of black nails, swung open with a squeak. Angela hesitated; then, taking a deep breath, she crossed the threshold into her new life.

Coolness embraced her, for the sunshine seeping through the windows to brighten the diamond patterns of the marble floor was swallowed by the massive space. A pair of brass chandeliers hung an unbelievable distance over her head. Gilt shone on the metalwork along the banister. The ornate staircase divided into twin staircases as it reached up from the ground floor. The stone steps led to a half-landing where a full suit of armor sat atop the steel that would have protected the knight's horse. Weak sunlight sparked off the hilt of the sword.

Angela pressed her hand to her heart, wanting to be certain it was still beating as she entered this extraordinary fantasy world where no mere human should dare to trespass. She had called at elegant houses in London before she had cut her single Season short to tend to her dying mother. Those houses would be envious of this ancient grandeur.

"Good afternoon. Are you Miss Needham?"

At the elderly voice, Angela forced her gaze away from the glorious entry to look at a graying man. His livery was a brilliant blue which matched the tiles edging a hearth set between two doors to her left. As he walked toward her, she realized he was no taller than she was. His sunken eyes and withered face bespoke his age.

"Yes, I am Angela Needham," she answered, noting how her voice vanished in the emptiness.

"I am Hervey, His Grace's butler, miss." When he held out his gnarled hands, she slipped her shawl off her shoulders. He took it, then, with an expression of distaste, handed the dusty lace to a young woman who popped out of the shadows beneath one arch of the staircase.

With a shiver, Angela wondered what or who else might hide there. Sternly she told herself not to be fanciful. Her mother had related wonderful stories of her months at Oslington Court. Angela was sure she would enjoy her tenure at the grand house as much.

"This way, Miss Needham," the *major domo* said. His

deep voice resonated along the high corridors opening off
the foyer. "Please do not delay to gawk. His Grace expected
you nearly an hour past."

"I am looking forward to meeting His Grace." Angela
would save her explanation for the duke.

When she said nothing else, the hunched man pointed to
a door on the left; she walked in that direction. Hervey was
silent while he led her past doors that provided glimpses of
glorious rooms resplendent in crystal and marble and fine
wood polished to reflect the few candles that were lit against
the coming of night. When she realized that each room's
hearth and mantel were unique, she longed to stop and examine them. She promised herself that she would succumb
to that temptation later. For now, she must be sure that she
made the best possible impression on the duke.

As they passed a looking glass, she sought to spy her
reflection. The fancy pier mirror, with gilt fruit capping the
top, was set too high on the wall. Looking at the dust clinging to the hem of her gown, she guessed the ribbons on her
bonnet were as uncomely. Mayhap even worse, she feared
the flowers on her bonnet had been battered by Lord Harrington's butterfly net. Blast that man! He should have been
watching his young friend more closely. The remnants of
her irritation were not eased as she pushed her hair back
into place. She was as skimble-skamble as the viscount, for
she should have thought to ask Hervey for a chance to wash
the grime of the road from her face before she met the duke.

If only Lord Harrington's boots had not sprayed dust all
over her!

Angela's steps faltered as the peculiar viscount intruded
on her thoughts yet again. She did not need that enigmatic
man clogging her head now. Yet the warmth in his emerald
eyes, when he had been concerned for her well-being, refused to be forgotten. Nor could she push aside the memory
of his hands, strong and at the same time gentle.

Hervey glanced back with a disapproving frown. Hurrying to where he stood by a closed door, Angela silenced a
tremor of dismay. She must focus on this introduction to the

Duke of Oslington. His Grace would send her back to Town posthaste if she acted as unsettled as the young miss he hoped she would guide into the Season.

The butler opened the door, which was as silent as his disapproval. Crossing the parquet floor, the old man did not turn to see if Angela was following.

She did at a slower pace, for her eyes were caught on every step by something else in the fabulous chamber. Two walls were hidden behind huge, glass-fronted cases filled with books of every size. The single window had diamond-shaped mullions marching across its breadth and splashing the long shadows of sunset on the roughly hewn hearth. As she edged around benches and tables, Angela smiled. A trio of leather chairs were set in a corner beneath the window. It was perfect for an indulgent afternoon of reading.

Hervey paused by a chair, which was turned so she could not see its occupant. "Your Grace, Miss Needham has *finally* arrived."

"Needham?" came back an impatient voice. "I know no one by that name."

The butler bent toward the chair. Although Angela did not hear his words, she guessed the butler was reminding the duke about the companion for his ward. She squared her shoulders as she wondered if the man was always so forgetful. That was sure to make her life more difficult.

"Oh, *that* Miss Needham," the man said in the same rich, tenor voice. "Thank you, Hervey."

The butler backed away and looked toward Angela with a frown that ordered her to come forward to present herself. Wondering what sort of tyrant the Duke of Oslington might be, she took a single step toward the chair, then paused as His Grace stood.

This was not the crotchety man she had imagined. The duke was handsome. His jaw was firm, and he possessed sternly chiseled features. A hint of gray lightened his brown hair near his temples, and lines were drawn into his sun-darkened skin. She recalled the duke had written that he had returned recently from India, so she guessed the deep tan came from his long sea voyage.

The heels of his knee-high boots tapped the parquet floor as he came toward her, but she barely noticed the sound. The fine cut of his navy coat and the cravat at his throat went unseen as she was caught by his appraisal. His gray eyes swept along her, inspecting her as if she were one of the sepoys under his command.

"You are Miss Needham, the Miss Needham I contacted to be my ward's companion?" He picked up a silver snuffbox from the table by his chair. Opening it, he removed a pinch.

"I am Angela Needham. It is my pleasure to be able to help in this way, Your Grace."

The duke put the snuffbox onto the table and his handkerchief beneath his coat. "Miss Needham," he said coolly, "when my mother suggested that I might contact you to help me solve this problem of bringing my ward into the Polite World, I was of the mistaken understanding that you were more than a chip."

"I can assure you, Your Grace, that I am no longer a child."

"You look it."

Astounded by his want of civility, she wondered if all men in Northumberland suffered from a lack of manners. First she had been accosted by Lord Harrington and his butterfly net. Now the duke was acting as if she were unsuitable to be his ward's companion. She quelled the shudder flying along her back as she envisioned him giving her her leave. She must avert that disgrace, if it was still possible.

"Your Grace," she said, fighting to keep her voice serene, "I celebrated my sixth-and-twentieth birthday less than a fortnight ago."

"Is that so?" Again he looked her over from head to toe. He nodded.

She started to ask him what he meant when she heard footsteps fading behind her. Looking over her shoulder, she saw a woman in a gray dress hurrying out of the room. The duke's silent message had not been for Angela, but for this servant she had not heard enter.

Motioning toward a chair, the duke continued, "Do sit, Miss Needham."

"Thank you. I trust I shall soon have the opportunity to meet your ward."

"In due time." He inclined his head again toward the chair next to where he had been seated.

Angela recognized that as a command. Even though she was exhausted and her head ached and she was so thirsty she could have downed half the North Sea, she sat with every bit of grace she had left. She was too aware of the handsome duke gauging every motion she made. She must prove to him that she was fit to teach his ward proper behavior for *Le Beau Monde*. Folding her hands in her lap, she waited for His Grace to speak.

He dropped into his chair. "I must own to being grateful that you could come to Oslington Court on such short notice, Miss Needham. It is most fortunate that you had nothing to compel you to remain in London."

"I was able to arrange matters quickly," she answered, not willing to own to this cold man that she had been glad to leave her brother's home.

"As I said, most fortunate." His fingers played with the tooled edge of the book on the table by his chair, and she guessed he was anxious to return to his reading. "Few women of your age and class would be willing to leave Town during the Season."

Angela bristled as his words echoed Lord Harrington's comments. It was no concern of either man why she had decided to come to Oslington Court. She did not need anyone to remind her that her life had taken a turn she could not have imagined when she had been as young as the duke's ward. Then she had dreamed of a glorious Season that would end with a loving marriage.

Taking a deep breath, she forced herself to swallow her anger. The duke could not guess how his words resurrected the grief and frustration she tried to forget. When she spoke, she was pleased with her even voice. "Your Grace, it was my pleasure to be able to accept your kind offer to act as companion to your ward."

"I must own, Miss Needham," he said with a sudden fervor, "to being very eager to do the best I can by Leonia. Her father was my commanding officer at Fort St. George in Madras, and he was a man who accepted nothing but the very best effort. I vowed to oversee Leonia's future, and, as Leonia's companion, I shall pass part of that burden and that obligation to you."

"She has been educated?"

His laugh was as sharp as the coachman's whip. "Fort St. George was no wilderness. I think you would find yourself quite at home among the English in the compound."

"Then you wish only for someone to ease her way into the Polite World?" Angela was disconcerted anew. This man was almost as bothersome as Lord Harrington. If the duke had been a bit more forthcoming in his letter about his expectations and his ward's background, she would not be so awkwardly uneasy now.

"I wish, Miss Needham, to find her a husband."

"That, no doubt, is the wish of any guardian who fires off his ward."

His dark brows reached toward each other as he scowled. "I see you find the straightforward speech of a soldier disturbing. You need not worry. Leonia is far more pretty-mannered than I." He gave another cold laugh. "And as I am not in need of a husband, you should concern yourself only with her."

"If you wish to succeed in your quest, Your Grace," Angela returned primly, "you shall see that a potential husband may have parents who concern themselves as much with you as with the bride-to-be."

"True." Leaning back, he pyramided his fingers in front of his nose. "I can see that we have much to learn from you. You shall find me appreciative of your hard work and dedication to your task." He picked up the book. "Do you read Scott, Miss Needham?"

"I have," she answered, startled at his abrupt question.

"This is one of his latest. *Rob Roy.* It is pleasing enough, but I preferred *Waverly.* I assume you have read the latter." Without a pause, he asked, "Do you speak French?"

Angela stiffened her back as she answered in that language, "I have learned enough to allow me to converse with some skill."

His expressive eyebrows arched before settling back into place. "As I can see. You seem to have had a satisfactory education, and your manners, in spite of every provocation I have made to unsettle them, are as excellent as my mother had led me to believe. I suspect you and I shall work well together in this enterprise."

"I hope so, Your Grace."

"Have you—?"

Angela was not certain what the duke might have asked her next, for he interrupted himself. She followed his gaze to see a young woman walking toward them. The sunlight caught fire on her red hair and accented her pert nose. A few freckles marked her porcelain skin, and, as she neared, Angela could see the young woman's eyes were as blue as the ribbons on the bodice of her stylish gown. Angela was astonished to note that the young woman wore her hair loose along her back as if she were still a child.

"This is Leonia Sutton, your charge," the duke said. "Leonia, please greet Miss Angela Needham, your new companion. I trust you will make her welcome at Oslington Court."

Angela waited for the young woman's reaction. It would be her first clue to the relationship she would have with the redhead. If Leonia Sutton was as bewildering as her guardian, this position might prove to be intolerable.

Her anxiety was groundless, for Miss Sutton rushed forward to take her hands. Squeezing them, she exclaimed, "Miss Needham, I am so glad you are here at last! Rodney has insisted that I stay in the nursery until you arrived. How I have tired of being treated like a child!"

"I am glad to be here." The girl's effusiveness contrasted

with the bleak temper of her guardian. "You should ask His Grace's pardon for your unthinking words, when I am sure he was thinking only of your comfort."

Miss Sutton blinked, but proved she had had a good upbringing when she turned to the dark-haired duke and said, "I meant no offense with my words, Rodney."

"You are forgiven." His riveting gaze returned to Angela. "You can see the chore ahead of you, Miss Needham. My ward possesses an enthusiasm that I do not wish to have curbed, merely muted. To fire her off will require many lessons on your part and much attention on hers."

Angela replied, "I have no doubts that both Miss Sutton and I shall be equal to the task." She was rewarded with a brilliant smile from the young woman.

The duke reached for his book again and opened it. "Leonia, acquaint Miss Needham with the Court."

"But, Rodney—"

"Do as you are told like a good child," he said without looking at her, for his concentration had returned to his book.

Angela hoped that was the only reason he did not acknowledge Miss Sutton's woeful expression. If he was being intentionally indifferent to his ward, Angela had traded a horrible existence at her brother's home for worse at Oslington Court.

Again Miss Sutton's reaction was reassuring. Her smile returned as she led Angela out of the room. As they walked along a dim passage, she glanced shyly at Angela. "I am pleased you are here. Rodney said that once you arrived, I could begin to make calls. Do you think we could visit one of the neighbors tomorrow? I do love to make a look-in on a neighbor, Miss Needham. At Fort St. George, I visited with one nearly every day. Do you suppose I could have some *cartes des visites* made? I know I should wait until I am part of the Season, but it would be so much fun."

"I think the first thing we should do is get to know one another." Angela could not keep from smiling back at the enthusiastic girl. She wondered if Miss Sutton was always such a prattle-box. If so, Angela must work on tempering that aspect of Miss Sutton's warm personality.

"Oh, that would be glorious! And you shall get to know us." She put her hand on the thick banister of the other set of stairs. "Do not let Rodney distress you. He does not mean to be cold. He simply is so busy thinking of important things now that he is a duke and has to tend to the welfare of Oslington Court."

"You seem to understand him well."

"I have known him since I was no more than a babe. When my mother died, Rodney was there to help Papa." Tears filled her sapphire eyes. "Oh, forgive me, Miss Needham. I still think of Papa often."

Angela patted her hand. "As I think of my mother who died last winter."

"Oh, I am sorry." Again she grasped Angela's hands. "But now you are here with us. For that, I am very, very glad."

Instead of answering, Angela followed her up stairs that were almost as wide as the ones by the main entrance. The stone walls and dark paneling would have been dreary if the floors had not been brightened with Oriental rugs. Hallways erupted in every direction from the top of the stairs, but Miss Sutton gave Angela no chance to peer down any as she walked to the right. All the doors were closed, and the window at the far end of the long corridor could not light the passage.

"If you get lost," Miss Sutton said with a chuckle, "do not despair. I had to have the servants direct me back to the main wing twice during the first week after we arrived here." Her smile broadened as she swung open a door. "Look!"

Angela could not silence her gasp of astonishment as she followed Miss Sutton into the elegant room. The chamber was as light as fairy's wings, a contrast to the dreary corridors. Cream silk over the walls matched the coverlet on the cherry tester bed. A dressing table, an armoire, and a pair of settees and a chaise longue upholstered in gold-

and-white stripes were arranged on a rug that was too large to fit in her brother's parlor. Here, there was room to show-case the parquet edging the rug. A pair of windows, with gauzy lace beneath gold velvet draperies, swept from floor to ceiling. When Miss Sutton rushed to push them aside, Angela realized they were French windows that opened onto a balcony.

When Angela walked out onto the balcony, the evening breeze caressed her face. She smiled at the gardens vanish-ing into the twilight along the curve of the hill. Outbuildings were lumpy shadows, but the faint odor from the stables wafted to her. Beyond them, trees marked the edges of the fields. She could see little more, for the setting sun had vanished after painting the clouds a red as garish as Lord Harrington's coat.

Angela's fingers tightened on the iron railing at the edge of the balcony. She was being silly to let the peculiar vis-count dally in her thoughts. She might have been able to forget him if he was not a puzzle that teased her to solve it.

Hearing Miss Sutton call, Angela went back inside.

Miss Sutton was sitting on the bed. It was so high her feet hung in the air. She ran her fingers along the coverlet and said, "This is one of my favorite rooms in the Court. That is why I chose it."

"This is lovely," Angela said. She considered asking Miss Sutton if she knew of the eccentric viscount and her opinion of him, but that would require explaining how Angela had chanced to encounter him. That she wanted to avoid doing.

Jumping down from the bed instead of using the steps, Miss Sutton nearly skipped to Angela. "So you like it?"

"Of course, and I can understand why you do. The ground floor is so dark. This is like emerging into the sky."

Miss Sutton dropped to the chaise longue, her dress riding higher. When she saw Angela's dismay, she rearranged her skirt. "The sky is still far above us. I have thought it a shame that there are so few windows in the attics. Shall I take you there? They have many interesting spaces. We can explore the storage rooms. I suspect there are trunks that have not been opened since before Rodney was born. Think what treasures we might find."

"Another time." Angela loosened her bonnet ribbons and lifted it off her head. She tried not to wince when she touched a lump near her right ear. No wonder her head continued to pound with pain.

"Are you unwell, Miss Needham?"

"I do not wish to be curt, Miss Sutton, but I am fatigued after my journey from Town. If you would be so kind as to show me to my room—"

Miss Sutton laughed. *"This* is your room!"

"This?" Angela's voice came out in a squeak. If this grand chamber was set aside for a servant, she dared not imagine how magnificent the other bedrooms were.

"Oh, Miss Needham, you must not be such a straight stick. Esther will delight in taunting you."

"Esther?"

"My little sister." Her nose wrinkled, even as she smiled. "Esther is a trial, although she can be a dear when she wishes. She is almost twelve. When my brother was that age, I discovered it is a most intolerable period."

Angela smiled at Miss Sutton's attempt to make herself sound older than her years. "I had no idea that you had siblings. His Grace mentioned nothing of it in his letters."

"Oh, yes." Her martyr's sigh was ruined by an assertive knock.

"Is Miss Needham here yet, Leonia?" came a whisper from the door.

"Do come in," Angela said.

The door opened to reveal a girl, who must be Miss Esther Sutton. Her hair was a ghastly red, which Angela hoped would darken to the color of her sister's. More freckles than could be counted pocked her plump cheeks, and her bright blue eyes sparkled with mischief. The hem of her dress drooped on one side. Leaves tangled in her stockings and hair.

"Esther, you are filthy!" Miss Sutton cried with despair. "Have you been climbing trees again?"

The girl pointed an accusing finger at Angela. "She is as mussed as I."

"Miss Needham has been traveling from London. You have been no farther than the fields." Pressing her hand to her breast, she added, "Or have you?"

"Is *she* Miss Needham?"

Angela almost smiled at the child's refusal to own to any wrongdoing. "I am, and may I assume you are Miss Esther Sutton?"

Instead of answering, Miss Esther turned around, and Angela saw another shadow by the door.

"You may as well come in," Angela called. "Skulking about will do none of us any good."

A lad edged into the room. His reddish-blond head was bowed so she could not see his face. He was thin from too much growth in too few months.

Angela stared as Miss Sutton asked, "Thomas, whatever is wrong?"

He looked up and whispered, "I am glad you are here and unhurt, Miss—" He flushed as red as his sister's hair. "I mean—I am sorry, Miss Needham. I did not see you. I—"

"Thomas, what is this bibble-babble?" Miss Sutton asked, again assuming the tone she clearly hoped would make her sound more mature. "I do not understand."

Angela understood. Even if she had not heard his name, Master Thomas's flustered words identified him as the wielder of the butterfly net. Taking sympathy on the lad, who could be no more than two years older than Miss Esther, she said, "Miss Sutton, your brother and I have already met."

"You have? Where?"

She smiled. "You can rest assured, Master Thomas, that neither I nor my bonnet were damaged badly by your enthusiastic sport."

"What sport?" Miss Esther demanded. "Why are you always leaving me out of the fun?"

Master Thomas asked at the same time, "Will you tell Rodney?" He gulped, his Adam's apple bouncing wildly.

Now Angela was bewildered. "Is there a reason why he should not know you were chasing butterflies?"

"Butterflies?" Miss Sutton gasped. "Thomas, were you with Lord Harrington again?" Shaking her finger at him, she said in a scandalized tone, "You know Rodney has forbidden you to go to Harrington Grange."

"We were not at the Grange," he returned, but lowered his head again. Poking his toe at the fringe on the rug, he sighed. "Leonia, I had told Justin that I would go with him before Rodney gave that order. Papa always said a man is only as good as his word. What good would I have been if I had left Justin waiting at the gate for me when I told him I would be there?"

"Justin?" asked Angela, as she sat on a chair next to the dressing table. "Is that Lord Harrington?"

"Yes," Miss Sutton said softly, as if she feared being overheard. Angela understood when she added, "But please do not speak of him. Rodney wants no one in this house to have anything to do with him." She fired a frown at her brother. "Ever!"

Three

The next morning, Angela woke, certain she would find the household much more ordinary. She dressed in her favorite green sprigged muslin gown. Fresh flowers had been left on her dressing table, so she pinned a single rose to the modest curve of her neckline. The pink flower matched the line of embroidery decorating her bodice.

She checked the glass. Last night upon her arrival at Oslington Court, she had looked as bedraggled as Miss Esther. No wonder His Grace had questioned her ability to serve as Miss Sutton's companion. Now her hair was curled around her face beneath her lacy cap, and the green ribbons on her gown showed no sign of the days they had spent in her box while she traveled north.

Angela sighed. By the end of her first day at Oslington Court, she must be termed a success. She had created a poor first impression, which she must rectify at her earliest opportunity. Although she had befriended Miss Sutton, neither Miss Sutton nor her siblings would explain why the duke insisted upon them staying away from Harrington Grange.

That puzzled her. Lord Harrington might be bizarre in his interest in capturing butterflies, but his defense of Master Thomas had been heartfelt and logical. She hoped today would bring answers instead of more questions.

Angela smiled as, picking up her lace-edged parasol, she wandered out onto a broad stone terrace. She heard a distant clip-clop of horses' hoofs. Taking a deep breath of the dew that still clung to the grass, she smiled more broadly when she saw her hired chaise driving away from the house. Its leaving severed her last connection with London, and she could not be sorry about that.

She saw a form, long and slender as a cat. That must be Master Thomas Sutton. He was walking toward the gate and the road leading past Oslington Court.

Hurrying from the raised terrace, she set her parasol on her shoulder as she crossed the neatly trimmed yard. She did not pause to admire the shrubs or the fruit budding in the trees. Master Thomas was just the person she needed to talk with. She hoped he would be able to answer the questions taunting her. Miss Esther was too young, and Miss Sutton had resisted explaining why she was so distressed by a mere glance from her guardian. There were too many mysteries in this huge house, and she wanted to have some of them resolved so she could do her best to guide Miss Sutton.

Angela reached the gate exactly at the same moment Master Thomas did. Her smile became a frown when she saw the butterfly net he was carrying propped on his shoulder and the stubborn set of his jaw. Miss Sutton had been mistaken. Her brother had not set aside his propensity for trouble-making with his adolescence.

"I thought your guardian requested that you refrain from calling on Lord Harrington," Angela said with a sigh. She did not want to give him a dressing-down, but she had a responsibility, as did everyone in Oslington Court, to see that the children obeyed the duke's rules.

Master Thomas kicked one pebble toward the gate, then another. He stuck his hand into the pockets of his dark breeches, causing his short coat to hang at an odd angle. Reluctantly he answered, "Rodney said Justin was not to come chasing after his 'blasted butterflies'—his words, Miss Needham, not mine—on Oslington land. As you can see, I am meeting Justin on the other side of the gate. On the public road. Off Oslington land."

She plucked the butterfly net from his hand, surprising

him. "If His Grace gave you such an order, you know he intended you to keep it both on Oslington property and off. Did you tell him that you would obey him?"

"Not exactly. I said—"

"That your father told you a man was only as good as his word. If you gave His Grace your word, in any form, then you should recall both that and your father's advice."

He snatched the net back. His chin jutted defiantly. "I never said anything about meeting Justin on the road."

"Master Thomas—"

"Why are you chasing after me? You were hired to watch over my sister." He grinned. "You are watching over her like a guardian angel, aren't you?" He laughed, clearly delighted with his own *bon mots* as he continued, "You are my guardian's Angela. Go and bother Leonia. She is your charge, not me!"

Taken aback by the venom in his voice, Angela knew she must not yield at this point. "Master Thomas, if you would explain to me why His Grace has—" When she realized he was not listening, but looking past her with a sudden grin, she turned and gasped as she bumped into Lord Harrington.

"Miss Needham." He tipped his tall hat to her. As when she had seen him the previous day, he was dressed well. He wore a russet coat over his light brown leather breeches that accented the subtle strength of his body. In one hand, he carried a small basket, which Angela suspected had something to do with the butterflies he hoped to snare with Master Thomas's help.

"Lord Harrington," she said as coolly as the last time they had spoken.

He smiled, setting his eyes to twinkling again with the humor that had both infuriated and charmed her the previous day. "I see I have no need to atone for the discourtesy of failing to introduce myself properly yesterday. My reputation precedes me, as they say."

"Do they?"

His green eyes narrowed as he set the basket on a low section of the wall by the gate. "Are you always so imperturbable, Miss Needham? Or do I rate a special conde-scension from you?" Not giving her a chance to answer, he continued, "No doubt, by this time, Oslington has filled your head with all kinds of pap about me."

"You flatter yourself, my lord," she answered. Tilting her parasol, she watched his face tighten into stern lines as she added, "His Grace has said nothing of you in my hearing."

"And beyond it?"

She heard a muffled laugh and tensed. Not only was he exhorting a child to disobey, he was teaching Master Thomas to be disrespectful of his guardian. She must put a halt to this posthaste. "Master Thomas, I have asked you to return to the Court. Please do so."

The lad hesitated, then glanced at Lord Harrington. Angela's hand clenched on the parasol. No matter what the viscount thought of his neighbor, he must realize that the duke expected that his wards would obey his rules.

"Go along, lad," the viscount said, but his eyes refused to release Angela's gaze. "I wish to speak to Miss Needham now. There will be other days we can spend in the mead-ows."

"There will be no more," Angela said as Master Thomas walked past her, his head down, his whole pose filled with disgust. "His Grace wishes to put an end to Master Thomas's association with you. The duke shall not be half pleased to discover Master Thomas has gainsaid his orders."

"And that is that?" Lord Harrington demanded, the heat in his voice matching the fierce fire in his eyes. "He has trained you quickly if you fall in line like one of his sepoys. I had thought you to be a woman of some strength of will."

"It is not my place to countermand the duke's rules for his wards. I am sure His Grace has a reason for his rules."

Lord Harrington held out his arm. "I am sure, too."

"Then—"

"Shall we discuss this while we walk?"

"I should not."

"Are you subject to his rules as well?"

Angela glanced at the huge house beyond the stone walls

as guilt flooded over her. "I should be spending time with Miss Sutton. After all, that is why I am here."

He drew her hand within his arm, his smile returning. "My dear Miss Needham, if you are here to teach Miss Sutton how to deport herself in the company of Town, you would be wise to be an example for her of how to listen politely to someone who wishes to ask of your welfare. Such as now, when I want nothing but to ask you how you fare after yesterday. May I say you look no worse for the experience, although I must own to missing that smudge of dirt you had on your cheek then. It accented your guinea-gold hair."

Angela drew her hand back with a gasp. This man was as unmannered as a conveyancer plying his horrible trade along the road. If Lord Harrington thought he could ply her with compliments in order to convince her to be an ally in whatever battle he was waging against the duke, he was wrong.

"Come now, Miss Needham," he continued when she was otherwise silent, "surely you enjoy adulation as much as the rest of us."

She hesitated on her answer, and the viscount took her hand again and settled it on his arm. As if she had agreed enthusiastically to his offer, he led her on a lazy stroll along the road. He began to whistle, startling her. The tune was cheerful and jaunty and the perfect tempo for a walk, but she guessed it was his way of keeping her from asking the questions she must. If he thought she could be halted like this from asking those questions, he must be shown how mistaken he was.

"Lord Harrington, I wish to speak with you of this serious matter," Angela said.

"And are you always serious?"

"Are you ever?" she retorted with abrupt heat.

Pausing beneath the shade of a large oak, he did not release her arm. His fingers brushed her hand, and she fought to silence her gasp at the unexpected pleasure wafting up her arm. When his lips tilted in a genuine smile, she knew she had not concealed her response to his touch. She was ready to remonstrate with him at his boldness, but her words melted, unspoken, when she was captured by the uncompromising flame in his eyes.

Slowly he raised her fingers toward his lips. He bent, but did not kiss them. When he looked past her hand to her wide eyes, she saw the challenge in his smile.

She should pull away. She knew that, but she continued to stare up at him, caught as utterly as she had been in the net yesterday. Lord Harrington was not handsome when compared to the duke's classic features. His smile was a bit crooked, and there were lines about his eyes that suggested he smiled often. Yet there was something in his face that drew her as butterflies were lured to a fragrant flower. Something so alive, something so restrained, something that urged her to discover more.

"An apology," he murmured, the deep, rough sound of his voice caressing her ears.

"For what?"

"For teasing you yesterday when you clearly were not yourself." His eyes glittered with mischief as he added, in his normal voice, "You are more yourself today, I would wager, and I see you are not the shy flower you seemed upon our first meeting."

Angela pulled her hand out of his. He was hoaxing her yet again. What an addle-cove she was to be taken in by his glib prattle! Lifting her parasol off her shoulder, she turned to walk back to the gate. His laughter followed her, but she was shocked when his hand settled on her arm.

"Lord Harrington!"

"I was not finished apologizing to you. You do not wish to leave until I am finished, do you?"

She hated the blush that burned on her cheeks as she answered, "Say what you must."

"I shall." His hand curved around her elbow to steer her hand back onto his arm. "I trust Thomas has apologized for entangling you in his net yesterday."

"Yes."

"Probably nicer than I did . . . yesterday."

"Without a doubt."

"Ah, honesty!" He laughed. "That is a charming change, Miss Needham. I own that I thought you would cut me quite to the quick yesterday with your cold comments."

She dared to meet his eyes again. "My lord, you must own as well that I had a reason for being distressed yesterday."

"Why?" he asked in the same infuriatingly reasonable tone. "If your life is so boring that such an incident upsets it past repair, you need to do something to create a bit of excitement in it."

"My life is none of your bread-and-butter."

"True, but I hate seeing anyone moldering away in ennui, especially when that someone is a lovely young lady who has fled the excitement of Town for a reason she keeps hidden behind a cool smile and beguiling blue eyes."

Angela pulled her hand away. Lord Harrington was impossible! His comments were impertinent. This walk and this conversation must come to an end.

Her exasperation faltered when she was caught again by his eyes that were as cool and mysterious as polished jade. Around her, the silence was filled with the buzz of summer bees seducing pollen from the flowers and the distant song of a lazy bird. The breeze touched her cheek, teasing her hair from beneath her bonnet. Everything was just as it should be, save for how each breath seemed to catch on her swiftly beating heart.

A dozen questions battered her lips, but she could not voice a single one. She wished to know why the Duke of Oslington despised his neighbor. Yet, most of all, she yearned to find out why Justin Harrington fascinated her so completely that he had plagued her thoughts for the past day.

When Lord Harrington took a step toward her, her breath refused to escape. She could not free it, any more than she could free herself from his compelling gaze.

"Look," he whispered as he pointed past her.

Angela turned, but saw nothing between the road and the wall surrounding Oslington Court. The field was as empty.

"There," he said in the same low tone, but his voice was tinged with a fervor she had not heard before. His warm breath brushed her nape as delicately as would have the wings of the butterfly, which was sitting on a flower. The butterfly opened and closed its golden feathers as if it wished to give her the chance to admire the dark specks across them. "Miss Needham, that is a pearl-bordered fritillary, the *Argynnis euphrosyne,* if you prefer the Latin name. It is one of my favorite species, for it was the first one I captured and studied when I was no older than Thomas."

The mention of the lad's name broke the bewitching spell he was spinning around her. Stepping away, Angela faced him. "You were free to study butterflies in your youth, my lord, but Master Thomas is not. I must ask you to refrain from convincing him to ignore his guardian's dictates."

"I have left that to Thomas to decide, as you and Oslington should." Lord Harrington's eyes sparkled, but not with the amusement she had seen before. As hard as faceted stones, they became slits when he added, "The lad is nearly a man. It is time for him to decide what rules he will or will not follow."

"That is for His Grace, as his guardian, to decide."

Striding past her, Lord Harrington grabbed his basket from the wall. "I thought you would be different, Miss Needham, when you snarled at me yesterday, but you are like everyone in that stone mausoleum. Not an ounce of spirit in you. No wonder Oslington obtained you as his ward's companion. You can teach her to be as bland as the rest of you."

"That is unfair," she fired back, stung by his words. "You know nothing of me."

"And I find I have no wish to learn more. I bid you good day, Miss Needham, and goodbye." He nodded toward her before leaving her to stare after him in astonishment once more.

Four

"Now we both are in trouble," grumbled Thomas as he slipped out of the gate once more to stand in the middle of the road.

Justin Harrington wanted to agree wholeheartedly. It was trouble he was calling upon himself. When he had seen that pretty Angela Needham was heading toward Oslington Court, he should have steered both himself and young Thomas far from her and her broken-down coach. Instead, while Thomas had been skulking closer to the road to find out what had happened to the carriage, Justin had let himself be drawn to her by how the light played on her tawny hair and how her eyes shone like the deep blue of a shadowed pool.

Her name might be Angela, but there seemed to be little that was angelic about the strength of will in Miss Needham's eyes, and she certainly had the devil's own way of making a man think of things he should not. He had intended to do no more than plead for her to understand how Thomas needed to leave the doldrums of Oslington Court and his grief behind. Instead, the conversation had gone in directions he had not planned because he could not keep from admiring her lush curls and even lusher curves that were accented by the single flower on her bodice.

"She will go straightaway to Rodney," Thomas continued. He kicked a pebble along the road.

"Mayhap so, mayhap not."

Thomas looked up, his eyes wide. "How can you say that? She wants to impress my guardian."

"I suspect she already has."

"How?"

Justin smiled and ruffled Thomas's hair. He was not going to share with the boy thoughts of how Miss Angela Needham had intrigued him so much that he had anticipated the chance of seeing her today more than he had collecting butterflies. She had been in a near pelter over Thomas's antics, but she had not swooned away as many a woman would have upon finding herself captured by a butterfly net and dependent upon a stranger to help her escape.

"Don't fret about Miss Needham," Justin said. "I doubt if she will last much longer than any of the others your guardian has tried to hire. There are not many young women who are willing to hide away in that mausoleum while Oslington decides what he wants to do with the rest of his life."

When Thomas frowned, puzzled, Justin knew he had said too much. Egad! After all this time, he should have learned to guard his words. He knew Oslington believed that Justin had struck up a friendship with Thomas simply to create trouble for the duke and his household. Nothing could be further from the truth, but Oslington never changed his mind once it was made up. No matter how many facts might come his way.

"Miss Needham is not like the others." Thomas drew a circle in the dirt with his toe. "She does not get angry and yell or look as if she is going to cry like Mrs. Meyer does when I disagree with her."

"I suspect Miss Needham is not at all like your governess."

"She is prettier."

Justin laughed at Thomas's clearly reluctant words. Clapping the boy on the shoulder, he said, "You should return to the house."

"But I thought we were going to—"

"You will not help yourself in your guardian's eyes if you linger here where you have been told twice over, if Miss Needham is to be believed, you should not be."

Thomas grumbled again, but went back through the gate at a run.

Moving so he could view the front of the grand house, Justin watched the boy disappear among the trees. How many years had it been since Justin had raced among those trees? They had seemed as high as the walls then, but the trunks had grown even thicker with the passing of the years. He chased those thoughts from his mind. Memories of Oslington Court were tainted now, and he wanted nothing to do with them. If he had half the wit of a goose, he would confine his search for butterflies to the fields on the other side of Harrington Grange and avoid this place.

A rapping cut into Angela's sleep. She forced her eyes open, but saw only darkness. At first, she could not recall where she was, for the shadows were different from the ones in her bedroom in her mother's home and the ones in her brother's attic. Then, seeing the reflection of the moonlight in her dressing table mirror, she realized she was in her chamber at Oslington Court.

Who was knocking in the middle of the night?

Images of a dozen catastrophes burst through Angela's mind as she groped for her wrapper. Flinging it around her shoulders, she hurried to the door.

Darkness shrouded the corridor, for only a single sconce lit the expanse. Angela saw no one. A shiver sent frosted fingers down her back as she imagined a ghostly caller that walked endlessly through these old corridors.

Hearing a whimper, Angela pushed aside her superstitions. She knelt by the crumpled form and put her hand on the child's back. It quivered as if with a fever. Her breath caught, but Miss Esther's skin above her thin nightdress was not heated with fever.

"Miss Esther?" she whispered. "Are you all right?"

Her only answer was a half-swallowed sob. Putting her arm around the trembling child's shoulders, she drew Miss Esther into her room to sit next to her on the chaise longue.

Softly Angela chided, "You should not be out of the nursery at this hour. Did you have a nightmare?"

Gulping, Miss Esther nodded.

"Why didn't you go to Mrs. Meyer?"

"She will not listen. She just sends me to bed, and the dream could come back."

"What about your sister or brother?"

"Thomas sleeps so deeply, it takes forever to wake him. Leonia . . ." She began to sob again.

"Do you want to tell me about it?" Angela hid her surprise that Miss Esther had sought her out when the child believed no one else would help her. She silenced the momentary thought that this was another of the child's pranks. The tears on the little girl's face were real.

Miss Esther shook her head, then murmured, "It was horrible, Miss Needham."

"Mayhap not talking about it is best."

A motion caught Angela's eye, and she gasped when she noticed, by the door, a little boy bouncing from one foot to the other. Since she had arrived here almost a week ago, no one had mentioned to her that there was a fourth Sutton child, but she could not doubt this youngster, who could claim no more than six years, was a sibling to the other Sutton children. He had the same round cheeks and freckles and blue eyes and ruddy hair.

"And who are you?" Angela asked.

"That is Seth." Miss Esther frowned at him. "Why did you follow me here?"

"You were bawling like a ewe." He came forward in his long nightshirt. "I thought you were sick. I thought you might toss up your dinner and—"

"Enough," Angela said, glad that they could not see her roll her eyes as she stood. These children would challenge the patience of a saint. Going to her bed, she took a pair of pillows and a blanket. "Do you want to stay here with me tonight?"

As she started to spread the blanket on the chaise longue, Miss Esther whispered, "Can I sleep *with* you?"

"Of course. Master Seth, you can sleep on the chaise longue."

With a cheer, he jumped onto it and curled up beneath the blanket.

Shaking her head in amazement, Angela held out her hand. Miss Esther put her fingers on it and smiled weakly. Angela smiled back. She was unsure if Miss Esther would be any more accepting of her when the sun rose, but she dared to believe it was a beginning of easier times to come.

Morning brought the return of Miss Esther's easy grin and mischievous laugh. When Angela sent her to the nursery, she left only after obtaining a promise from Angela that they would go for a walk with Master Seth that morning before her lesson with Leonia.

Miss Esther had chuckled when Angela agreed, so Angela was uncertain what to expect when, after a quick breakfast tray, she met the children in the foyer. Angela kept her blue silk parasol over the flowered brim of her poke bonnet. Walking in the grass beside the road beyond the wall, she protected her satin slippers from the dust raised by the children's exuberance. The lazy sunshine urged her to sit on a low wall and enjoy the day, but she must not let the children out of her sight. Devilment was clearly a part of Miss Esther, and Angela was resolved the little girl would have no chance to exult in her naughty behavior.

When she heard hoofs on the road, Angela called, "Miss Esther! Master Seth! Here by me."

Master Seth ran to her, but Miss Esther hesitated. As the rider came over the rise in the road, the little girl scampered to join them. Angela was about to chide her for her recklessness when she heard the horse slow.

"Good morning, Miss Needham. May I say that the country seems to be agreeing with you?"

At Lord Harrington's voice, Angela looked up to see his eyes crinkled in amusement. He dismounted with the ease of a man accustomed to the saddle. He greeted the children.

"I am not supposed to talk to you," Master Seth announced with the disdain of a king speaking to his lowliest subject.

"Me neither!" Miss Esther boldly stared at the viscount. "Rodney says you are bad for us."

"Miss Esther!" Angela scolded.

Lord Harrington chuckled, but his laugh had a strained sound. "Do not fault the child for her guardian's sins, Miss Needham. Have you been forbidden to speak to me as well?"

"Of course not."

"Then, if I may have a few words with you . . . alone."

Angela pointed to a nearby stile. "Miss Esther, Master Seth, why don't you see what wildflowers you can find in the field? Some of them would brighten the table in the nursery."

She smiled as they scrambled over the wall. When the viscount lashed his horse to the railing on the stile, she was not surprised when he lifted his butterfly net off his saddle with one hand and offered her his other arm. What astonished her was that he led her over the stile and followed the children at a slower pace.

"You have forged an attachment to these children very quickly," Lord Harrington said.

"I enjoy them, their enthusiasm, and, yes, even Miss Esther's teasing. She and I take walks together, usually in the gardens, but occasionally we go farther afield. Then she tells me about places she has seen, places I long to visit."

Lord Harrington smiled. "You wish to suffer the heat of India? Or could it be that you yearn for a bit of *mal de mer* as you travel the conflicting currents of the seas?"

Angela faced him. "My lord, I do not understand why you are belittling my dreams."

"No? Odd, for you have voiced your derogatory opinions of what brings me enjoyment."

She flushed and was as vexed at her coloring as at Lord Harrington. Then she realized he had a right to chide her, for she *had* labeled his avocation an eccentricity.

"Forgive me," Lord Harrington said when she did not reply. "I did not mean to put you to the blush. Before today, you seemed to be a person who appreciates plain words."

"I do . . . except when they remind me of my own folly." She smiled, pleased how easy it was when he grinned back. "In town, I grew tired of the words that meant less than their sound. That is one of the reasons I was happy to come here."

"Just one of the reasons?" He paused near where the stone wall twisted back toward them. "You steal my romantic notions, Miss Needham. I had imagined that you were fleeing an amorous suitor who was determined to go to any lengths to have you as his wife."

"That is no romantic notion. That is a fairy-tale."

His eyes widened at her tone, which was sharper than she had intended. "I can understand your anxiety to escape Town and its accompanying circus. I enjoy my days at Harrington Grange."

"But don't you wish to see beyond your home and the moor?"

"To where? I vow, Miss Needham, that after years of being obligated to be away from my home, I am quite convinced that the Grange is the place in this whole world where I can be happiest." He paused to peer into a bush by the wall. When a butterfly rose on the light breeze, he smiled. "A common sort," he said, but adding, "I see no reason to wander beyond the shire. So many things wait here for me to discover them."

Angela could not keep from blurting, "But, my lord, I would have thought you might be inclined to travel across the Channel or to Africa or even as far as the Spice Islands to find even more exotic butterflies to study."

"You thought that, did you?" He strode along the wall

toward where the children had found a patch of yellow flowers. She hurried to catch up, but his back was to her as he said, "Like you, I have my reasons for preferring the serenity of the country." Turning toward her, he smiled. "Or I should say, I did prefer it. Since the arrival of the Sutton children—and you—things have been less serene."

"How can the children bother you? I thought they were forbidden to call at Harrington Grange."

"Even if they do not present themselves at my door, I hear their enthusiastic play from across the fields."

Angela heard his odd wistfulness. Did he wish for children of his own? He had been more than kind to Miss Esther and Master Seth despite their rude words, and Master Thomas clearly doted on him and looked forward to any chance to join the viscount to watch an insect embroidering its bright colors across a summer sky.

Quietly she said, "If you wished to speak of an important matter without young ears overhearing, you should do so before we reach the children."

"I do not wish to burden you with what bothers me."

"You do not. I realize you are concerned about whether you will be able to continue your friendship with Master Thomas."

"Do you?" He looked back at her and quickly away.

"Your interest in him is exemplary."

He paused beneath the shade of an ancient tree reaching its branches from one field to the next. "I hate to see his interest wasted. If I did not think it would be futile, I would suggest that you speak to Oslington of Thomas's interest in studying butterflies."

"I mean to, but I have not had a chance." She smiled. "Miss Sutton took most of my afternoon yesterday. She has so many questions. She is a dear young woman. Her warm reception helped persuade the other children to welcome me."

"You sound as if you do not pity these children."

"Pity?" asked Angela, astonished. "That is the last thing they need."

"I agree. They need a firm hand—of which I believe you have two—and a warm heart."

"Of which you are less certain I possess?"

"Thomas professes to being confused about you." Lord Harrington took her fingers between his broad palms.

Angela would have retorted if she could have formed a thought of something other than the delight of his touch. His fingers were pleasingly warm—as warm as his gentle smile. She noticed, for the first time, a small scar near his right ear. It was no more than a short line, but her fingers itched to touch it, to discover if all his skin was as intriguing as his hands.

She was saved from such foolishness by the shout of "Justin!"

Lord Harrington released her hands and turned to wave.

Angela's shoulders stiffened when she saw Master Thomas running toward them. He hesitated when he saw her, then nodded condescendingly toward her before turning to the viscount.

"Justin, I am sorry I am so late," he said, excitement bursting on every word like fireworks on a holiday. "I wanted to check a book in the library. The butterfly we saw yesterday afternoon—" He glanced guiltily at Angela.

"Master Thomas, this is appalling," she said. "Your guardian has forbidden you from calling at Harrington Grange."

He hung his head and mumbled, "I know."

"What you do not know is that I plan to intercede on your behalf with your guardian."

"You do?" He looked to the viscount to confirm her words.

"That is what she tells me," Lord Harrington answered.

Angela bit back her exasperation. "Sneaking off to meet Lord Harrington behind your guardian's back may jeopardize my efforts."

"I do not need your help!"

"Thomas!" Lord Harrington's smile vanished. "You may

be angry with Miss Needham, but you must never forget your manners with a lady."

"She is not a lady. She is my sister's companion."

"You know what I mean. Apologize."

Master Thomas grimaced, then muttered, "Sorry, Miss Needham."

Suspecting she would have to be satisfied with that less-than-sincere apology, Angela nodded, then called to the younger children.

"Must you leave so quickly?" Lord Harrington asked.

"It is apparent that neither you nor Master Thomas believes that I aim to keep my vow to speak to His Grace until I have proven that I have."

"How do you propose to *prove* that?"

"When His Grace . . ." She could not promise the duke would rescind his order to the children.

As her gaze was caught by the viscount's again, she wished she could be honest. She abhorred the regret she had seen in Master Thomas's eyes, but it hurt doubly strong when she viewed it in Lord Harrington's. Somehow, the duke's intentions to protect his wards from more grief was having just the opposite effect. She wished she knew how she might persuade him to change his mind.

Five

The surprising summons came when Angela was attempting—yet again—to write a note to her brother to let him know of her safe arrival in Northumberland. She had tried to pen the note more than a dozen times since she had arrived at Oslington Court, but interruptions had become commonplace. Usually from Miss Esther, who saw her as a playmate in the games that led her on adventures throughout the Court. The little girl, unlike her siblings, could not hide the fact that she missed her parents.

She was also interrupted often by Miss Sutton, who sought her out to discuss the Season she hoped to enjoy in London or to bring her a picture of a frock from the latest edition of *Ackermann's Repository*. Miss Sutton seemed interested in nothing else.

Master Thomas never came to see her. She had spoken to him only once since she halted him from going with Lord Harrington. He slunk through the rooms, a gloomy shadow. Not that the duke seemed perturbed by the boy's silence. The duke spent most of each day in his book-room, reading.

That was why she was startled when a footman came with the message that Mr. Weare wished to speak with Miss Needham immediately. Closing her bottle of ink, Angela rose. She had met Master Thomas's tutor only once, but he had not seemed to be the sort of man to make such demands lightly.

Angela had been astonished to learn that Master Thomas was still being taught at home instead of being sent to school. Miss Sutton had explained that His Grace wanted the children to become acclimated to England before being separated.

"But Master Thomas is so unhappy *here*," Angela said as she climbed the narrow stairs to the uppermost floor to the nursery. Master Thomas would welcome her compassion as little as he had her interference in his friendship with Lord Harrington.

"Blast him!" Angela muttered as she walked along the upper corridor. When a maid glanced at her—aghast at her unseemly language—Angela hurried to the nursery. She had been brought to Oslington Court to refine Miss Sutton, but the uncomfortable situation was quickly ruining Angela's manners.

Entering the classroom, Angela did not see Mr. Weare by the two low tables. Miss Esther shared one with her younger brother while Master Thomas worked alone. Miss Sutton continued to study French with the tutor every other day.

"Mr. Weare?" Angela called, hoping the tutor had not gone in search of her. They could spend the afternoon wandering through the halls of Oslington Court and never find each other.

"Just a moment, Miss Needham," came his scratchy voice from an inner room.

As good as his word, the tutor appeared right after his reply finished echoing along the high ceiling. Mr. Weare had a long nose and the unfortunate complexion left from a youthful bout of smallpox. His black hair was the only color on his features, for his skin was sallow from too little contact with the sun. Dressed in a coat and breeches that strained across his bulk, he was far from a fearsome creature. Yet the children offered him a respect that Mrs. Meyer had been unable to win.

He smiled, but Angela sensed tension in his motions that were as jerky as a hangman's rope. "I am so pleased you could come quickly, Miss Needham."

"Your message suggested that what you wish to discuss is a matter of some import."

"I wish to discuss Master Thomas."

Angela nodded. When the schoolmaster motioned for her to sit, she chose one of the hard benches. He leaned against his high desk and sighed.

"Mr. Weare," she said, having sympathy for him, "I know Master Thomas has been sullen since I—" She clamped her lips closed because she had said nothing to anyone about the conversation with Lord Harrington by the gate. Her hope that her silence would convince Master Thomas that he could trust her had failed.

"I know he has developed an antipathy to you that is in direct contrast with his siblings' opinions. That is why I was curious as to the sudden change in him."

"There has been no change."

Again he sighed, his bulky shoulders rising and lowering slowly. " 'Tis as I feared. I found it odd that he asked to be excused from working here this afternoon because he planned to join you and the younger children exploring the gardens and the outbuildings."

"Master Thomas has as little to do with me as possible. I fear we got off to a very poor beginning when I prevented him from doing something he wished to do."

"You need not explain. Lord Harrington!" He clasped his hands behind the back of his funereal coat. "Damn that man!" His wan cheeks became a more lively shade. "Forgive my fervor, Miss Needham, but I believe the viscount is leading Master Thomas down a very unrosy garden path."

Angela set herself on her feet. The tutor's words told her what she should have guessed. Master Thomas must have decided to sneak away to visit his friend. She suspected the prohibition by the duke was only strengthening the bond between the boy and the viscount.

"I could speak to—"

If possible, the tutor's face grew even more pallid. "I implore you to refrain from bringing this to His Grace's attention. The duke has made it clear from my arrival at the Court that he has no taste for his neighbor. I believe that is why he has forbidden the children from calling there."

Angela went to the room's sole window. Beneath the heavy clouds and across the meadows dotted by puffs of sheep, she could see the roof that belonged to Harrington Grange. "Master Thomas heeds little that I say," she said without turning. "If I ask him again to obey his guardian, I doubt he will listen any better than he has in the past."

"You know the viscount, don't you?"

"I have spoken to him two or three times." She was glad her back was to the tutor, for she did not trust her face. It might betray how her heart beat faster at the very recollection of those brief conversations.

"Would you consider going to him and asking him to end his relationship with Master Thomas?"

Angela faced Mr. Weare. "I already have asked that."

"Oh." His mouth worked as if he were about to weep.

"If you wish, I will speak with him again. I fear it will do no more good than it did before." She bit her lower lip. Why had she offered to do *that?* She had enough to do with preparing Miss Sutton for her Season.

With a sigh, he bent to sit on a bench. "Thank you, Miss Needham. I would not ask, save that I am desperate for a solution. If Lord Harrington fails to heed you this time, I suspect I shall have no choice but to go to His Grace." Raising his gaze to meet hers, he said, "I fear *that* will cause even more trouble."

Angela nodded. "I understand."

"May I ask one more favor of you?"

"Of course."

"Please, as soon as you return, let me know how your call goes with him this afternoon."

"This afternoon?"

He came to his feet. "I thought you understood the urgency, Miss Needham. Master Thomas may be on his way to the viscount's house even as we speak."

As she emerged from Oslington Court into the misty afternoon, Angela wondered if she should have suggested waiting a bit before giving chase. Not wanting to alert His Grace to her destination, she had refrained from calling for a carriage. By the time she was halfway across the field to Harrington Grange, the mist had congealed into rain. She should return to the comfort of her rooms and spend the afternoon in pleasant conversation with Miss Sutton. Her duties were only, as Master Thomas had stated in anger, teaching the young woman how to make an entrance into the Polite World.

She paused by the low gate in the stone wall which was almost concealed by rose vines that twisted along and over it. Harrington Grange was not the cottage she had expected from seeing its thatched roof through the trees. It was the breadth of a half-dozen town houses in London, but only three stories high. Dozens of windows glowed with lamps that were fighting back the thickening storm. Outbuildings were gray lumps through the rain.

Her hand trembled as she reached for the latch on the gate. Bother! She could not call upon Lord Harrington when she was trembling like a frightened child or a young miss breaking the rules of Society. Yes, she was calling without a chaperon, but she was here on the duke's behalf. If Master Thomas was here against his guardian's wishes, then Lord Harrington must be set to rights about aiding the child in disobeying.

Closing the gate behind her, Angela grimaced as she stepped into a puddle. Her slipper soaked through instantly. She swallowed the curse that ricocheted through her mouth. How she would enjoy putting this all on Lord Harrington's head!

She walked along the path between rows of flowering shrubs. Why had the viscount allowed his garden to appear so untamed? Mayhap he hoped to entice butterflies—and Master Thomas—into it.

The thought spurred her up the pair of steps to the simple door. She let the brass knocker fall against it, hoping that someone would answer it before she was completely soaked.

The door opened. A lanky woman peered out and gasped,

"What are you doing out on such a frightful day? Do come in."

As she entered, Angela was careful she did not brush the woman, for the black-haired woman's bones were so sharp, Angela feared she would be cut. The foyer was as unadorned as the door. A single chair waited by the door. Framed paintings were hanging along the wall, shadowed by the dark day.

"You must be Miss Needham," the woman continued.

Startled, Angela said, "Yes, I am."

"Thought so. Master Thomas has been talking up a storm about you." She smiled and winked at Angela, astonishing her more. "I must say that the lad has a good eye for such a young sprig. Not that he looks at the ladies much, being still a lad, but he described you well." Her smile wavered as she tapped a long, bony finger against her gaunt cheek. "Or mayhap it was his lordship."

"Is Lord Harrington at home?" Angela asked, hoping her question would put a halt to the woman's discomforting comments. The idea that the viscount might have discussed her with his household was unsettling when she was already uncomfortable with calling on the viscount uninvited. Then, she reminded herself again that this was no social look-in.

"I am sure he will be glad to speak with you, Miss Needham." Taking Angela's wet cloak, she shook water from it gently and hung it on a peg that Angela had not seen by the door. Another set of pegs closer to the floor pushed out the hem of her cloak. "I am Mrs. Graves, his lordship's housekeeper. Come with me. I believe he is in his book-room. He usually is at this hour."

Although she would have preferred that the woman speak with the viscount before announcing her, Angela followed. The more quickly she completed her errand, the more quickly she could return to Oslington Court.

Mrs. Graves led her along the uncluttered hallway to an arch that opened into a room that offered an immediate sense of welcome. Several overstuffed chairs were pushed close to the walls and the wide window with dozens of small panes of glass in a rainbow of colors. Beams crisscrossed the ceiling, making it appear lower. A fire lilted to its own silent song on a hearth edged with blue and white tiles. In front of it, his stockinged feet propped on a three-legged stool, Lord Harrington sat. He stared at a piece of paper. With his coat tossed onto another chair, his hair appeared even darker against his high, white collar.

Angela knew she should not stare, but she could not halt herself. His strong features were highlighted by the glow from the hearth. As his forehead wrinkled when he turned the page over, a strand of hair fell forward. He ignored it, but her fingers trembled as they had by the gate. Not with disquiet now, but with an incomprehensible desire to smooth aside that vagrant strand.

Mrs. Graves cleared her throat, and Angela flinched. The housekeeper glanced at her as the viscount looked up. His expression changed rapidly from a smile to a taut astonishment as his gaze settled on Angela. Coming to his feet, he said, "Miss Needham, this is, indeed, a surprise."

"Am I interrupting something important?" Angela asked.

He glanced at the page he held, then placed it on a table by his chair. " 'Tis nothing of import. I own that I am overmastered at the idea of having you calling on such an afternoon." His smile returned, but it was a cool one. "Or any afternoon, to be honest."

"My errand is an important one," Angela answered with a coolness that matched his.

Lord Harrington motioned toward a chair where a bright red petit-point cushion leaned against the back. "Please be seated. I prefer to enjoy this fire and watch the storm through a window today. Mrs. Graves, I trust Miss Needham would like something to warm her. Brandy, Miss Needham?"

"My lord, I need to speak to you about—"

"About brandy? I had no idea you were a connoisseur of spirits and enjoyed talking of such things."

"Not brandy." Angela bit back her next words when she saw the twinkle in his eyes. He was jesting with her again in hopes of making her so ill-at-ease that she would bumble her way through this conversation. She must not allow him to have the upper hand. "I would prefer tea or hot chocolate."

"I believe Mrs. Graves has tea at the ready."

"Then tea would be fine."

He turned to his housekeeper. "Please bring tea for Miss Needham and me."

"Yes, my lord." The thin woman glanced back over her shoulder as she went back out into the dusky hallway.

Angela sat. Lord Harrington was so different from his neighbor. The duke had not made a humorous comment in her hearing, and it seemed that Lord Harrington was seldom serious.

She wondered if he had heard that thought, for his face took on somber lines as he picked up the paper he had been reading. Folding it, he placed it under a book on the table. Was he determined that she would not read it or did he simply not want it to be misplaced? She was curious what it might contain, but reminded herself that the viscount's concerns were not hers except when he helped Master Thomas ignore his guardian's decrees.

He took his chair and set his feet on the stool again. Wiggling his toes, he smiled. "Now, Miss Needham, you obviously are eager to tell me something. I can imagine no other reason why you would journey through this inclement weather to call upon me."

"Mr. Weare—the tutor at Oslington Court—"

"I have heard of the inimitable Mr. Weare."

"From Master Thomas, no doubt."

"No doubt."

Realizing he did not intend to make her task any easier, Angela squared her shoulders. "My lord, Mr. Weare is highly distressed."

"A most unfortunate set of circumstances."

"Yes." She would not let him change the course of the conversation with this feigned pity. "Most unfortunate for Master Thomas. It is not right for the boy to be false with his tutor by telling Mr. Weare that he is going to be taking a walk with me in the Court's gardens when he obviously

intended to slip away to spend time with you and your bizarre hobby."

"Collecting butterflies is not what I would term bizarre.
Carrying tales for a boy's tutor is."

She clasped her hands tightly in her lap. "I am carrying
no tales. I wish only to ascertain if Master Thomas is here.
If he is not, even you must own 'tis a matter of grave concern
for his guardian that Master Thomas is unaccounted for."

"So Oslington is not aware of Thomas's apparent bangers
about being with you instead of at his lessons?"

"No."

Lord Harrington rested his hand on the wooden arm of his
chair, but his fingers tapped it. She sensed he was hiding
something. Other than the fact that Master Thomas was or
had been here? That was no longer a secret. If Lord Harrington
was trying to conceal something else . . . She told herself not
to be fanciful. She should care only about finding Master
Thomas. She should not be thinking of how she was fascinated by the many moods conveyed by his expressive eyebrows.

"Of course, you are correct, Miss Needham. The boy
must spend his time with his tutor in order to get a basic
education. Do you wish me to speak with him?"

"He might listen to you as he will not to Mr. Weare or
his guardian."

"Or you?"

"He does not heed me, my lord. Nor should I expect him
to. I am not his governess."

"True. However, the lad has developed keen insight into
the people around him as well as the world around him."
He laughed. "My dear Miss Needham, please dispense with
that unflattering frown. I meant no insult to you. Only that
Thomas would be want-witted not to believe that you will
join forces with Oslington's other staff to prevent him from
coming here."

"As I should."

"That I shall not debate with you when you have heard
only Oslington's side of this argument."

"His Grace is Master Thomas's guardian. Not you."

"Do you always delight in repeating the obvious?" Standing, he gave her no chance to answer. "Mayhap you would like to see what your charge's brother has been up to in my laboratory here at Harrington Grange."

"I thought—"

"Capturing the butterflies is only part of the course of scientific study, Miss Needham." Holding out his hand, he said, "Allow me to show you what the lad is learning. Then you may wish to reassure Mr. Weare that Thomas's time is not completely wasted during his visits to the Grange."

"So he will join me in trying to persuade the duke to let Master Thomas come here on occasion?"

"I have already told you that no one has ever persuaded Oslington to do anything once he has set his mind upon a course of action. Not even logic will jostle him from that stance."

"Nor you from yours."

"That also is quite true. Shall we?"

She raised her hand to place it on his. As his long fingers closed over hers, she did not come to her feet. Instead she found herself lost once more in his green eyes, warm as the velvet on the chair where he had been sitting. After their previous conversations, she should have been inured to the powerful emotions in those enigmatic eyes, but each time she was held by them, she found it more impossible to escape. The warmth seeped through her, tingling along her skin to where his fingers held hers.

"Miss Needham?" he asked softly.

"Yes?"

"Shall we?"

Justin kept his smile to himself as Miss Needham blinked as if she were waking from a deep sleep. Too easily, he understood her reaction. His own clear thinking was muddied whenever he was in her company.

It made no sense because she was so blasted sensible. He had had enough of pragmatic people in his life. All those nosy souls who had a comment about anyone who did anything they deemed improper. After so many years of trying to please them, he had learned it was impossible without giving up all he was. So he had taken the biggest risk of his life, the one everyone said he would fail at. He had not, but the happiness at proving them all shortsighted had been too short-lived.

"Thank you," Miss Needham said as she stood.

"You are welcome, Angela."

Her head snapped up and her fingers froze where she had been dabbing at the wet spots on her skirt. The warm, wide pools within her eyes enticed him to explore more deeply. Again he was tempted to laugh. He might be foolhardy, but he was not fool enough to delve into them.

"I doubt you will convince young Thomas to change his mind any more quickly than you will Oslington," Justin said, keeping his smile cool. "I suspect we shall be having enough conversations to make it appropriate for me to call you by your given name and you to offer me the same intimacy."

She folded her arms in front of her, accenting her delightful curves. "You like trying to startle people with your ways and words, don't you . . . Justin?"

"Ah, you have discovered the truth with such speed." He laughed.

"It is not difficult when you make every effort to unsettle me."

"To the contrary. I wish only for you to be yourself as I take pride in being."

Her tone became prim when she said, "You were going to show me what work Master Thomas has been involved with here at Harrington Grange."

"Certainly." With a half-bow, he motioned toward the door.

"You know I must be honest with both Mr. Weare and the duke."

"Must you?"

Whatever she might have said was halted by Mrs. Graves returning with the tea tray. Asking his housekeeper to keep the quilted cozy over the pot so the tea would remain hot, he motioned again for Angela to precede him out of the room. By Jove, the sway of her skirts could catch the attention of a monk. And he was no monk. A wry grin tugged at his mouth. Or mayhap he had become one since his life had been turned inside out by the whims of cruel fate. He glanced toward the stairs. At this hour, Delicia would be taking her nap, so he could concentrate on one problem at a time.

All urge to smile disappeared. He wanted to think about the only true problem he had. Oslington's dictates to his wards did not matter as much as the recommendation from the latest doctor Justin had contacted. Under no circumstances would he put Delicia in an asylum. The child deserved better than that, although he was not sure how he could guarantee she would receive it.

"Justin?" Angela's impatient tone suggested she had spoken to him without him noticing.

"This way." He opened a door at the end of the corridor. He needed to get his thoughts under control with all due speed, and Angela's call must not waylay him from what was truly important.

Angela fought to keep from frowning. Justin had flouted the canons of Society, but he had never been so rude as to refuse to answer her question. And it had been an innocuous one about the drawing of a butterfly that was hanging on the wall.

As he gestured for her to precede him through the door, she ignored a twinge of disquiet about what his failure to answer might mean. Her eyes widened when she saw the trio of tables in the middle of a room that was smaller than his cozy book-room. On the tables were mounted butterflies and open books and drawing materials. She crossed the room to look at an easel where a half-drawn picture was unquestionably of a butterfly similar to the one Lord Harrington had pointed out to her the day after her arrival. The style matched the one she had seen in the hallway.

"Did you draw these?" she asked.

"Not me."

"Master Thomas?" She carefully picked up a finished

painting from the table. Tilting it toward the window, she marveled at the fragile lines of the butterfly's sketched wings. Even in the dim light, the watercolor tints on the outspread wings and the curve of the antennae had an aura of life. "This is wonderful."

"He has a true gift."

"I am sure if the duke knew of this, he would change his mind about Master Thomas studying with you."

"Oslington knows."

Angela lowered the painting and looked at Justin. His jaw was as rigid as Master Thomas's had been when she spoke to him by the gate. Glancing at the beautiful paintings, which exhibited both an artistic beauty and a technical perfection, she shook her head. "If His Grace saw one of these paintings, I cannot believe that he would not sanction Master Thomas continuing this work."

"I am quite certain that Oslington has seen the boy's work, and you know his decision." Justin's eyes were icy cold.

Slowly she turned away to put the painting back on the table. "I would be glad to speak to His Grace."

"You would be wasting your time."

"It is mine to use as I see fit."

"True." His shoulders sagged from their stiff pose. "Forgive me, Angela. You are not the one I should be furious with."

She glanced back at the paintings. "Master Thomas needs to have an opportunity to explore his talent."

"Your opinion and mine, but you shall never convince Oslington of that."

"I can try. There must be—"

"Nothing you can do." His smile returned, but was as cold as the duke's. "Don't you understand, Angela? You will not change Oslington's mind on any matter concerning me. Not ever."

Six

Angela hurried through the gracious foyer of Oslington Court and toward the stairs. She needed to talk with Mr. Weare about what she had learned about Master Thomas at Harrington Grange, but first she must sort out her thoughts. How could she express her thoughts to the tutor and Master Thomas's guardian and not appear to be helping Master Thomas ignore the duke's commands?

"Miss Needham," said a footman who rushed into the entry hall. "Master Thomas wishes to speak with you."

"He does?" Knowing her shock that Master Thomas had sought her out was unseemly, she took a steadying breath and asked, "Where?"

"On the glassed-in terrace, Miss Needham."

"Thank you." She paused. "Where is the glassed-in terrace?"

With the directions from the footman, Angela went through the twisting halls. She tried not to think that Master Thomas had conspired with the footman to get her lost. When she saw the lad waiting for her on a terrace enclosed by three walls of glass lined with the falling rain, Angela took a deep breath. This conversation would be no easier than the one with Justin. Both Master Thomas and the viscount were stubborn.

"I know Mr. Weare sent you to Justin's house in hopes

of catching me where I was not supposed to be," Master Thomas said in lieu of a greeting.

"That is true." She could be as forthright.

"I was not there."

"That is true, but it is also true that you have called there often since the duke requested that you stay away from Harrington Grange."

Master Thomas crossed his arms in front of him and raised his chin. "You should not be chasing after me. You are my sister's guardian angel." He paused, but she did not reply to the name he seemed to have decided to use whenever he wished to vex her. Disappointment blossomed in his eyes that he had not sent her up to the boughs. "I wish to know what you plan to say to Rodney about this."

"I plan to say that you are a talented artist and that your skills should be given a chance to be refined."

He stared at her in astonishment, and she knew this was not the answer he had expected. "Will you really? You really think I have talent?"

Angela smiled when his pose changed from a young tyrant to a child eager for a compliment. "Yes, Master Thomas, I think your work is exceptional. I would be glad to speak to your guardian about obtaining a drawing master for you." She paused, then added, "If you will recall your promise not to pay calls to Harrington Grange."

"That is blackmail."

"I am not trying to coerce you into doing something you should not do. I am trying to convince you to do what you should do."

"Obey such a jobbernowl order?" He flung out his hands in frustration, then jammed his fists against his hips.

"You told me that you promised your father that you would be true to your word, and you gave His Grace your word."

Master Thomas's lip quivered, revealing the vulnerable, grieving child beneath his cocky disregard. Tears filled his eyes. She took a step toward him, holding out her hand, but he backed away, once again defiant. "I do not need your pity."

"Good, because I was not offering it. However, you do need my friendship."

"I do not need that, either."

"You do, if you want an ally to help persuade His Grace that you have true talent as an artist."

"Why do you want to do that?"

Angela hesitated. She could not tell him the truth of how her own dreams of meeting a man who would travel the world with her had been squashed by her sister-in-law's assumption that Angela would be a servant in her brother's house. Banished to dusky corners when her brother and sister-in-law entertained, she had known that she must set aside that silly hope. She did not want Master Thomas to suffer the same disillusionment.

"It is what friends do," she replied simply.

He gave her another peculiar glance. She did not give him a chance to ask more questions. Walking back into the house, she sighed. This was going to be even more difficult than she had guessed when neither of them—Justin nor Master Thomas—trusted her.

Angela hoped today would be better than yesterday had been. Everything she had done, everything she had tried to do, had been far less than successful.

She went out onto the balcony opening from her bedchamber. The sun was barely over the horizon, but already the voices of servants drifted about the gardens. This was her favorite part of the day, a time before the hubbub began. Mayhap that was why she never had been able to keep to Town hours during her short Season. With a smile, she leaned on the railing. Mayhap it was as simple as she feared she would miss too much if she stayed abed even a minute longer.

Or was it that she wanted to avoid having another dream about Justin Harrington? Dash that man! He found a way into her thoughts far too often. His charming, lopsided grin that suggested he was no older than Master Thomas contrasted with the strong passions in his eyes, passions that belonged to a man. He seemed determined to do everything he could to unsettle her . . . and he was doing a fine job of it if her dream last night had been any example. She had been walking with him across the moor, looking for a rare butterfly. When, far from both his house and Oslington Court, he had drawn her into his arms, she had offered up her lips eagerly, wanting to sample his kiss.

She wrapped her arms around herself and shivered, although the sensation that raced through her was most definitely not cold. His touch had been heated and her response as fervid.

Was she out of her mind? Her employer insisted that his wards remain far from Harrington Court. He would not be pleased to discover the direction of her dreams.

"Don't be silly!" she chided herself. "One cannot control one's dreams." That was true, but her thoughts that wandered toward Justin too often when she was awake were being rebellious.

Angela's eyes were caught by someone waving wildly from a window set in the uppermost floor of a tower across a narrow court. Hearing a shout, she could not understand the words, but was sure it must be Miss Esther. She wondered how the solemn duke managed with such a flamboyant child. Then she recalled how little time he spent with the children. Otherwise he would have understood how talented Master Thomas was, as Justin did.

Egad! She had to put Justin Harrington out of her head.

She waved back and laughed when the little girl whistled before closing the window. There was something definitely delightful about such enthusiasm. She must find a way to make Miss Sutton and her family suitable to be welcomed into the *ton* without curbing their wonderful spirits.

Angela faltered in midstep. In disbelief, she realized Miss Esther's tune was the same one Justin had whistled during their walk beyond the gate the day after her arrival at

Oslington Court. Was Master Thomas the only one paying calls at Harrington Grange?

She tried to leave that thought behind her with all other thoughts about Justin as she went down the stairs to the breakfast-parlor on the east side of Oslington Court. Its wide windows were thrown open to the morning light, which washed over the surprisingly modest oak table that could seat no more than a dozen people. The sideboard was carved with leaping stags and vines and roses. Atop it awaited a generous selection of breakfast-foods.

An apple-cheeked woman popped into the room and smiled. "Good morning, Miss Needham," she said with a hint of a lisp.

"Good morning, Mrs. Seger." The cook had been one of the first to welcome her to Oslington Court.

Angela looked around the otherwise empty room, then back to the gray-haired woman wiping her hands on her apron. "Has Miss Sutton eaten?"

"She is taking her breakfast with the children in the nursery today." Mrs. Seger gestured toward the table. "Help yourself to breakfast while I bring you some coffee. Make it nice and dark, I do. His Grace likes it that way." With a friendly wink, she pointed to a pitcher. "There is cream if you want it less strong. Help yourself to some kippers and eggs. Biscuits and jam, too. If you do not mind me saying so, you are too thin, Miss Needham. It would be good for you to eat some food that would stick to your ribs."

"Thank you," Angela said when the garrulous cook paused to take a breath.

Only when Angela had taken a plate and started to fill it from the salvers on the sideboard did the cook seem satisfied. When the door had closed behind Mrs. Seger, Angela looked down at her plate with dismay. It contained twice as much breakfast as she customarily ate. She began to spoon some of it back into the serving platters when assertive footfalls echoed from the corridor.

Consternation cramped through her. If the duke saw her standing by the sideboard, putting eggs back like a naughty child, he would question anew his decision to hire her to be Miss Sutton's companion. She sighed and carried the plate to the table. It was her fault that she had allowed the cook to intimidate her. Now she must pay the price.

Angela was spreading sweet butter on a blueberry muffin when the duke entered. Under the arm of his dark green coat, he carried a newspaper. He nodded to her before serving himself. Setting the newspaper by his plate, he sat across from her. His eyes widened when he looked at the amount of food on her plate, but he said only, "I see you have made yourself quite at home here."

As heat rose along her face, Angela said, "I was unsure if I should wait for anyone else this morning. If—"

"We keep the hours we wish here in the country, as you have no doubt seen, Miss Needham." He opened the folded newspaper and raised it in front of him. "I trust you will eventually accustom yourself to our ways."

Angela could not tell if he was jesting, for the newspaper remained between them. His even voice gave no hint, and she wondered, despite Miss Sutton's assertions to the contrary, if this stern man ever smiled.

"Your Grace?" she asked.

"Yes." He still did not lower the newspaper.

"I wish to speak to you about Master Thomas."

"What has the boy done now?"

"Done?" She wished he would look at her instead of the tiny print on the pages between them. "I wish to speak to you of his drawing skills. Your Grace, he is very talented."

"So I understand."

"But I thought you had seen his work."

The duke finally lowered the newspaper and regarded her steadily. "Who told you that?"

"Just—" She bit back Justin's name, which would cause the duke's brows to lower even farther. " 'Tis just an assumption."

"Making assumptions is not a wise thing to do."

Heavy footsteps stopped by the doorway and halted Angela's answer. A generously proportioned woman wrung her hands over her dull gray uniform that matched the streaks in her hair. The keys at her side identified her as Mrs. Burkhardt, the housekeeper. She glanced at Angela, then, dampening her lips, said, "Your Grace, that beast is loose in the conservatory again."

Angela looked from the woman's scowl to the duke's newspaper. He did not lower it as he said, "Mrs. Burkhardt, send someone to have Esther remove it immediately. She knows there may be plants in the conservatory that would not agree with it."

"But, Your Grace, she—"

"Take the message yourself, Mrs. Burkhardt, if you feel she will heed you more than anyone else. If not, send for Mrs. Meyer. After all, it is her duty as governess to keep track of that imp." He raised the newspaper and, turning a page, leaned back in his chair. Without waiting to see if his orders were carried out, he added, "Miss Needham, I fear Esther has an endless aptitude for mischief."

Angela's gaze remained on the housekeeper, who was clearly torn between obeying the duke and urging him to help her. Taking pity on the poor woman, Angela said, "If you wish, Your Grace, I shall assist Mrs. Burkhardt."

"You?" He kept on reading, but she heard his amazement. "I believe you have scant idea of what an adventure you might be setting upon."

"Your Grace—"

The duke interrupted Mrs. Burkhardt again, "Do go and find Mrs. Meyer if you feel unequal to the task, Mrs. Burkhardt. Tell her that she should collect her charges and be done with this idiocy before the household is disturbed more."

Angela watched the housekeeper's face blanch as she edged out of the room. Staring at the newspaper's bold headlines, Angela asked, "What sort of beast does Miss Esther have?"

"A monkey."

"A monkey?" she gasped.

He set the newspaper on the table and sighed as if he

were greatly set-upon to have to speak to her during break-fast. "Miss Needham, you need not look so aghast. It is no great African ape. Merely a small monkey like those pos-sessed by many children in India."

Angela was unsure how to reply. Could it be that he was hoaxing her? She negated that thought, for she had seen no signs that the duke had a humorous bent. Even with the collection of children he had had foisted on him, he acted as if his household were very much an ordinary one.

Mayhap it was . . . to him.

"The beast runs tame about the house?" Angela asked.

"Climbs about the house would be a better description." He glanced at the newspaper and jabbed it with his forefin-ger. "By the heavens, here is yet another tale of the Prince Regent's wife's endless adventures on the continent. When will these papers realize no one cares about her behavior?"

"I trust the Prince Regent does."

He affixed her with a stern glower. "That, Miss Needham, goes without saying. Clearly the Prince Regent's concerns are the cause of this rigmarole."

When he bent to read the newspaper again, Angela re-leased the breath she had not known she was holding. What a bizarre place Oslington Court was! Not only was there an Indian monkey roaming freely, but the duke chided her for the poker-talk that had been enjoyed in London. She was beginning to despair that she never would get used to this curious family.

Before Angela could speak, Mrs. Burkhardt returned, her face even paler than before. "Your Grace, forgive me for another interruption."

"What is it now, Mrs. Burkhardt?" He grumbled some-thing else under his breath, but it seemed to be aimed at whatever he was reading.

"I fear the beast is still creating undue havoc in the con-servatory. Miss Esther is trying to retrieve him, but her ef-forts have been less than effective."

The duke pushed back his chair. "I shall talk to the child myself and remind her of her promise to watch over the creature. Come along, Miss Needham, so I may introduce you to your folly of believing you could handle this. You have only begun to find out what this household is truly like, I fear. The sooner you learn to deal with these crises, the sooner I may turn my attention to other concerns."

Angela rose, nodding, then paused. She was to be Miss Sutton's companion, not a governess to these ungovernable children. When she saw relief on the housekeeper's face, she realized that everyone in the house had been asked to try to restrain the youngsters. They had failed, and now Miss Needham was going to be given her chance to bring them to heel. That was fine, because this might give her the opportunity to persuade the duke to heed her about Master Thomas.

She simply must be cautious not to mention Justin's name. If she did, everything she was trying to do for Master Thomas would be ruined.

The conservatory was reached by going through another of the dark corridors, but its wide doors opened to a chamber built into the sunniest corner of the Court. Squeals of excitement welcomed Angela into a large room smelling of stagnant heat. Greenery sprouted wildly in every direction, and she wondered if the duke was trying to recreate India in here.

The gravel around the plants crunched, and Angela turned to see Miss Sutton running toward them. "Esther refuses to leave until Wallah is safe. Wallah will not come down while Esther is racing about."

"Wallah is the monkey," the duke said, staring through the overgrown garden.

"I suspected as much," Angela replied. When he glanced at her, astonishment on his face, she kept hers expressionless. Let him think what he wished about her cool answer. "Where is Miss Esther?"

"Behind the palm," Master Thomas replied, peeking out from behind a large bush.

Although Angela was not sure which plant was a palm, for the leaves were so tangled she could not tell where one began and the next ended, she followed Miss Sutton's finger that pointed to the left corner.

"Do come away, Seth," the duke said in a resigned voice. "Your shouts are sending the poor beast up to the highest boughs."

Miss Sutton giggled, but stifled the sound when the duke gave her the same glare he had shot at Angela. She blinked sudden tears, and Angela was astounded. She had not thought the vivacious young woman would be so cowed by her guardian. Then she realized how little, even after more than a week here, she knew about any of these people.

Seth ran to the duke and flung his arms around his guardian's legs while Miss Esther babbled about how the monkey had escaped from the nursery when she had been sure the door was shut. Hushing Miss Esther, the duke plucked the child from his legs. "Young man, there is no need to race after Wallah as if you are both being chased by a *bagh*." Glancing at Angela, he added as if an afterthought, "A tiger."

Angela's answer was silenced when the duke strode toward the tangled vines where the monkey could be seen at the top of the branches near the glass roof. He held up his hands and said something in a language she could not understand.

"Wallah always listens to him because Rodney speaks to him in Tamil," Miss Esther whispered. "Wallah misses India."

Putting her arm around the child's slim shoulders, Angela said, "I am sure the duke will persuade your pet to heed him today, too."

Miss Esther fired a vexed frown at her, then tugged away. She gave a joyous cry as she ran to where her guardian had coaxed her pet down. Taking the creature, she cradled it in her arms as if it were a baby. She turned to Angela while she cooed to the beast.

"Some people say he is ugly, but I think Wallah is pretty." She looked up at Angela, her large, blue eyes sparkling with the remnants of her fearful tears. "You think he is pretty, don't you, Miss Needham?"

"I doubt if there could be a prettier monkey," she said, not wanting to hurt the child's feelings by speaking the truth. The creature's face reminded her of a dried fig and its coat was matted with something that looked suspiciously like strawberry jam.

Angela put her fingers out to pat its head. When it spat, she leapt back. The children laughed. Mortified, she looked at the duke. He merely arched an eyebrow and started to walk out of the conservatory.

"Remember when the colonel came to visit and Wallah stole his quizzing glass?" Master Seth asked with a low chuckle. He tugged on Angela's skirt. "Do you wear blinkers, Miss—?" A perplexed expression crossed his face that still resembled the baby he must have been such a short time before.

"Needham," whispered Miss Esther.

"No, I do not wear glasses," she answered.

"Wallah does not like strangers," Miss Esther said unnecessarily.

"So Miss Needham can see, Esther," the duke replied. Without even a pause, he added, "Miss Needham, your comments about Thomas's artwork leads me to believe that *you* have seen his work."

"Yes, Your Grace." Why had he chosen this time when the children were listening to broach this subject?

"Where?"

"At Harrington Grange." She refused to be false. That would be a bad example for Miss Sutton and the others.

The duke glanced at Master Thomas, then turned back to Angela. "Your words, Miss Needham, suggest that you believe Thomas has skill in this direction."

"Yes, Your Grace."

"Under Harrington's tutelage?" He looked again at the boy.

Master Thomas nodded.

"I see." The duke clasped his hands behind his back. "It

seems that you have chosen, Thomas, to disregard my request that you not go to Harrington Grange. I see that, like your father, you insist on discovering the truth for yourself. Very well. If Miss Needham is willing, you may pay a call to Harrington Grange for two hours each week." He tapped his chin. "On Thursdays."

"Why that day?" Master Thomas asked.

"It fits well with your schedule and Mr. Weare's." He took a deep breath and released it slowly. "Will you give me your word on this, Thomas?"

Angela wanted to put her arm around the boy, who seemed to be torn between relief and despair. He looked at her and away as he said, "Yes, Rodney, you have my word on this."

"Good. If that is settled . . ." He turned toward the door.

"This will be fun," Miss Esther said. "Wallah will enjoy an outing. Isn't that right, Leonia?"

"Yes."

At Miss Sutton's distracted tone, Angela saw her charge watching the duke walk away. Miss Sutton's sigh was so low that Angela was sure only she had heard it. There was something amiss between the duke and his ward. It would behoove Angela to discover what it was and help heal the rift before their relationship became even more strained with the stress of the Season. If she did not, she suspected her sojourn at Oslington Court might come to an abrupt end.

Seven

Angela glanced at the clock on the mantel in the small parlor. Miss Sutton should have been here by now for her next lesson in deportment. If the lesson went well, Angela would use the rest of the afternoon to give Justin a look-in and explain the duke's offer. She tried to ignore the suspicion that there was a reason for the duke's choice of Thursday other than the convenience of the children's tutor. Accusing the duke of an ulterior motive would be unthinkable, so it would be better to ask Justin for an explanation.

When Miss Sutton did not arrive, Angela went in search of the girl. She had to ask a servant where Miss Sutton's private chambers were, for she realized she had never been there. The woman eyed Angela with candid curiosity, but explained that Miss Sutton's room was on the uppermost floor. The maid's gaze poked Angela's back until she went down the stairs toward the kitchen.

Angela climbed the stairs and was astounded to discover Miss Sutton's bedchamber was in the nursery wing along with the other children's. She knocked on the door, and it opened.

Miss Sutton smiled, motioning for her to come in. The small white room was not spartan, but contained little beyond a bed and a chest of drawers. Curtains on the pair of octagonal windows were of chintz, as was the coverlet on the bed. The bright splash of red flowers brightened the otherwise dreary room, but did not flatter either Miss Sutton's hair or the pink gown she wore.

"Let me get you a chair, Miss Needham," Miss Sutton said. "There is one in the nursery."

"Thank you." Her reply was to Miss Sutton's back, because the young woman ran into the nursery across the hallway.

Coming back, Miss Sutton could not hide her eagerness about what Angela might say first.

Angela smiled as she sat on the short chair that left her knees nearly to her chin. Folding her arms on them, she watched as Miss Sutton sprawled in an unladylike jumble across the bed. She was about to chide the young woman, but hesitated. If Miss Sutton's heart was as fragile as her siblings', Angela must be careful not to speak too harshly.

"You are late for today's class," Angela said, smiling. "I wanted to make certain nothing was amiss with you."

"Oh, dear! I was reading and lost track of the time."

"Reading is exemplary, but you must not skip your lessons."

"Do I have so much still left to learn, Miss Needham?" Miss Sutton asked.

Instead of answering with the obvious, Angela said, "The first thing is to move you out of the nursery."

Miss Sutton sat up, her eyes sparkling. "Do you think you can convince Rodney to let me do that? I have implored him repeatedly, but he has insisted I stay with the others."

"You no longer need Mrs. Meyer's supervision—"

"That hornet!"

"Miss Sutton! Comments like that are what persuade your guardian to treat you as a child. If you wish to be fired-off into society, you must practice restraint at all times. A member of the *élite* does not use such language about a servant."

"I have heard Rodney say worse."

"His Grace is a man," Angela answered, hoping her calm voice would hide her amazement. She could not imagine the duke reacting to anything so inconsequential. "He is excused such language. A lady must never speak so."

"What is London like? Is the Season as glorious as they say?"

"London is wonderful. You have never seen houses as wondrous as the ones along the squares when they are decorated for a *fête*."

"The buildings in India were grand and very old. Not that we saw them very often. We usually stayed within the compound."

Not wanting to let the conversation veer away to another topic, Angela said, "We must obtain the services of a good abigail. You have lovely hair, but you need a woman to help arrange it."

Miss Sutton clasped her arms around her knees. "Rodney offered to have one of the girls assist me. She was so bothersome that I sent her back to the kitchen. Although Mrs. Burkhardt said she would find me a replacement, I urged her not to. Will you help me?"

"For now." She smiled, not adding that a companion's duties were different from a personal maid's. "When you marry, you will need to supervise a whole staff of servants. Learning to deal with your abigail will help you."

Miss Sutton leaned across her bed again and rested her chin on her palms. "You know so much about what I need to know. You must have had a Season."

"I did."

"Then why aren't *you* married? You are quite pretty."

"Thank you."

"You are not answering my question."

Angela stood. "Because I have no answer other than I am not married because I have never met a man I wish to marry."

"What about Rodney?"

"The duke?" she gasped.

The young woman laughed. "You act so awed when you speak of him. You really should not be."

"He deserves the respect I offer him."

"That is true," she mused, as if confronting the idea for the first time. "You must realize, Miss Needham, that—"

"You may call me Angela, if you wish. After all, we shall be spending much time together, and I would have us be friends."

"I would like that, and you must call me Leonia. And stop calling my little brothers and sisters 'master' and 'miss.' " Two dimples punctuated her smile.

"That is the proper address."

"True, but we are accustomed to the informality of family. Seth, in particular, is bothered by it."

"As you wish." Angela would relent on this, because she needed to concentrate on more important lessons with Leonia.

"As I was saying, you must realize, *Angela,* that I have known Rodney almost all my life. He was Papa's secretary in the sepoy company. They went on a few campaigns, but usually they were garrisoned at Fort St. George."

"Where is that?"

"Near Madras on the southeast coast." She sat and wrapped her arms around her knees again, and Angela began to despair that she would never teach Leonia to sit still.

Mayhap contemplating the task would push thoughts of Justin out of her head. Angela frowned at the thought. She must not let the eccentric viscount keep sneaking into her mind.

Leonia continued, "I know both Papa and Rodney were frustrated that their unit was seldom called to defend the East India Company. When Mama died several years ago— Seth was just a baby—Papa seemed more content to stay in garrison."

"But the duke never was?"

"Never." She shook her head. "Thank goodness he was there when Papa was hurt." Lowering her eyes, she whispered, "I am sure you know that Papa died because of a bizarre accident. Who would have guessed that his horse would panic at the sight of a runaway bull and throw him?"

Sitting on the narrow bed, Angela put her arm around Leonia, whose cheeks were lined with sudden tears. "You need say no more of it."

Leonia turned her head against Angela's shoulder. "I want to speak of Papa. Rodney refuses to. He leaves the room if one of us mentions Papa. I know he looks at us and remembers Papa and their friendship. That makes him sad. I believe he mourns Papa's death more than his own father's." Raising her head, she added, "Rodney came—even before Papa's funeral—to oversee our household, although it was not necessary. Our *ayahs* would have helped us."

"*Ayahs?*"

"The maids in our household. Rodney refused to let us be alone. He was sure he would be appointed to succeed Papa, but word came from England that *his* father had died. Rodney was now the Duke of Oslington with responsibilities here."

"So he sold his commission and returned?"

"With us." She ran her fingers across the coverlet. "He takes his appointment as our guardian seriously."

"As he does everything."

Leonia's eyes widened. "Serious? Rodney?" She laughed, startling Angela. Sliding across the bed, she set herself on her feet. "You have seen him only as he is now. You should have known him before he took on the burden of us. I daresay Rodney was the most dashing officer in Fort St. George. He has a lively wit, and I never danced with a man who possesses his grace."

Angela tried to readjust her appraisal of the duke. The somber man did not seem the type to whisper court-promises to the ladies when he asked them to stand up with him. Even more bizarre was the thought that he might be as unhappy here as the children. His stern façade could be a shield to conceal his pain. Any man who took on the obligation of four high-spirited children and gave up a career he had devoted years to must have more to him than the spiritless wraith who hid behind the newspaper at breakfast.

"If you have such insight into His Grace's thoughts," Angela said when Leonia paused in her praise of her guardian, "you should be able to charm any young rogue interested in finding a wife."

"I am not sure I want a husband now."

"You are young, but obviously His Grace feels the time has come for you to consider buckling yourself to a husband."

"Thomas wishes for me to marry Lord Harrington."

Angela flinched. She could not halt herself as she imagined Leonia as Justin's bride. It could heal whatever breach there was between the duke and Justin. Yet, the idea bothered her. She did not want to explore why, because the very idea led her in the dangerous direction of recalling her dreams of being in his arms.

Leonia nodded as if Angela had spoken. "You are right to be upset. Because Thomas likes Lord Harrington is no reason for me to marry that air-dreamer. After all, Rodney has told us that the viscount is not fit company for any of us."

"Why?"

With an indifferent shrug, she said, "It does not matter. Rodney must have a good reason. He always does." She clenched her hands by her sides. "Let Thomas leg-shackle himself to that widgeon. I shall not!"

She ran from the room in a flurry of pink muslin to leave Angela more betwattled than ever.

When Angela drew the pony cart to a stop before the gate to Harrington Grange, she was certain her appearance was more fitting than during her last call in the drenching rain. She appreciated Mrs. Meyer's offer of the cart, even though Angela had not told the governess where she planned to go.

She lashed the reins to an iron ring on the wall and opened the heavy gate. An extravagance of color welcomed her into the house's chaotic front garden. On a stool by the door, a little girl, her raven curls contrasting with her white dress, rocked a doll on her knee.

Angela smiled. The child could be no older than Seth, but Angela could not imagine the boy playing so quietly. "Good afternoon," Angela said as she came closer.

The little girl did not look at her.

"Good afternoon," she repeated.

Again the little girl did not reply.

Angela tapped her on the shoulder. With a gasp, the child jumped to her feet and stared at her, her hazel eyes wide in shock.

"I am sorry if I disturbed you," Angela said with a smile. "I—"

The child turned and fled into the house. The door slammed.

Angela sighed. She had not meant to alarm the child.

The door opened again. Mrs. Graves peered out and tried to smile. "Good afternoon, Miss Needham. His lordship is out, but I expect him back soon. Would you like to wait?"

"If I may use the time to apologize to the little girl I just frightened." Angela lifted her hand to her waist. "About this high."

"Oh, you must mean Delicia."

"What a charming name! And it is perfect for such a shy child. Is she your daughter?"

Mrs. Graves wrinkled her apron. "Will you sit, Miss Needham?" She motioned with her head toward a cast iron bench set within an arbor.

Angela could not mistake the disquiet in the house-keeper's voice. Bees buzzed through the flowers on the vines, but Mrs. Graves said nothing while Angela sat.

"Miss Needham, I had thought that you would have known by this time. Few things stay quiet in this shire."

"Known what?"

"About Lord Harrington's tragedies."

"What sort of tragedies?" she asked. She had never guessed that Justin's easy grin hid anything but his needle-wit.

"About Delicia and her mother."

"He is married?" That odd, wrenching sensation twisted through her as it had when Leonia spoke of marrying him.

"Was. His wife died more than five years ago, right after Delicia was born. It has not been easy for his lordship to raise such a child alone, so she was often with his mother until the dowager viscountess died last year."

Angela recalled how during her first visit to Harrington Grange, Justin had been perusing a page while he wore a troubled expression. Had that been about his daughter?

"He must be delighted to have his daughter with him again," she said when she realized Mrs. Graves was waiting for some sort of response.

The housekeeper crossed her stick-thin arms on her chest. "Do not think that I am overstepping myself, Miss Needham, when I say 'tis time she came here. This is where the poor lamb belongs."

"With her father."

Mrs. Graves's forehead threaded in bafflement. "I meant here in the country where she can grow up without being an embarrassment to him."

Angela knew she should keep her tongue in her head, but she asked, "Why do you say that? She is a beautiful child and a gentle one as well. I could see that from the way she handled her doll."

"I am only speaking the truth. There is no place for that poor, deaf child in a decent household in Town."

"Deaf?" Rising, Angela kneaded her fingers together. "That explains why she was so startled when I touched her. She did not hear me."

"Her grandmother kept her away from strangers to protect the child from the cruelty of pity."

"Pity? That is the last thing she needs." Angela shuddered as she recalled saying nearly the same thing about the Sutton children. "Delicia needs to be with other children."

"That is impossible."

"Of course it is possible."

"Miss Needham, that is her papa's decision."

Knowing she should not probe more with the housekeeper, Angela whirled as she heard the gate creak. Justin strode along the walk, carrying his net and basket. When he saw her, he smiled and waved.

"How could you be so heartless?" she demanded.

His smile faded as he looked from her to Mrs. Graves. The housekeeper mumbled something as she went into the house. Tossing his butterfly net and the basket onto the wall, he asked, "Can I believe you might once greet me with something as mundane as a 'good afternoon?' "

Angela flushed. Caught up in her shock about Delicia Harrington, she had let her mouth rule her head. "Good afternoon."

"Good afternoon, Angela. May I inquire what has brought you here today?"

"His Grace has agreed to allow the children to make a call here for two hours on Thursday afternoons—"

"Dashed benevolent of him, knowing as he apparently does that I often go on Thursdays into the village to have tea with the vicar and talk about the study of nature. I shall change the day for our discussion and accept Oslington's paltry benevolence."

"He is more benevolent than you are!" Angela fired back.

"You are in quite a pelter today, aren't you?" He laughed without humor.

"I find it unconscionable that you are imprisoning your daughter behind these walls."

Justin took off his hat and set it on the wall. Resting one booted foot beside it, he arched a single, ebony brow. She did not want to admire how smooth each motion was and how his arms, which had held her so close in her dreams, were now crossed across his broad chest. "I trust by your heated words that you have met Delicia."

"Met her and learned of the poor child's situation. Mrs. Graves was kind enough to enlighten me."

"You should know that Mrs. Graves does not speak for me."

"I should have, but . . ."

He smiled grimly. "It appears Mrs. Graves has convinced you to share her conviction that I am hiding Delicia because I am ashamed of her."

"Yes." Angela bit her lip. "Mayhap I have jumped to conclusions unwisely."

His voice hardened. "Mayhap you have. I should have guessed that you would have little pity for anyone you thought had abandoned a child. Apparently you have developed the same pity for the Sutton children, for, in spite of the fact Oslington has a governess and a tutor to oversee the education of his wards, you seem to have taken them on your own responsibility."

"The topic of this conversation is your child, not—"

He gave a terse laugh, then sat on the wall. Looking up at her, he did not apologize for his lack of manners. Instead he said, "I have not abandoned my child. Not now. Not before. I sought the best medical care for her after the fever claimed my wife and left Delicia without her hearing. When I learned there was nothing that can be done, I brought Delicia back here, although she often visited her grandmother, whom she adored. Since my mother died, Delicia has stayed here all the time with me."

"With you, yes." She did not wait for an invitation, sitting beside him as she asked, "But why won't you allow her to play with the Sutton children?"

"Me allow?"

"I told you," she said with rare exasperation, "His Grace has consented for the children to pay calls on Thursday afternoons. If *you* agree, they may call here. Delicia and Seth are nearly of an age. They could—"

"What? Play? Can you imagine Delicia with them?"

"Yes."

He stared at her with astonishment. "I thought you were a practical woman, but I clearly was wrong. Delicia cannot hear. She cannot speak. She certainly cannot take part in any games."

"How do you know?"

"I . . ." His smile did not lessen the iciness of his green eyes. "I understand your ploy. You wish me to say 'I don't know.' Then you can persuade me to let the children play together."

Angela rose. Her gaze remained locked with his as he

stood. "Why not try once? It cannot hurt. Say yes, and I shall bring the children to call on Thursday next."

He took her hand. When he raised it to his lips in a gentle, questing caress, she was sure a flood of warmth had dissolved every bone within her. A soft gasp bubbled from her as he placed a swift kiss on each knuckle of her fingers.

Just as he had in her dream . . .

Unnerved by the sudden yearning to be even closer to him, Angela drew her hand away. She struggled to make her voice sound serene, but—as she saw the knowing smile on his face—she knew he had sensed her pleasure with his touch. Just her pleasure . . . or his, too?

"If you will say yes, Justin, I am sure the children will be delighted to call upon your daughter."

"Bring them on Thursday," he said softly. "I see getting into a brangle with you is useless. You have a delightful method of getting your way."

Angela nodded and turned to leave, fearful of what might happen if she lingered so close to him in the empty garden. As she reached for the gate, he called her name.

She turned to discover him right behind her. Taking a step back, she paused before her gown could snag on the vines twisting along the wall. "Yes, Justin?"

"You make it easy to say yes to things I have not considered for many years." He smoothed a strand of her hair back beneath her bonnet.

"We should not be talking like this. Without a chaperon, we—"

He laughed as the door opened, and his daughter rushed out to embrace his legs just as Seth had the duke's. Setting one hand on Delicia's hair, he put his other under Angela's chin. He tipped her face closer to his. "We have a chaperon now."

"A little girl."

"But a little girl who reminds me that I should not put into action the thoughts I had when I saw you here amid my overgrown garden."

"Thoughts?" She should not let this conversation continue, but she could not bear to bring it to an end when she was able to look up into his emerald eyes.

"Do you really wish to know how I could not decide if I would rather admire your pretty lips or your prettier curves? Do you want me to say how I cannot wait for the next time your eyes snap at me with fury because your fiery spirit enthralls me? Do you want me to say anything?" He bent toward her as his fingers trailed up her cheek. "Or do you want to be done with talk altogether?"

Delicia pushed between them, and Angela stepped back. The child might not be able to hear or speak, but she seemed to understand the inherent danger of Angela remaining so close to her father. She gazed up at Angela with an expression that matched Justin's most obstinate one.

Kneeling, Angela said, "Delicia, I am sorry I startled you."

"She cannot hear you." Pain blared from his voice.

"I know, but she can read what is on my face."

"You can only assume that. At least one of the doctors we took her to believes that she has no more wit than a rambunctious pup."

"Nonsense!" She kept her smile in place, but Delicia pressed back against her father's legs. Coming to her feet, Angela added, "Do you need further proof? She must be able to discern something because she just reacted to the anger that must be in my eyes."

"They are snapping in righteous fury." His frown eased into the cockeyed smile that did such strange and wonderful things to her heartbeat. He cupped her elbow and drew her nearer again.

Once more, she drew back, although she had to fight every longing in order to force her feet to move. "I need to return to Oslington Court. Leonia is expecting me to give her another lesson today." That was not the truth, but she could not speak the truth of how she yearned to slip into his arms and to stay there more than a few moments.

"Thursday then?" he asked, reaching over Delicia's head to curve his fingers along Angela's cheek.

"Yes."

"I will look forward to Thursday then." He gave her the teasing wink that had irritated her before.

Angela hurried through the gate. As she stepped into the cart and sent it back toward Oslington Court, she was glad that—for once—she had not spoken the words battering her lips. Then he would have known how disappointed she was that he had kissed only her fingers. She would be a fool to let *that* dream come true.

Eight

Justin dropped into the garden on the far side of the wall that surrounded Oslington Court. Wiping dirt from his hands, he chuckled quietly. He had not guessed he would ever sneak over that wall again.

Looking around, he saw that little had changed since he had last come here. The hedges might be an inch or two taller. The trees in the orchard were more gnarled with age, but the pond and the ducks and a pair of aristocratic swans were the same as they had been when he was a boy. The same as they probably had been since this house had been raised and its gardens built to hold back the wild moor hundreds of years before.

He strained for any sound. From the right, he could hear the voices of the stablemen. He sought a different voice, one that was higher in pitch and stirred his blood far hotter than it should. Thomas had told him that Angela often took a walk in the gardens during the afternoon.

The orchard would offer no shield from anyone looking out the windows of the grand house, so he walked along the hedges toward the white garden. Or it had been the white garden when he last had visited here . . . could it be over five years ago? That one attempt to ease the enmity had been thrown back in his face. He had vowed not to return.

He would not have, either, if he had not had a compelling reason to call here. Again he glanced at the house that hunkered down on its garden like a great stone monster that had climbed out of some break in the moor.

"What are you doing *here?*"

At the gasp in the voice he had been hoping to hear, Justin smiled at Angela. She was a pattern-card of prettiness with her tawny hair refusing to remain beneath her bonnet that tied beneath her chin with ribbons the exact sapphire of her eyes. Her light blue gown had a hint of a green stain just over her left ankle, so it must have brushed against one of the bushes.

"Justin!"

Was that impatience that he had not answered or distress that he was here in her voice? He pulled his gaze from the beguiling sight of that green spot flowing over her slender ankle to meet her wide eyes. "Good day, Angela."

Taking his arm, she tugged in the direction of the front gate. "His Grace has made it more than clear to the children that you are not welcome here."

"I did not come here to see the children. Nor did I come here to see Oslington. I came here to see *you.*" He led her past the hedge to where he knew a low stone wall edged a drop to a pool. He sat and drew her down to sit beside him, out of view of anyone in the house. "Angela, I know I overstepped the boundaries of propriety when you last called at Harrington Grange."

"Yes, you did. A gentleman would never have . . ." Angela looked away when the twinkle reappeared in his eyes. "You did not come here to apologize, did you?"

"I did nothing for which I am sorry. I have come seeking you to discover if you can say the same."

"For what do you think I should be sorry?"

"That you rushed away so quickly."

"If I had stayed, who knows what might have happened?"

"Exactly."

She could not keep from staring at him in amazement. His slow, easy smile matched the warmth in his eyes. He was like no one else she had ever met. Instead of calling to offer his abject contrition for bringing her into his arms, he dared her to own that she had wanted to stay there.

"You are a prime rake, Justin Harrington."

"Not for many years." He chuckled. "Mayhap never, for I was never one for dallying with a young woman unless there was interest on my part."

"And have you changed?" She put her fingers to her lips, shocked at her own outrageous question.

With another laugh, he drew her fingers away and folded them between his. "There are those who will tell you that I have never changed, that I was always an air-dreamer who thought less about nothing-sayings and the gossip at my club than I did of my interest in butterflies."

"An interest you have inspired in Thomas."

"Actually, Thomas was studying a butterfly when I first met him. I was amazed that he knew the species of the butterfly he had captured, both its English name and in Latin. Then I saw his sketches, and I was further impressed with his skill." He glanced at the house, then back to her. "I offered to teach him more about butterflies if he would teach Delicia to draw."

"So Thomas has already met your daughter?"

"Of course. As many times as he has been to Harrington Grange, it would have been peculiar if he had *not* seen her."

"Why didn't you mention her to me before?"

He stroked her hands, but the intensity had returned to his voice. "Mrs. Graves denounces me as overprotective of Delicia, but I will do what I can to safeguard her from the cruel comments of others. She may not be able to hear them, but you are right. She seems to be a good judge of what is being said by reading a person's expression."

"Do you think I would have been cruel?"

"No." He laughed wryly. "You have opened your heart to the Sutton children as if they were your responsibility instead of Oslington's."

"But you do not trust me."

"It is not that, either." Shrugging his shoulders, he said, "I think rather it has been that you and I seldom speak of anything but the rift that has kept the Sutton children imprisoned behind these walls."

Angela frowned. "That is not true. They are quite free to go wherever they want."

"Even to Harrington Grange for a sparse two hours one afternoon each week."

"We will be able to call only if I can persuade Esther to leave her monkey here at Oslington Court." She shuddered. "Do you realize Esther insists on taking that creature in a perambulator on our walks about the garden?"

"I understand that Wallah is very dear to her."

"I know the beast was given to her by her papa. Yet she risks its safety when she takes it outside. It runs away all the time, and it pays no attention when she calls it. She would be better off to have a dog."

"Do you know what the word 'wallah' means?"

"I assumed it was an Indian name."

"It is an Indian word, not a name. Thomas told me it means 'person.' From what he has said, that is how Esther thinks of her monkey. As another person. You are asking the impossible if you suggest that she set the beast aside."

With a sigh, she said, "I try to understand her affection for it, but I find it difficult when the creature spends half its time doing things too disgusting to discuss."

Justin laughed. "My dear Angela, you are charmingly naïve."

"I know."

"You do?"

She pulled her hand from between his as she flung them out. "There is so much of the world I wish to see and learn about. I would like to see it all."

"I have seen enough to be glad to be at Harrington Grange where I can immerse myself in the life I have chosen."

"That is fine as long as you do not stay here simply to hide."

"Hide?" He shook his head. "I have nothing to be

ashamed of, Angela. If Oslington has told you otherwise, you should not heed him. He is—"

"My employer." She came to her feet. "A fact I should not forget. As he does not wish you to call here, I must ask you to leave."

"After." He stood.

"After what?"

"After this." He grasped her arm and spun her up against his chest. His mouth covered hers before she had a chance to protest.

But she did not want to protest. As he kissed her gently, she wanted to be nowhere else but here. Her arms curved up around his shoulders as he deepened the kiss until she could not still the quivers rushing along her. She had imagined being kissed, but her fantasies had been insipid imitations of this splendid delight.

When he raised his lips away, she did not step back. She reached up and ran her finger along one of his dark brows. He smiled, tilting his head to press his lips to her palm. That sent a surge of the feverish fire through her again, but it was not what she yearned for. She guided his mouth back to hers. He tugged her to him, even tighter, until she was unsure if the frantic heartbeat throbbing through her was hers or his.

She eased away, dazzled by the emotion sweeping over her. Her breath thudded in her ears, and she had to fight her desire to rush back into his arms. When he uncurled his fingers along her cheek, she closed her eyes and savored the rough texture of his skin.

At a childish squeal, Angela stiffened. She could not move before Esther came around the hedge, racing after her monkey. Grasping Justin's arm, Angela pointed toward the gate. Oh, why had he lingered here? She should have insisted as soon as she saw him here that he leave posthaste.

She gasped in astonishment as Wallah jumped up onto her arm and raced along it to perch on Justin's shoulder. She reached for the monkey, but it shrieked at her as it buried its face in Justin's hair.

"Don't hurt him!" Esther cried as loudly as the monkey's shriek.

"Me or your pet?" Justin tried to untangle the monkey's tail from around his neck.

"Wallah is just showing you how much he likes you."

Angela said, "Esther, convince Wallah to go with you. Lord Harrington must be on his way."

"Yes, he must," said the duke, coming around the shrub. "We do not welcome trespassers at Oslington Court, Harrington."

"Is *this* your way of proving that? Setting monkeys upon them?" Justin returned, a cold tone that Angela had never heard tightening his voice. Squatting, he added, "Miss Sutton, if you will please retrieve your pet, I would be greatly in your debt."

Esther faltered, looking up at her furious guardian. When Angela motioned to her, she edged closer and picked up Wallah. The monkey clung to her and chattered.

"Thank Lord Harrington for helping you keep Wallah from escaping from you again," Angela murmured.

"Thank you, Lord Harrington," Esther said, oddly dutiful.

"Take Wallah back inside."

Esther nodded and rushed toward the house.

Angela wished she could follow because the rage between the two men was almost visible. They stared at each other like hissing cats seeking any weakness. When she started to speak, Justin put his hand on her arm.

"I will take my leave, Oslington," he said.

"You will not return."

"I have no interest in returning, but I want you to understand that no one within these walls invited me. When I chanced upon Miss Needham, I took the opportunity to engage her in conversation." Turning, Justin did not smile at Angela. "Until we have a chance to speak again." He picked up her hand and bowed over it as if they were the least of acquaintances. Out of view from the duke, his thumb stroked her palm in a sinuous circle. "Good afternoon."

"Good afternoon." She struggled to keep her voice even, but it wavered on the two words.

Justin walked away.

The duke said nothing as he watched his neighbor disappear among the bushes that framed the garden. He looked at Angela. "Miss Needham, I will see you in my book-room for tea this afternoon."

"Your Grace, I would be glad to discuss this with you now."

"Now would not be wise." His mouth worked as he looked in the direction Justin had walked. "Not wise at all. By tea, I shall be composed enough to speak to you of this unfortunate incident." He walked toward the house.

Angela sank back onto the low wall. The duke was enraged to discover his hated neighbor here with her and Esther. He was sure to demand an explanation, and she must give him one that would keep him from turning her off from Oslington Court.

But what could it be? To speak the truth would guarantee that she was banished back to London. She closed her eyes and clasped her hands together over her heart. She would be condemned to return in disgrace to her brother's house. And, so much worse, she might never see Justin again.

The book-room was nearly lost to the soft hush of a twilight that claimed it. Sunlight had been banished to hide beyond the thick drapes drawn at the windows. With the servants retired on the far side of the green baize-covered doors to their section of the house and the children confined to the nursery and their teatime rituals, Angela could believe she was the only living soul in Oslington Court. Although Hervey had not abandoned his obligation to wait outside the book-room for the duke's next command, the butler seemed as ancient and unmovable as the stone walls of the house.

The duke looked up from his book when Angela entered the book-room. She was struck anew by the contrast between him and Justin. Even in the informal privacy of his book-room, the duke wore a dark brown coat, his collar held tightly in place by an elegantly tied cravat. He did not rest his feet on a stool, but sat as straight as if he were watching his company pass by on parade.

"Miss Needham," he said with a nod as he set himself on his feet.

"Your Grace, if this is a convenient time, I would like to speak to you."

"If this is about this afternoon and . . ." He grimaced, and she guessed he did not wish to speak Justin's name. "I have given the incident much thought, and I find that I have no wish to discuss that matter further as long as you assure me that you had no foreknowledge of Harrington's visit."

"No, Your Grace." She kept her eyes lowered, glad that he could not read her thoughts within them. Did her eyes still glow with her delight at Justin's kiss? Had they been alight with elation when she had stood between the two men in the garden? Impossible! She had been so distressed then that there should have been no hint that she had been in Justin's arms, his lips over hers. Now the joy was like a slow-boiling pot within her, a bubble rising now and then, unbidden, from her very center to spread a smile across her face. She must not let her own happiness betray her.

"Esther told me that you had asked Harrington to leave."

"Yes, Your Grace." How much else had the little girl been privy to? If Esther had seen Angela in Justin's arms, surely she would have mentioned that to her guardian.

"Then I have nothing else to say to you on this."

Angela nodded, knowing that she had been given a reprieve from being sent from Oslington Court in disgrace. "Thank you, Your Grace." She hesitated and raised her eyes toward his, unsure if he wished her to leave.

He flinched as their gazes met. He looked at his book, then back at her, once more composed. "I should ask you, I collect, for a report of how Leonia is progressing with her lessons."

"She has mastered the art of paying calls with ease, and we are working on developing her skills with conversation."

The duke motioned for her to be seated. When she was perched on the very edge of a green settee, he took his chair again. The tea tray was on a table beside him, but he did not reach for the pot. "I am pleased to hear that. She will need to know every intricacy of what is expected of a young woman when she goes to Town."

"We have had our sessions at least twice a day, but she needs to practice those skills with someone other than the members of this household. She should call on your neighbors."

"She is my ward, and many of the ladies in the shire possess a higher rank than her late father's. They should call here first."

Angela smiled. "So I told Leonia when she asked me impatiently when she could begin to use her *cartes des visites,* which arrived yesterday. She informed me that many of your feminine neighbors called shortly after her arrival at Oslington Court. No doubt, they are waiting for her to return the calls."

He picked up his book, obviously desirous of returning to his reading, and tapped his fingers on its spine. "Then do what is required, Miss Needham, to initiate the process. I trust you will oversee Leonia's calls."

"Certainly. They will be simple, for she has yet to have her coming-out." She smiled and rested her elbow on the arm of the chair. "I suspect that she will do little more than leave her card to announce her call."

With a low chuckle, he crossed one leg over the knee of his pale breeches. "Pray do not suggest that I set up a weekly at-home to welcome Leonia's callers here."

"She must learn how—"

"Spare me the intimate details, Miss Needham. I have weathered a Season or two, so you need not try to teach me what I already know. If you deem it a necessity, Leonia may have an at-home once a month here for any of the gentry in the shire."

Angela hesitated, knowing she chanced destroying the

small gains she had won, but she asked, "Any of the gentry?"

The duke's smile vanished, as she had feared. "You know who is welcome and who is not."

"Does that mean that you do not wish the children to call at Harrington Grange as you offered?" She hoped once more that her face did not reveal the truth. She could not let the duke view her dejection at the thought of not seeing Justin tomorrow.

"Quite to the contrary, Miss Needham." He set himself on his feet. "As I told you, I have given this matter much thought. 'Tis my opinion that if I allow the children to call on Harrington, they will soon grow bored with visiting him. I recall from my own youth that, for a child, what is prohibited becomes enticing."

"That is true." Wishing he did not stand in front of her, his hands folded behind his back, as if she were a raw recruit under inspection, she said, "You have told me you wish the children to have a normal English childhood. Part of that is learning to get along with their neighbors."

"*Other* neighbors are more appropriate to be receiving my wards." He frowned. "Mayhap I am wrong in thinking they will grow bored with visiting *him*."

"May I ask what the source of the enmity is between you?"

"I will not bother you with all the dreary details. Suffice it to say that he has proven too many times that he is not a man of honor. That he has persuaded Thomas to break his word is another example of how cheap he considers any vow."

Angela tried to grasp for any words to reply. She should say something. Anything. But she could not agree with the duke, for she had learned today of the agreement for Thomas to teach Delicia Harrington to draw. Thomas would have considered that offer an obligation he could not ignore. Defending Justin would be silly. So many questions pelted her lips, but she did not speak one. The duke's comments suggested that he had no interest in answering them. She should concentrate instead on the other issue—the children calling at Harrington Grange.

"Your Grace, I believe, if you do not make an issue of this," she said before the duke could persuade himself to change his mind, "you soon shall discover visiting Harrington Grange is no longer a point of contention between you and Thomas. He is eager to gain your respect, and he would very much like to show off his art for you. It would mean so much to him." She took a deep breath. "More than showing it off to Lord Harrington, for the boy admires you greatly."

His face lost its hard edge as he sighed and walked toward the window. "You seem to have much more insight into a child's mind than I do. However, you know less about a man's."

"I know you would be forcing the children to violate your rules by putting a treat in front of them and then denying them the chance to sample it." This time, she did not lower her gaze from his scowl. "As you felt when you were kept in garrison while other units had the chance to defend the East India Company's interests."

"I apparently was wrong, Miss Needham," he said. Pinning her in place with his ebony gaze, he smiled. "You do know the state of a man's mind. Very well. You may tell the children—including Leonia—that they may call on any of our neighbors, as I previously agreed, each Thursday afternoon for two hours, but only under your direct supervision."

"Mine? Your Grace, I—"

"Yours, Miss Needham." His smile grew taut. "You know, as I do, Mrs. Meyer is a blithering cabbage-head who is overmastered by the children. I can trust her to govern the nursery, but I am sure that she will make a jumble of a matter as delicate as this. I do not want Leonia making a bad first impression on those she will encounter again in London. Do you accept my terms?"

Sure that she was being manipulated, but having no idea how to convince him to change his mind about Mrs. Meyer taking the younger children on their calls, Angela said, "You leave me little choice."

"I leave you many choices. You may disagree with my terms and keep the children away from Harrington Grange as I requested in the first place."

"I find that choice even less acceptable, for I know it will create more problems for this household."

"So?"

"I will oversee the children when they call on your neighbors."

"Save for Leonia, who may make her calls as you see fit, the children may make their calls only on Thursday afternoons for no more than two hours."

Knowing she had to be grateful that she was being given this duty instead of being sent from Oslington Court, she whispered, "Yes, Your Grace, save for Leonia, the calls will be only on Thursday afternoons for no more than two hours."

When he smiled, she wondered if this was what he had intended all along. If so, especially in the wake of the icy words in the garden this afternoon, she did not understand why.

Nine

The room Angela chose for Leonia's new bedchamber was cramped with furniture that waited to find its rightful place between the one long window and the smaller one with its stained glass throwing a pattern of light across the rolled-up rug. As Angela worked with Mrs. Burkhardt to supervise the arranging of the bed, the tables, chairs, and dressing table, Leonia whirled about the room like a feckless windstorm, getting in the servants' way and asking dozens of questions Angela had no time to answer.

"Leonia, why don't you get some flowers from the garden to brighten your room?" Angela suggested. "Some daisies. They will look lovely with your yellow rug."

"But, Angela, I want to watch!"

With a laugh, she tugged Leonia toward the door. "You must trust Mrs. Burkhardt. You have given her your instructions. Now allow her to see the servants fulfill them." Linking her arm with the girl's, Angela smiled. "While you are in the garden, I shall check with Shelby and see if she has arranged to have your clothes brought here."

Leonia smiled at the mention of her newly appointed abigail's name. Angela was sure Leonia would be happy with the bubbling sprite Mrs. Burkhardt had recommended. Although Angela had hoped for a more mature woman to guide Leonia, she had agreed that the two young women would do well with each other as they learned together under Mrs. Burkhardt's watchful eyes.

Satisfied that Leonia would be kept busy collecting flowers from the garden, Angela hurried up another set of stairs. Her light spirits plummeted when she saw a man standing at the end of a dusky corridor. He did not move, but continued to stare. Not that she blamed him, for she was acting the muttonhead to halt in the middle of the passage and gape at him.

"May I help you?" she asked uneasily.

He gave her no answer.

A twinge of fear clamped around her. The man's faded clothes were not the color the staff wore. Since Justin's visit, the duke had made it clear that no one uninvited was to be granted admittance to the house. This man who remained in the shadows seemed to want to avoid being seen. She did not want to insult a guest by sounding the alarm.

"Sir, if you are lost," Angela said in the calmest voice she could manage, "I would be glad to help you."

Again he was silent.

Her disquiet became suspicion. The man had not moved his arms, nor had his gaze shifted from hers. Taking a deep breath, she walked toward him and laughed when she realized she had locked eyes with a life-size portrait. Not a painting, but needlework created with the tiniest stitches she had ever seen. A plank propped him against the wall. Although she had never seen one, she had heard of how these figures were used in country houses to add some "life" to the long corridors.

Hearing laughter behind her, she whirled to see a child's lacy skirt flit around a corner. She considered giving chase after Esther—for it must have been the little girl—but she could spend hours searching without ever finding the child. Smiling, she shook her head. Esther was a high-spirited child who needed to have her energies focused on something positive.

Continuing along the corridor at an unseemly pace, Angela halted when she saw another tall form in the doorway of Leonia's new room. This silhouette was unmistakable, for the duke's brown hair was the perfect foil for the navy coat he wore over casual, gray pantaloons. He carried a finely bound book. When he turned to face Angela, his face was as stern as always.

"Miss Needham, you are making quite a few changes in my house," he said in lieu of a greeting.

Silencing her first impulse to apologize, Angela tilted her chin so she could meet his eyes. "A change, Your Grace, which was long overdue."

"How so?"

"Leonia is not a child any longer."

"No?"

When he looked past her, Angela glanced over her shoulder to see Leonia, who rushed into a door on the other side of the room with a bowl of flowers. She laughed softly. "Mayhap I should have said, she is nearly an adult. To become what she must be, she must sample a woman's life and responsibilities."

"I know nothing of what a young woman needs." A slight smile pulled at his lips. "Ask me how to outfit any member of the company I once led, and I can give you a good answer. For this, I fear I am as naïve as Leonia herself."

"You must think of Leonia's firing-off much as you would any battle you might engage."

Bafflement stripped the most austere edges from his face. "How so?" he asked again.

"She must be armed with knowledge of the *élite*. She must possess the proper uniform—in this case, dresses that are *à la modality* and the accessories which announce her standing as the ward of the Duke of Oslington. She must know the rules of the battlefield upon which she is about to engage her life. She must—"

He laughed, startling her, for she had never heard the sound, which was surprisingly lighthearted. "Well said, Miss Needham, although I own I have never heard the Season described so."

Walking beside him toward a bench built beneath a tall

window topped by a half-moon glass, Angela said, "A young woman is trained to be prepared for the Season and the life she will have beyond it. Leonia will do very well."

"I suspect so." He continued to smile as he gestured for her to sit. Holding the book behind his back, he regarded her with honest bemusement. "She has told me of your lessons. She assures me, as you have, that she is cognizant of the intricacies of making calls and what to say when she has her coming-out. One thing you have not changed—and I fear no one can—is her impatience."

"She is young. Time passes more slowly for her."

"Than for an ancient like yourself?" Again he laughed, but with a restraint that suggested he was determined to keep his emotions in check. "Miss Needham, although Leonia has pestered me as annoyingly as a mayfly in October to bring her out in the Little Season, I intend to delay until the spring."

"That is wise."

"It shall take a unique chap to see the charm beneath her exasperating ways."

"Your Grace, Leonia will do well when she is fired-off. If you have any doubts, a small hop at Oslington Court would be a good idea. You could watch how she handles herself with young people from the shire. I believe that would quell many of your concerns."

"A hop? Here?" He shook his head, his smile gone. "You forget, Miss Needham, that this house and these children are in mourning."

"I never forget that, Your Grace. Nor do I forget your wish to have Leonia brought out in the spring. You must decide if the past or the future is more important to you."

The duke did not answer, and Angela suspected that she had overstepped herself. The plainspoken habits of her own childhood should not have been allowed to loosen her tongue during this conversation. As she began to apologize, the duke waved her to silence.

"You are correct yet again, Miss Needham." He bowed

his head toward her. "How odd that you should choose words so strikingly similar to Colonel Sutton's!"

"I consider that a compliment."

"You should." He looked out the window beyond her, and she guessed he was seeing a vista of distant India. "I never met a finer man than the colonel. It has been my greatest honor that he selected me to safeguard the future of his children."

"And to see they are happy?" she ventured.

"If possible."

"You have certainly done that for Thomas. He has been as chipper as a robin since you agreed for the children to—"

"Spare me any mention of that decision!" His voice was once more frigid. "Miss Needham, I have decided that I will allow this single visit. Then I will reappraise the situation."

"Your change of plan will break Thomas's heart. He—"

"Angela!" Leonia's plaintive call resonated along the corridor. "Oh, Angela, do come and explain to this nod-cock what we planned with the dressing table!"

"Leonia needs you more than I, Miss Needham," the duke said icily. "I trust you will help her sort out the mess you have created for *her.*"

Angela clenched her hands in frustration as he strode away. For a moment, she had seen the charming man Leonia had described, but he had vanished as soon as she broached the subject of Thomas and—although his name was never uttered—Justin. What was the true reason for the antipathy between the two men? She was resolved to discover what it might be.

When Angela sent for Leonia to come down to the foyer, she was not surprised to discover that Leonia was vexed at the idea of making a call at Harrington Grange. Leonia seemed to agree with everything her guardian said.

"Angela," she retorted in a whining tone, "I wish to continue with the unpacking in my room. I have no interest in calling on that bothersome man."

"Bothersome? I did not know that you had met Lord Harrington."

"Once. When I went to tell Thomas that he must return here posthaste." She frowned. "I do not understand why Rodney acquiesced to Thomas's demands that we pay Lord Harrington a visit."

"This call upon Lord Harrington will be excellent practice for you."

"In making calls on folks I cannot tolerate?"

"Leonia!"

The young woman sighed and flounced back toward the stairs. "Why must I call there when I truly want to visit Mrs. Raleigh and her daughters? They have recently arrived from Town, and I am sure that they must have the latest copies of *Ackerman's Repository*."

"The fashion-plates will be waiting when we look in on them next week. By then, you will have had this chance to use your new skills at Harrington Grange."

"I called upon them in India many times."

"But this is not India."

"I believe I noticed that."

Angela sighed. Leonia was being as petulant as Thomas today. "You must understand that while Mrs. Raleigh might condone a *faux pas* or two because you are so newly arrived from the East, the rest of the Polite World will be less forgiving. Before you give anyone beyond your closest neighbors a look-in, you must be well-versed in all the nuances of making a call."

Leonia grumbled, "But Consuelo Raleigh will have chosen all the best designs by then and will have requested her *modiste* to make them. If I want something that is not just like hers, I shall have only the leftovers."

"I doubt Mrs. Raleigh will grant her leave to order every gown she wants."

"But if we go to Harrington Grange, we shall have to listen to Thomas and the viscount's bibble-babble about butterflies."

Angela smiled. "And that will provide you with an excellent lesson to prepare you for your entry into the *ton*. Not every conversation you will be part of during the Season will be scintillating and interesting, but, as a guest, you must not reveal that." She patted Leonia's shoulder. "The cart is waiting. Please get your sister and brothers. Then we can go."

"If you wish . . ."

Angela was glad that Leonia's eyes remained downcast, because her own must be glittering with the anticipation of talking with Justin again. The mercurial man might today be a jesting fool or the man who spoke with such fervor of his hobby of chasing butterflies across the moor. Or he might be the beguiling man who had swept all thoughts from her head with his ardent kisses. Whatever he was, she was drawn back to him.

Her hope that the other children would be more eager to get out of the grand house vanished as soon as Esther ran down the stairs to her. Seth was on her heels and copied Esther when the little girl clamped her arms together in front of her and regarded Angela with ill-concealed irritation.

"Mrs. Meyer says Wallah must remain here," Esther said with a scowl. "If Wallah cannot go, I shall not, either."

Looking past the little girl to where the governess was shaking her silver-gray head in dismay, Angela said, "Esther, there are many plants in the garden at Harrington Grange. Any of them could be lethal to Wallah. Once you have looked at the plants there and checked them in one of your guardian's books to identify them, then you can be sure Wallah will be safe."

"You want me to do all that work? It sounds like what Mr. Weare makes us do."

"If you wish to take Wallah out beyond Oslington Court's gardens, you must be certain he is safe."

Esther's stance grew softer, but she mumbled, "He had better be invited to go with us next time."

Seth seconded her sentiments by nodding and following her toward the front door.

"Where is Thomas?" Angela asked.

"In his room," Mrs. Meyer said, adding in a near whisper, "He is no happier about going to Lord Harrington's than the younger ones."

"No happier?" Angela had been sure Thomas would be ecstatic about the chance to visit his friend without skulking across the fields. "Why not?"

"Because I am going to have to share the scanty time I have with Justin," snapped Thomas as he came down into the foyer. "I thought you were supposed to help me, Miss Needham."

"This was the best I could do. Your guardian was emphatic that all of you or none of you would call at Harrington Grange." She did not add that she believed the duke hoped to put an end to any calls there after today. "His Grace has said we can call for two hours, which will give you time to retrieve some of your artwork to show him."

"Two blasted hours," he grumbled, "and I have to share them with my prattling sisters and my cabbage-head brother."

"Thomas!"

The ginger-hackled boy scowled at her, then strode out of the house.

Angela sighed as she had so often since she had come to Oslington Court. She had not guessed that Thomas would be so jealous of the small amount of time he had with his friend. If only he would realize how fortunate he was to have this opportunity, but his frustration had blinded him.

The ride from Oslington Court in the pony cart was as gloomy as the day was bright. Angela's few attempts at conversation were met with silence. She wondered if she should turn the cart around and simply send word to Harrington Grange that they must postpone their visit. This would not be the best way for the children to meet Justin's daughter. She resisted giving in to defeat. If she hesitated now, she suspected both Justin and the duke would rescind their agreements to allow the children to visit.

At the gate of Harrington Grange, Esther and Seth tumbled out of the cart. Angela thanked Thomas for handing her down, but his only reply was a mutter, warning that he

had not changed his opinion about this call. She had no time
to watch him assist his sister, for the younger children
launched into a brangle. They were debating—ever more
loudly—which one of them could run faster and reach the
end of the garden wall first.

Angela said, "Do have a race, and be done with it."

If they were startled by her vexed tone, she gave them no
time to comment. She walked through the gate, wishing she
could convince the children that this visit to Harrington
Grange was so very important. Not just to them, but to
Justin's daughter. She had explained nothing to the Sutton
children, because, until she was sure how Delicia Harrington
would react to meeting her neighbors, she did not know
what to say. How could she prepare these children when she
was so uncertain herself?

Her heart banged against her chest so fiercely that she
was amazed that neither Leonia nor Thomas said anything
about the frantic sound. She could barely hear past its thud.
Even more than the children's meeting, she was unsure about
how to act when she saw Justin for the first time since he
had kissed her. More than once in the past few days, she
had considered what a skimble-skamble she had made of
the already tenuous situation by letting him seduce her into
his arms at the very time he had come to apologize for being
so bold as to kiss her hand. Her hand? 'Twas her lips that
ached for his kiss now.

Angela looked around the small garden. She had guessed
that Justin would be waiting for them. When she saw no
one, she wondered if he had become immersed in his studies
and forgotten that this was Thursday and the Sutton children
were to meet Delicia.

Or had he remembered, but changed his mind about the
call? She could not forget the fury in his eyes when they
had locked with the duke's.

Her hands fisted by her sides, but she forced her fingers
to loosen. She had no reason to believe Justin would renege
on his promise. That he had welcomed Thomas to Har-

rington Grange showed that Justin would not feel compelled to obey his neighbor's orders.

Angela knocked on the door, but received no answer. Hearing uneasy rumbles from the children, she forced a smile. "Leonia, if you would please take the others to sit in the arbor by the garden path, they might be more comfortable. This sun is very bright."

"Is something wrong?"

Wavering between a falsehood and the truth, Angela had no chance to answer. The garden leaves rustled, and the barebones housekeeper emerged from the overgrown vines.

"Mrs. Graves!" Angela could not silence her shock to see the housekeeper sneaking through the brush.

Mrs. Graves glanced toward the house, then at the children standing beside Angela, their mouths wide with amazement. "Miss Needham, may I please take a moment of your time?"

"Of course."

"Alone?" When Angela frowned at the peculiar request, the older woman hurried to say, "I needed to speak to you before his lordship brings Delicia out."

Angela nodded. "Leonia, please take your sister and brothers and sit in arbor."

"But, Angela—"

"This will take but a moment."

Leonia scowled, but herded the others ahead of her through the garden. The look she shot back at Angela announced that *this* was not her idea of how to pay a call. Nor was it Angela's.

"Is Delicia ill?" asked Angela as soon as the children were out of earshot.

"No, but I beg you to reconsider your plans for today," Mrs. Graves answered, wringing her hands in her apron.

"Why? Lord Harrington has approved of them."

The older woman shuddered. "Mayhap he does not fully understand their import."

"Import? I realize he and the duke have a long-standing

feud, but that should not preclude the children from playing together."

"Delicia is not at all like the Sutton children."

Angela smiled as she glanced at where Seth and Esther were busy swinging on the gate. Their laughter and shouts filled the garden, and she did not have the heart to remonstrate with them for disobeying her request to sit in the arbor. "I doubt if there are many children like these. They are so rambunctious, and their manners can be abominable. However, they have warm hearts, so you do not need to fear on Delicia's behalf. I know they will be eager to meet a new playmate, for they were accustomed to being with other children in India."

"Will they be so eager when they see how she is flawed?"

"Delicia cannot hear, but she is not flawed," Angela fired back. She struggled with her abrupt anger, for it would do no good to release it. Yet, she could not allow Mrs. Graves—who thought she was speaking out of love—to ruin this day and what might be the single chance for the Sutton children and Justin's daughter to meet. "You must not speak of her as if she is nothing more than a piece of furniture which should be hidden in the attic when it is no longer perfect. No child is perfect." Her smile returned as she heard the gate give a protesting creak before banging closed, but she became serious again when she added, "Delicia is a little girl who needs to be with other children, so she can learn to be a child just like them."

"She cannot be like *them*." Mrs. Graves's face grew long with dismay.

"She must have the chance to be as boisterous and play as a child should."

"If—" The housekeeper clamped her lips closed as the front door of Harrington Grange opened.

Angela was sure she had never seen a more charming *tableau* than Justin in the doorway, his hand in his daughter's. Seeing them standing next to each other, their kohl hair glistening in the sunshine, their eyes of the same seagreen shade searching the garden, she was surprised that she had not sensed the truth that Delicia was Justin's daughter from the very first moment she saw the child.

Delicia's bonnet tied under her chin with green ribbons that matched the ruffles on her skirt. Justin's single-breasted coat was as dark as his hair, but he wore a flowered waistcoat which was only a shade darker than Delicia's ribbons.

Angela was abruptly aware of the dusty state of the children she had brought with her. Patting at her hair, which refused to stay confined beneath her straw poke-bonnet, she brushed her hands against her pink muslin skirt. She took a single step forward, wishing someone else would speak first.

Kneeling, she smiled as she saw bafflement and uneasiness in Delicia's eyes. She held out her hand and said slowly, "Delicia, I am Angela."

The little girl put her fingers on Angela's lips, startling her.

"Say your name again," Justin whispered, as if his daughter would hear him if he spoke louder. "It gives her some comfort."

Angela resisted retorting that the child needed more than comforting, but pointed to herself and repeated her name. Then she pointed at Delicia and said the child's name. A wisp of a smile teased the little girl's serious face.

Standing, Angela motioned for the Sutton children to come forward. They were as silent as they had been during the drive to Harrington Grange.

Justin stayed close to his daughter, who stared at the youngsters flanking Angela. With a low laugh, he said, "We look like a group of widgeons when we stand here like this."

"Yes, we do." Angela drew Esther forward, then gave her a gentle shove toward the younger girl. "Esther, this is Delicia Harrington." Bending, she murmured in Esther's ear, "Say your name slowly. Delicia cannot hear when you speak."

"Cannot hear?" Esther's eyes were large as she looked from Delicia to Angela.

Seeing Justin tense, Angela hurried to say, "She lost her hearing when she was a baby. She is only a little younger

than Seth, so I thought you and Seth might enjoy playing
with her. Do you think she will like Wallah?"

Esther grinned at the mention of her pet. Stepping closer
to Delicia, she must have forgotten Angela's request to speak
slowly because she prattled like her monkey.

Angela was about to reprove Esther, but bit back her
words when she saw how fascinated Delicia was with the
other little girl. Esther held out her hand as Angela had,
never pausing in her chatter as she now related how she and
Seth had swung on the gate.

Delicia looked to her father. Justin nodded, and the little
girl clasped Esther's hand. When Esther led Delicia to meet
her siblings, Angela released a sigh of relief. The children
were not yet friends, but she could believe that was possible.

Thomas pushed past the other children. "Justin," he said,
unable to quell his excitement, "I want to show you the
information I discovered yesterday in Rodney's library about
that butterfly we saw when we went out for that walk last
week."

"Let us take care of one matter at a time," Justin replied.

Angela's frown returned. Justin was so busy watching his
daughter with Leonia and the youngest Sutton children that
he did not see Thomas's despair. She started to speak to the
lad, but he brushed aside her words. Striding through the
gate, he let it slam behind him.

Angela sighed. Keeping all the children happy at once
seemed an impossibility. Her delight at this first meeting
between Esther and Delicia was muted by Thomas's unexpected envy. Somehow she must convince the lad that Justin
would find time for both him and Delicia. Then she realized
she could not promise Thomas that. She had no idea what
Justin—or the duke—planned after this single call.

As Esther led the way to the gate, Angela followed.
"Swinging on the gate is not a good idea."

"It is fun!" said Seth stoutly.

"But you may break the gate."

"You are no fun, guardian's angel!"

Justin laughed. "What did you call her?"

"Guardian's angel." Seth stood as tall as he could. "That is what Thomas calls her. She is our guardian's Angela, so . . ."

Justin did not hear the rest of what the little boy had to say. *Our guardian's Angela?* The very sound of those words bothered him, threatening to resurrect the past that he had believed buried with his late wife. That had been before Oslington had returned to his family's estate, bringing the obligation of four children with him along with a daily reminder of the past.

As he walked beside Angela as she steered the children out of the garden to play in the field that separated Harrington Grange from Oslington Court, his fingers rose to caress her cheek. He pulled it back. Did she have any idea how difficult it had been to walk away and leave her standing by Oslington in the garden? Every step had been shadowed by the craving to turn around and demand that she stay far away from Oslington. She had not appeared to notice how Oslington had inched closer to her during their brief exchange. The duke had made it clear that he considered Angela his.

Guardian's Angela.

He cursed under his breath, wishing he had never heard those two words together.

"Why are you so dour?" Angela asked. "I would have thought you would be happy to see how well Delicia and the others are getting along."

"I am."

"Then . . ."

"Mayhap I am like Thomas."

"Jealous that the other children are intruding on your time with him? Thomas needs to learn that he must share his time with you if he hopes to have any time here."

"I am jealous of how the children are intruding on my time with you." He was glad that he could smile. The sweet flavor of truth whetted his hunger to sample her lips.

"You are being ridiculous."

"Me? What is ridiculous about that?"

She lowered her voice. "I saw your reaction to what Seth called me. I know you are bothered by it."

"You are insightful. I should always remember that." By Jove, he must be more cautious around her, but how could he think about hiding his thoughts when each one was about her?

He drew her hand within his arm as they continued along the dusty road. The scent of summer flowers hung thickly in the hot air, but a gentle breeze was seasoned so lightly with salt from the sea not so many miles away. While Esther and Seth raced over the stile and into the field, Leonia followed more slowly, holding Delicia's hand. Where Thomas might be, he could not guess.

Nor did he wish to spend time considering that. He wanted to be here with Angela's fingers on his sleeve and her steps matching his. Even more glorious than the aroma of flowers was the ethereal perfume she wore. It was intoxicating, urging him to throw aside common sense and pull her into his arms again.

"Do not fret so, Justin." Angela's words drew him out of his mesmerism with the fantasy of holding her.

"Fret? Me?"

She laughed, and he was pleased that the sound was not too strained as she climbed the stile. "You cannot deny the truth."

"Nor can you. In your eyes, as you brought Esther Sutton forward, I saw my own anxiety that all of this must not be allowed to explode into more problems."

"Esther is always an uncertain variable, but she is a kind child. Delicia is, you must own, neither salt nor sugar. She will not melt at the first touch."

"True, and I must allow her to live as normal a life as she can."

Angela smiled, and he followed her gaze to where Esther was kneeling to point out a clump of wildflowers peeking through a bedding of leaves. A nearly identical expression of delight and eagerness brightened Delicia's face. Tagging after them, Seth was distracted when a dragonfly buzzed past him.

"What is wrong?" he asked when he saw Angela's smile waver.

"I wish Thomas was here to make the group complete."

"He will come about when he learns what he is missing." He chuckled when Seth took Delicia by the hand and tugged her with him to chase after the dragonfly.

"See?" Angela patted his arm. "Children take to one another without needing a common language."

"You are a wise woman, Angela Needham."

"A compliment from you?" She laughed. "This is a rare pleasure."

"Not as rare nor as pleasurable as when I kissed you in Oslington's garden."

The children's voices grew distant as she turned to face him. There was no mistaking that she shared the yearning that had kept him from sleeping each night since he had left Oslington Court. When her hand brushed his cheek lightly, his arms were around her, tugging her to him, before he had time for conscious thought. Within him, there was only the need to savor her mouth and delightful curves as he was caught up in a sweet web of happiness. He bent toward her, eager to satisfy this hunger for her lips.

Angela flinched when she heard a throat being cleared behind her. Pulling away from Justin, she turned to see Mrs. Graves's disapproving face.

The housekeeper held out a basket. "You forgot this, my lord."

"Thank you, Mrs. Graves," he replied.

His housekeeper strode away, as candid in her dislike of the situation as Thomas had been.

"Pay her no mind," Justin said with a sigh. "Mrs. Graves can be as grim as her name. She has become very attached to Delicia and is determined to see that nothing bad will happen to her."

"Or to you." Angela turned as Esther shouted her name.

Waving to the little girl, she said, "I was wrong when I said we needed a chaperon."

"It seems we have too many."

"Mayhap not."

"What?" His dark brows lowered.

"Justin, the children should remind us that I am here to be Leonia's companion."

"Instead of mine?"

She gasped at his bold words, but was unsure if he heard her, because Delicia ran up to him. He did not look at Angela as he followed his daughter to where she was gesturing to something on the ground.

Had she misunderstood his words? He had been jesting with her. Had her heart sought a meaning that he had not intended? She was afraid so, for she was discovering, only now, how her heart longed to be his. She could not imagine anything that could complicate her life more.

Ten

"Isn't it wonderful?" gushed Leonia as she rushed into the small parlor where Angela was waiting for their next lesson.

Angela struggled to keep a stern expression in place. "Leonia, I have told you several times that you do not come into a room as if you have been shot from a cannon."

"But this is so important!" She grasped Angela's hands and tugged her to the pale green settee between two tall windows that reached to the ceiling. The shadow from the rafters that dropped from the peaked ceiling created a striped pattern on the flowered wallcovering and across the green paisley rug.

"Leonia, the import of a message does not grant you leave to forget your manners." Sitting, she smiled up at the agitated young woman. "However, it seems that you will burst with the tidings if you do not speak them soon."

Dropping inelegantly to the cushion beside Angela, Leonia winced when Angela scowled again. "Sorry, but I am so excited that I cannot calm myself."

"Take a deep breath."

Leonia tried, but it puffed out in a wild explosion as she said, "I just spoke with Rodney, and he has received an invitation from a friend who served with him in India. Lord Milborough. He lives not far from Edinburgh. He is getting married. We are invited. Angela! What will I wear? The wedding is only ten days from now. Can I get a gown ready for it? Can I wear my hair up? I know I am not out yet, but can I have a gown made like the one I saw in the pattern-book during our last call at Mrs. Raleigh's? The one that had ribbons woven through the lace on the sleeves? Can I—?"

"Whoa!" Angela held up her hands. "Leonia, please allow me to answer one question before you pelt me with a dozen more."

"It is so exciting!"

"That it is, but the first question must be: Is the duke planning to accept the invitation to the wedding?"

"He must!" Leonia's face bleached with horror.

"That is his choice." Angela hated to have to pop Leonia's bubble of joy, but the duke seemed to enjoy the quiet of his book-room and seldom wandered beyond Oslington Court's gardens. "If he chooses to go, he may choose to go alone."

Leonia jumped to her feet. "He would not!"

"That also is his choice."

"Then we must make sure he makes the right choice."

"Leonia—"

Angela sighed as the young woman raced out of the parlor at a pace even more indecorous than when she had entered. Standing to follow, she had not reached the doorway before Leonia returned . . . with the duke in tow.

"Tell him," Leonia pleaded. "Tell him how important this is."

Angela glanced from Leonia's hopeful face to the duke's vexation. That he carried a book under one arm was no surprise. She doubted if she had seen him more than a handful of times without something to read. His interests were eclectic, but usually focused on history and science. As she had before, she bit back her questions about why he and Justin were at such odds when they seemed to have so much in common. As she had before, she reminded herself that her sole concern here should be Leonia.

"Your Grace," Angela began.

"No need for *you* to apologize, Miss Needham," he said,

shaking his head. "It seems that both you and I shall get nothing else accomplished today until we iron out this matter of Milborough's nuptials."

Grasping his arm and regarding him with obvious hope, Leonia said, "Do say we can go, Rodney. There are certain to be many people there who were once stationed with us at Fort St. George."

"That is questionable." He looked over her head to Angela. "Milborough was an irascible man who preferred to ignore orders that did not suit him. Men of a military bent chose to avoid him."

"But he is getting married!" cried Leonia.

Angela stepped forward and drew her charge back from the duke, who seemed overmastered by Leonia's outburst. "Leonia, there is no need to lengthen this discussion by stating the obvious. You must let your guardian make his decision as he sees fit."

Leonia whirled back to the duke. "Do say we shall go."

"You would really enjoy that?" His smile was so gentle that Angela was astonished. This was not the cold duke who avoided any entanglements that stole time from his reading. "I recall you dancing in the shadows at the top of the stairs when you were younger than Seth."

"I still love to dance, Rodney." She laughed. "And you never told anyone that you had seen me there when I was supposed to be asleep."

"Not any of the times I saw you there." Again he looked past her to Angela. "Miss Needham, it might be an excellent opportunity for Leonia to meet some of the people she will encounter in London when she is fired off. Do you think she is ready to attend this wedding?"

Angela nodded. "There are more lessons she needs, but, if she concentrates on what she needs to learn, she should be ready."

"Very well." He patted Leonia's cheek lightly as he did the younger children. "Study well, Leonia, so you might be ready."

"I shall make you proud of me, Rodney," she asserted, her eyes glowing with happiness.

"I suspect you shall." He nodded toward Angela and walked out of the parlor.

Again Angela noted the wistful expression on Leonia's face. There was a candid longing in the young woman's eyes and more than a hint of sorrow. Sudden tears filled her own, because she wondered if Leonia was thinking of the past and her late father, who would never see her enter the Polite World.

But there was no time for melancholy. Clapping her hands, she said, "Leonia, we must get to work right away on a gown for you to wear to this wedding. It cannot be too ornate, because you are not yet fired-off. I believe I saw a white gown that you have in your cupboard that might be appropriate with some alterations."

"And what will you wear?" Leonia's sad face was now aglow with anticipation.

"Me?"

"You will be coming with us."

"The duke said nothing of that."

Leonia laughed and clasped Angela's hand. "Why should he have to when you know I shall need you there to help me avoid any *faux pas?*"

"Yes . . ." She doubted if Leonia noticed the lack of enthusiasm in her voice. While the young woman prattled about the wedding and who would be there and what she would wear and how she wished she could dance with all the guests, Angela sat and stared out the window in the direction of Harrington Grange.

Going to Lord Milborough's estate near Edinburgh would require at least a fortnight away from Oslington Court, and a fortnight would mean at least two Thursdays when she would not be able to take the children to play with Delicia. That meant missing two chances to spend time with Justin. She had not guessed how dreary that thought would make her.

*   *   *

The afternoon was perfect for dining *al fresco* beneath a gnarled tree by the stream that twisted through the meadow between Oslington Court and Harrington Grange. A rare summer heat had brought even the children beneath the shade for a respite from the sunshine.

The basket that had once been overflowing with food was now nearly empty. Crumbs from the delicious meat pies made in the kitchens of Oslington Court mixed on the trio of blankets with splatters of lemonade that Mrs. Graves had squeezed for them.

Seth was curled into a ball on one corner of the largest blanket, sound asleep. Beside him, Thomas was yawning broadly, but resisting the lazy day that suggested it was time for all of them to nap. His sketch of the stone wall and the bush beside it remained as unfinished as it had been a half hour ago, although he bent over the paper whenever anyone looked in his direction.

Handing Delicia an iced cake, Angela smiled as the little girl carried it to where Esther was sitting on the next blanket. Angela brushed more crumbs of cake from her apron as she said, "I was sure that Esther would be delighted with the chance to get to know Delicia. Esther does not tease to bring Wallah with us now, because she does not want to share Delicia with her monkey."

"She seems to have a habit of taking the defenseless under her wing," Justin said, drawing his pipe from beneath his navy coat.

Angela's smile faded when she heard regret in his voice. Closing the hamper, she said as he lit his pipe, "Delicia will remain defenseless if you keep her imprisoned here in the country, keeping her away from other children."

"Do you suggest I take her to Town for the Season?"

"Do not be absurd! I meant only that she should be allowed to have a childhood like any other child. That includes playmates her own age."

"Which you have so graciously provided." He scowled as he looked toward the roofs of Oslington Court. "For two hours each Thursday afternoon."

Softly she said, "That much was a hard-won victory."

"I have no doubts about that. Oslington has forever had a stubborn streak as grand as his conceit." His voice became less bitter as he said, "Now I have upset you, Angela. You must know that I do not fault you in any way for your association with that arrogant block."

"He is my employer, and I would ask you to refrain of speaking of him so."

His lips tightened, but he nodded. "As you wish." Resting his elbow on his drawn-up knee, he pointed with his pipe toward the stream. "I thought, if you were willing, I would take the children on a walk along the water next week. I saw some frogs a couple of days ago, and I collect Seth, Esther, and Delicia would be particularly delighted to chase a few."

"Next week, we will not be able to call."

"Oh?"

She knew she should take warning when he spoke with such an emotionless tone, but she had sought a way to tell him about the trip to Scotland since they had arrived at Harrington Grange almost two hours ago. If she did not tell him now, she would have no chance, because the Sutton children must be returned to Oslington Court soon.

"The duke is taking the children to a wedding at the home of a friend not far from Edinburgh."

"Is that so? Is this the interesting tidings you said, when you arrived, that you had to share with me?"

"No, that is something else, but I needed to tell you about this journey to Scotland so you will not plan on our call for the next fortnight."

His eyes narrowed as his gaze raked her face. "And I assume you will be going as well?"

"Leonia wishes me to be there, and, as her companion, it is my place to be at her side."

"But you are not today."

"She is having a fitting this afternoon for the gown she will be wearing for the wedding. The duke is indulging her in agreeing for her to have this dress that she will not be able to use again until she goes to London."

Justin came to his feet and held out his hand. When she slipped her fingers into it, he drew her up. "There are too many ears here to allow me to say what I wish to say."

"I must gather up the children and return to Oslington Court."

"Why disturb them?"

Angela looked across the blankets and smiled. Now all four children were asleep. Thomas's head was resting on his sketch, and she guessed he would wake with marks from the paper ingrained in his cheek. Esther and Delicia were huddled together like two puppies.

Turning back to Justin, she said, "You are right. There is no need to disturb them right now." She bit her lower lip, then added, "Especially when I have disturbed you so greatly."

He did not reply as he led her out into the sunshine. While they walked along the stream toward where several trees clumped by a shore embroidered with pebbles and rocks, he puffed on his pipe and said nothing. He kicked one of the stones into the water before propping his foot against a boulder. Facing her, he said, "If you wish the truth, Angela, I am not so much disturbed as worried."

"Worried? About our trip? I doubt there are many highwaymen on the road between here and Edinburgh."

"A knight of the pad is not what worries me." He set his pipe on the rock and put his hands on her shoulders. "Angela, I do not know what Oslington has said to you about me—"

"Very little. He avoids speaking of you."

"As I do him when at all possible, but you need to know that he is a man with a great and violent temper."

"The duke?" She stared at him, too amazed to say more. She could not imagine the duke being volatile about anything; then she recalled the tightly restrained fury in his eyes when he had encountered Justin at Oslington Court.

His hands on her shoulders swept down her arms. "Trust

what I tell you about this, if you never trust anything else I say to you. Even though you may not have seen it, that temper is there. I am sure the children have witnessed it."

"If so, they have shown no signs of being afraid of him." She took a step toward him, trying not to notice the incongruity of easing into his embrace as they spoke of the duke. "Mayhap he has changed."

"I have told you. Oslington *never* changes."

"And neither do you."

He brushed his lips against her cheek. "You may be right about that, although Mrs. Graves has stated more than once in the past week how you seem to be having a tempering influence on me."

"Tempering influence?" She laughed. "I would say it is quite the opposite. The children and I have created quite an upheaval in your life."

"I don't want to talk about the children. I don't want to talk about Oslington. I don't want to talk about anything."

His lips slanted across hers as his arm went around her waist and enfolded her to him. Her fingers sifted up through his hair, quivering as each strand slid through them. She longed for this kiss to last long enough so she could recall every moment of its pleasure when she was far from him.

"No," she whispered when he started to release her. "No, not yet."

His laugh was muffled against her mouth. His tongue slid along her lips, then between them. It stroked hers, and she could not silence the soul-deep moan of need that rushed from her. With her fingers clenching onto the back of his coat, she let the thrilling sensations engulf her.

He tilted her head back and smiled. "Thomas may call you his sister's guardian angel, but he is wrong. You are no angel."

"And you have the devil's own way about you."

"Mayhap, but I can tell you that your kisses are so heavenly that they would be enough to convince Old Scratch himself to give up his evil ways." Tapping her nose, he grinned. "Mayhap even persuade me to give up mine."

"Do you have evil ways, Justin?"

"More than you should know about." He started to add something else, but paused when a shout from the blankets warned them that the children had overcome the temptation to nap. Arching a single brow, he said, "I had hoped we could steal a bit more time before you had to leave."

"I know." Angela put her hand on his coat sleeve. "There is one other thing I wanted to share with you before we go."

He twisted a strand of her hair around his finger. "There is more than one thing I would like to share with you. Right now." His kiss was deep and tasted of the craving that was whetted with each touch.

Her breath was uneven when she stepped back. "Justin, I should not—we should not—"

"Of course we should." At another call from the children, he smiled wryly. "But I guess you shall have to wait for later for me to convince you of that." Taking her hand, he led her back toward where the children were rolling up the blankets. "What did you want to tell me?"

"I was reading the newspaper that the duke has delivered from London. There was an article in it about a school where they teach deaf children a way to use their hands to make others understand them."

"A school?" He faced her, but glanced at his daughter who was chasing Seth around and around the tree. He sighed. "I dislike the thought of sending Delicia away to school."

"I know." She reached into the pocket of her apron and handed him the article she had cut out of the newspaper. "It is so far from here."

"Where is it?"

"Near Paris."

"You want me to send her to *France?*"

Angela was taken back by his sharp tone. "I know it is a long way from here, but the war with Napoleon has been over for nearly four years. Many people are traveling to the Continent. If you take Delicia there, the school might offer her an opportunity for a normal life she could not have otherwise."

" 'Tis out of the question."

"But, Justin—"

Fiercely, he cut her off as he shoved the article back into her hand. "I said it was out of the question. As you have reminded me many times, let me remind you. Oslington hired you to intrude in his life, not mine."

"I did not mean to intrude. Only—"

"If you will excuse me, I think it is past time Delicia and I returned home."

A dozen questions begged to be spoken, but Angela voiced none of them as he walked to the tree where the children were playing. He took Delicia by the hand and led her toward the road. The little girl looked back, her baffled expression matching Angela's confusion.

Esther ran to Angela. Slipping her hand into Angela's, she said, "I wish they did not have to leave so soon."

"I know." She dared say no more because she feared her own distress would taint her words.

Justin had said many things to distress her, and she had irritated him often. But why had the mere mention of France unsettled him more than anything before this?

Eleven

Milborough Manor was perched high on a hill that would offer an excellent view of Edinburgh in the distance to the north. The original part of the house looked to be centuries old, and no effort had been made to match the old walls with the new sections of the house. The new wings had smooth stone walls, instead of being covered with gravel and lime like the center tower of what must have been an old castle. An elegant portico had been tacked onto the front of the ancient section, looking rather like an old dowager trying to dress like a young miss.

As Angela followed the duke and the children into the house, she smelled the odor of fresh paint. She stepped on something and looked down to see a forgotten nail beneath her shoe. Although the foyer was decorated with elegant furnishings, for there were benches with gold tufted cushions following the walls between the doors that must lead to other chambers, she guessed it had been chaotic just hours before the guests began arriving.

Quiet-footed servants led them up the stairs to where they could rest before the wedding later this evening. Angela's hand tightened on the oak banister as she looked at the duke. His face was still the odd shade of gray it had possessed for the past three days. When he called an early stop yesterday, she had expressed her concerns about his well-being. His sharp answers that he was well and she should focus her maternal concerns on Leonia had warned her not to ask again.

Yet, even the children were subdued, and she knew they shared her anxiety about the duke's health when they glanced uneasily at him when he was panting by the time they reached the top of the steps. Poor dears! If something happened to the duke, who knew where the Sutton children might be scattered? Few people were willing to take on the obligation of four recalcitrant youngsters and a monkey and all their other quirks.

Telling herself not to see the duke buried when he might be suffering no more than a head cold, Angela nodded when the duke turned to follow another servant and left her to herd the children ahead of her to the rooms they would share. They met no one else along the long corridor that led through the old section of the house. Looking back over her shoulder, she saw the duke disappear through the arch that led to the newer section. Lord Milborough was kind to give the duke a chance to enjoy the festivities without the children constantly underfoot.

Angela clapped her hands as she went into a large, circular room decorated in a brilliant red and gilt. Chairs were set by the bay windows, and the doors opening off the room revealed several bedchambers with walls as crimson. Blinking, for the very color burned her eyes, she pointed to which room each child would use. At first, she thought Leonia would protest sharing with her sister, but Leonia simply followed Esther into the room farthest to the right.

Sitting on a red tufted chaise longue, Angela sighed. Leonia's compliance bespoke the young woman's consternation about her guardian. More than once in the past few days, Angela had seen Leonia trying to ask the duke about how he felt. He brushed her aside with the same coolness as he had Angela.

Soft footfalls crossed the thick carpet. Esther put her head in Angela's lap.

"What is wrong?" Angela asked. "Do you miss Wallah?"

"Yes, but not as much as I miss playing with Delicia. It is Thursday, isn't it?"

"Yes." Would her voice sound faint to Esther, too, or just her own ears? She had struggled to ignore all thoughts of Justin. There had been so many. Everything she heard, everything she saw, everything she experienced reminded her of him. When the children said something amusing, she stored it away to share with him . . . then realized their Thursday outings might have come to an end, for the duke had hinted that they would be busy with other things upon their return.

"I wish we were home at Oslington Court, so I could play with Delicia," Esther whispered.

"We shall be returning there soon. A week, maybe two."

"But I will have forgotten what Delicia taught me by then."

"Taught you?" She lifted the little girl's head off her lap. "What did she teach you?"

"To help her understand what I have to say."

"How?"

Esther put her fingers on Angela's lips and then to her own. "Delicia does this and watches me. I try to talk nice and slow, and when she looks puzzled, I repeat myself."

"And she understands?"

"Of course, and she has taught me to understand what she has to say. She makes motions, and they mean things. I am afraid I will forget what they are by the time we get back."

"Just keep repeating them to yourself, and you will remember." Angela hugged the little girl. "You are a good friend for Delicia."

"And she's my best friend." She dimpled. "She and Wallah."

"Why don't you go and take a nap and dream of both of them."

As Esther skipped back into the room where Leonia could be heard pacing, Angela's smile was tainted with sorrow. Delicia Harrington must be a very intelligent little girl, for she was devising her own language. No wonder Justin had been intrigued with the idea of the school at first. Then he had abruptly changed his mind. Because it was in France? She shivered. There were many who could not set aside their hatred of all things French because of the long war with Napoleon, but Justin had shown no interest in politics. His focus was totally on his studies and his daughter.

None of this made sense. The missing puzzle piece was somewhere. She simply was not seeing it.

The house was no longer quiet. Voices came from every direction. The halls beyond the rooms Angela shared with the children were abuzz. From outside the windows covered with chintz drapes, more conversations mixed with the sounds of an orchestra tuning up. The wedding was over, and the festivities were about to begin.

She and the children had not attended the wedding in the tiny chapel somewhere on the ground floor of the house. That had been a wise decision, for, after the long trip, Seth and Esther had been even more unable to sit still than usual. Thomas had vanished to the conservatory somewhere else in the house, and Leonia had spent the afternoon lamenting about her hair.

Angela had been grateful for the excuse to retire to her own private chamber, a small room that barely had room for the tall tester bed and an oak cupboard. But being here alone, even with all the voices beyond the walls, brought forth more thoughts of Justin. If she had followed him and demanded that he explain why he had reacted so, mayhap her mind might be more at ease now.

"When did you start lying to yourself?" Her voice sounded strange in the small room. Thinking she could get Justin out of her thoughts proved she was out of her mind.

Tonight, she would have little time to think about him. The children were sure to be a handful during the party, because she had heard Seth and Esther discussing how big a piece of the wedding cake they should get and whether the frosting would be flavored. Between watching them and making sure that Leonia did not overstep the boundaries for a young miss not yet introduced to society, she would be too busy for anything but trying to stay one step ahead of them.

Angela took one last look in the glass to make certain that she looked her best. She touched the cream-white gown and the tiny yellow roses sewn into the ribbons dropping from the bodice. This gown was more splendid than anything she had worn during her interrupted Season. Not once, until the *modiste* had requested a final fitting the day before they left Oslington Court, had Angela guessed that Leonia was arranging for this gown to be made for her. It had been, Leonia had told her with a grin, a thank-you for persuading the duke to take the Sutton children to Scotland.

Going to the door that led to the girls' room, Angela knocked.

Esther opened it and twirled about, the ribbons on her dress matching neither the wallcovering nor Esther's hair, which was nearly the same shade. "Isn't this the prettiest dress you have ever seen?"

"Very nice," Angela said, vowing to speak to Mrs. Meyer about choosing colors more appropriate for Esther instead of the pinks that were all the rage.

"Leonia doesn't think so." Esther's nose wrinkled, blending her freckles together. "She won't let me look in the glass. All she wants to do is play with her hair."

"Go into my room and use the glass there. I am done with it for now."

Esther rushed out, then paused to say, "You look pretty, too, Angela."

"Thank you." Angela laughed and went to where Leonia was poking at her hair. Wishing that the duke had agreed to bring Leonia's abigail along, Angela picked up a comb edged with a light green feather that matched her simple gown. She quickly twisted Leonia's hair into place and affixed it with the comb, so it dropped down over her shoulders. Until she was fired-off, Leonia must continue to wear her hair simply.

"Perfect!" Leonia flung her arms around Angela, nearly upsetting them both onto the floor.

"It shan't stay that way if you do not curb your enthusiasm just a mite."

"I shall try." She spun about as Esther had, contradicting her own words. As Angela tried to redo the damage to Leonia's hair, the young woman said, "This is going to be the most glorious night I have ever had."

"You must remember that you are not yet fired-off, Leonia."

Touching the feather in her hair, Leonia hummed a joyous tune.

"What is that song?" Angela asked, startled. She recognized it. She had heard both Justin and Esther whistling it.

"I am not sure. I have heard Rodney humming it for as long as I can remember." She sat on the light blue chaise longue at the foot of her bed, which was draped in white damask, and ran her fingers along the ruffles on her skirt. "I do not remember a time when Rodney was not part of our family."

"Mayhap that is why it has been easier for you to leave India and come to England."

With her gaze still on the ruching on her gown, Leonia smiled. "I cannot tell you how glad I was, Angela, when I learned that Rodney had been appointed as our guardian."

"He is very fond of you."

"Do you really think so?" she asked, her face alight with joy.

"Yes, he has provided so well for you and the other children."

Leonia kneaded her hands together and stood. "The other children . . . Oh, yes, he has been very concerned with our well-being."

"It is a guardian's duty."

"Rodney always considers his duty before anything else."

She sighed and turned away, picking up a handkerchief edged with dainty lace.

Angela stared at Leonia in growing comprehension. When Leonia dabbed at her eyes, Angela turned to look out the window at the twilight sky. Why hadn't she seen before that Leonia had a calf love for the duke? Leonia glowed whenever she spoke of her guardian, but her high spirits vanished at any suggestion that the duke considered her a child like her brothers and sister. She wondered if the duke realized that Leonia had this affection for him. If so, he had shown no sign. He treated Leonia with the same gentle indifference and kind indulgence that he did all the children, except on the rare occasions when their paths crossed. In his mind, allowing Leonia to accompany him to his friend's wedding was a concession to keep her happy exactly as it had been when he allowed Thomas to call on Justin.

This complicated so many things. Wishing she could take Leonia by the shoulders and shake some sense into her head, she knew it was silly. A heart did not heed good sense, and Leonia's would listen to her no more than Angela's own did.

Angela pressed her hand over her heart—it was beating wildly. Had madness infected all of them? Leonia should know better than to have a calf love for the duke, and Angela was a beef-head to fall in love with Justin Harrington. Somehow she had to guide Leonia through this without being sure of the right path herself.

"Careful . . ." Angela held out her hands as if she could help support Esther and Seth, who were being picked up by two footmen. Both children had fallen asleep, with a great deal of reluctance.

"I will see they are tucked in," Thomas said. "You can stay here."

"Thank you." She did not smile, although she was tempted when she saw the boy's relieved expression. He had made it quite clear that he would prefer to spend the evening in Lord Milborough's library than here in the ballroom where music soared to a ceiling painted with a romantic image of the sky with cherubs peeking out from among the clouds. "Have the housekeeper send someone up to sit in our room."

He grinned and sped off to catch up with the footmen. With a maid overseeing the children while they slept, he could sneak back down to the library and peruse more of the books collected by their host.

That left her only one charge to be concerned with, and Angela guessed that would be enough. Leonia could barely conceal her impatience with the restrictions placed on her because she was not yet out. Her foot tapped the floor as others danced, and she wore a frustrated frown.

"Would you like some lemonade?" Angela asked quietly.

"I would like some champagne." Leonia's frown slipped away. "Oh, dear! I should not have said that aloud."

"As long as no ears other than yours and mine heard, there is no problem." Patting Leonia's hand, Angela said, "I know how difficult it is to want to participate fully, but not be able to because you are restrained."

"I know you do!" Leonia flung her arms around Angela, threatening both their appearances. "What would I do without you, dear Angela?"

Extricating herself from Leonia's earnest embrace, Angela rose. "I will get us some lemonade."

"*You* may have champagne."

"I do not want you to suffer alone."

As Leonia giggled behind her, Angela went to where glasses of lemonade were waiting as they had been since the beginning of the evening. She glanced back, but Leonia was sitting properly. When she saw the young woman eyeing two dowagers who were obviously talking about her, Angela chuckled. Leonia would curb her buoyant spirits under such watchful observation. Mayhap the Season to come would go more smoothly than the duke had hoped.

As if she had spoken his name aloud, the duke walked toward her. She no longer was surprised that he wore a serious expression. Leonia had commented that the Duke of

Oslington always kept his obligations in mind, and that explained so much. Engulfed with the abrupt responsibility of four vivacious youngsters, he was struggling to do the best he could for them, even if it meant keeping a grim frown in place.

"Where are the children?" he asked as Angela picked up two glasses of lemonade.

"The younger two are on their way to bed, and Thomas has gone with them." Lifting the glasses, she said, "Leonia and I are going to enjoy this."

He grimaced. "That there are so many glasses here suggests it is as tasteless as what is served at Almack's."

"I have never had the privilege of going there."

"You will when Leonia is fired-off." His mouth quirked. "I suspect I shall need your guidance with her for as long as you are willing to offer it. She seems to have developed an uncharacteristic inclination to pipe her eyes whenever I say more than a score of words to her. It is most peculiar."

Angela kept her sigh silent. The duke's remark told her that he was unaware that Leonia was sweet on him. Knowing she should keep her nose out of where it did not belong, she could not keep herself from saying, "It would not be inappropriate for you to dance with Leonia."

"She is not yet out."

"But you are her guardian. If her father were here, he could dance with her without anyone being aghast."

He sighed and straightened the front of his black coat. "I wish her father were here."

"You and Colonel Sutton were very close friends, I collect."

"He was my commanding officer." He arched a brow. "I would have died to protect him and his men. However, I never guessed I would become a surrogate father to his children."

"They consider themselves fortunate that you have assumed that responsibility." She kept herself from using the word "duty." Mayhap the duke would view Leonia differently if he saw her as a young woman falling in love with him instead of a mission—getting her fired-off—that must be completed with all alacrity and efficiency.

Angela turned to walk back to where Leonia was sitting. She did not look over her shoulder to see if the duke followed. There was no need, she discovered, when she approached Leonia. The young woman's eyes glittered with happiness, warning that her guardian was coming toward her.

Stepping aside, Angela waited for one or the other to speak. She nudged Leonia with her foot when the duke's face began to redden with discomfort.

Leonia glanced away from the duke, then nodded. "Are you enjoying yourself, Rodney?"

"It is pleasurable to see friends I have not seen in more than a year." He cleared his throat, then asked, "Are you having a pleasant time?"

"Oh, yes!" She nearly jumped to her feet with her enthusiasm, but seemed to catch herself just in time. "It is so much better to sit here and watch the dancing than to peek around the banister at the top of the stairs."

"Would you like to view it even more closely?"

"This chair . . ." Leonia looked at Angela in obvious confusion.

Quietly Angela said, "I believe your guardian is asking you to stand up with him for the next set, Leonia."

"Quite!" the duke said, his tone suggesting that he wished he had never come over to speak to his ward.

"You want to dance with me, Rodney?" Leonia's eyes glowed with such joy that every candle in the room could have been doused, and her happiness would still have been visible.

"If you would like to dance."

"Oh, yes!" This time, Leonia came to her feet so quickly that she almost splattered both glasses of lemonade over Angela.

"Put your hand on his arm," Angela whispered when Leonia faltered.

She guessed the duke had heard her as well, as she had

hoped, because he offered his arm to Leonia. When the young woman put her hand on it prettily, Angela smiled. Her fear that Leonia would forget every lesson at this important moment was for naught.

Sitting in Leonia's chair, Angela watched as Leonia danced with the duke. They were undoubtedly a well-matched couple, because Leonia's height complemented his. She tried to imagine Leonia in a gown that would be better suited for an evening with the *ton*. It was not difficult because Leonia had an air of sophistication as she followed the pattern of the simple dance.

Angela glanced around the ballroom and was glad to see that most eyes were focused on the bride and groom. Mayhap no one else would take note of how Leonia gazed with open adoration at the duke. This was something that Angela must speak to Leonia about as soon as they were home again.

"You seem to be able to convince Rodney to do just about anything." Thomas scratched the back of his neck and tugged on his collar.

"Why do you say that?" she asked, amazed because she had not guessed he would return here.

"He is dancing with Leonia, isn't he?"

She wagged a finger at him and chuckled. "Have you noticed how beautiful your sister looks tonight? If she were already out, I doubt she would have had a dance left free for her guardian."

"She always found a way to get under Rodney's feet whenever there was a gathering in India."

"So I have heard." She laughed. "Why are you here? I thought you would be poking through Lord Milborough's library."

"I did. He does not have anything else of much interest there that I did not already look at this afternoon."

"There are so many books. Have you inspected them all?"

"Most of it is poetry and ancient history." He grimaced again. "In French."

"Would you like some lemonade?" she asked, holding up the glass Leonia had not sipped.

He nodded and, taking the glass, wandered away. Although she should have called him back, she did not. She must keep a close eye on her charge tonight. Leonia was less likely to sit quietly after dancing, with the duke.

Angela learned how right she was when the duke returned Leonia to her care, bowed to both of them, and went to talk to his tie-mates. Leonia's smile fell away, and tears billowed into her eyes, making Angela wish she had never mentioned to the duke that dancing with his ward would be a good idea.

"Oh, Angela," Leonia bemoaned, "it is hopeless. He sees me as a little girl. Nothing else."

Taking Leonia by the arm, Angela drew her across the ballroom toward the hallway. She was glad no one seemed to take note of their leaving, although the room had grown so crowded with wedding guests that she had lost sight of Thomas as well. Seeing him talking to several men she did not recognize, she shook her head. One problem at a time.

The corridor beyond the ballroom was almost deserted. Leading Leonia to a shadowed corner by the staircase, she asked, "Leonia, has your guardian expressed any interest in a relationship other than as your guardian?"

"No." She slammed one hand against the other, startling Angela. "But that does not mean anything. Rodney has always been the epitome of a gentleman with me."

"Your father would accept no other behavior from a man under his command."

"How do you know? You never met my father."

Angela smoothed Leonia's hair back toward the comb pinned in it. "You have spoken of him with so much admiration. So has the duke."

Leonia moaned and hid her face in her hands. "I am being a fool!"

"I never meant to intimate that."

"But you think that I am silly to be so smitten with Rodney."

Putting her hand beneath Leonia's chin, she tilted the young woman's face up. "My dear Leonia, I would never chide you about anything you felt. However, you must understand that the duke may not share your wish to change your relationship. To him, you are the child of a man he admired greatly. He takes very seriously his duty to oversee your entry into the Polite World."

"His *duty!*" she spat. "That is all I am to him! An obligation he cannot wait to get rid of!"

"You do not know that."

"Yes, I do. While we were dancing, he quizzed me about my lessons with you as if I were a little girl reciting what she learned from her tutor." She whirled away.

"Leonia!"

"No, I cannot stay here and endure a moment more of this!"

Rushing to catch up with Leonia, Angela said, "You must learn, right now, to control these outbursts."

"How can I deny what I feel?" She backed away. When Angela started to follow, she pled, "I need to be alone now to sort this out."

"You need someone to talk to."

Leonia shook her head. "I will not do something skimble-skamble, if that is what you fear. I just want to go to my private chamber and . . ." Her face crumpled. "Esther is there."

"Go to my room. I will stay here for a short time longer. Then I will come upstairs, and we can talk."

Hugging her, Leonia nodded. She gathered up her skirt and rushed up the steps at an indecorous pace.

Angela sighed. How could she have imagined, when she asked the duke to allow the children to come here with him, that obtaining Leonia her heart's desire would break the young woman's heart? She must speak with the duke, but not tonight. Too many ears would heed what she must say. Tomorrow she might have a chance during the wedding breakfast. Now she must find Thomas and convince him to return to their private rooms.

How could she ask Leonia to change her heart? She wanted to laugh and to cry at the same time as she walked back toward the door to the ballroom. What a jest—on both her and Leonia—to think that was possible! If this evening had shown her nothing else, it had revealed that she had been right. Hearts refused to heed good sense.

"Excuse me!" she gasped when she bounced off a gentleman standing in the doorway. Bumbling about into Lord Milborough's guests as if she were foxed would make the situation even worse.

"No damage done." With a chuckle, the man turned and put his hands on her arms to keep her from walking past him.

In disbelief, Angela looked up into the green eyes that had been sparking with anger the last time she saw them. As her fingers were taken and raised for a kiss that wiped away any thought but of delight, she whispered, "Justin!"

Twelve

"What you are supposed to say next is: 'Why are you *here?*'" Justin smiled as he drew Angela away from the door. The light from the lamps glistened off the buttons on his gold waistcoat beneath his black coat. His breeches were the same white as his cravat.

"Why *are* you here?" She looked from his smile to his fingers that held hers as if they were as delicate as one of his butterflies. She doubted if she had ever seen him look so handsome.

"Milborough is a friend of mine as well. Rodney Abernathy and I have more in common than just the fact that we despise each other."

She sighed, her happiness vanishing before she had even had a chance to savor it. "Please do not inject that old anger into this evening. Tonight is about two people finding love and wanting to share that joy with their families and friends."

"As you request." He bowed his head to her, his manners as polished as any man within the ballroom. "You look even lovelier than usual tonight, Angela." His voice dropped to a rough whisper. "How did the rakes in London let you elude them?"

"They did not seem very interested in me."

"Proving that they are even more foolish than when I was last there."

"You as part of the London Season? That is the silliest

thing I have ever heard." She laughed, then put her fingers to her lips. "Forgive me, Justin. I should not have said that."

"Why not? I suspect, in your mind, it was quite the truth. You have seen me only in grassville, not being a dashing rogue." He struck a pose more suitable for a statue than a wedding guest.

She laughed again, and his smile warmed. "Are you suggesting," she asked, "that I know very little about Justin Harrington?"

"Not as much as I would like you to know." His fingers drifted across her cheek. In his eyes was a fire that gave his words an intimacy that created thoughts she should not be having. "And there is so much about you that I would like to get to know . . . much better."

She knew if she continued to gaze up into his eyes that she might not be able to turn down his unspoken invitation. She was as want-witted as Leonia, but she was not a young lass. Falling in love with Justin would prove she was a widgeon, even if her employer did not despise him. There were so many secrets that hid behind his volatile eyes, and he kept each of them hidden from her . . . as he had tried to conceal Delicia. She could easily forgive him for not mentioning his daughter because he wanted to protect the little girl from pity. Why was he keeping other truths from her? She knew she should ask that question and the ones he had not given her a chance to ask when he walked away from her without explaining why he had reacted as he did.

But all she could do was gaze up into his eyes and imagine him holding her close as he had by the stream. Far from all the other guests, she could gather him into her arms and offer him the chance to open his heart to her as she longed to open hers to him.

"Justin!" Thomas ran over and slapped Justin on the arm. "I thought that was you I saw talking to Lord Milborough! Why didn't you tell me you were coming here?"

"I was not so certain myself until I found myself on the way here." Justin saw Angela's eyes turn toward the boy, and he cursed silently. The children always found a way to intrude at the very wrong time . . . either his child or one of hers. Not hers! Oslington's! He silenced the shout of the duke's name to tell him to come and get Thomas. There were already too many people in this conversation.

Justin swore again, this time under his breath, when he saw Thomas's smile vacillate. He could not blame the boy for something that was not his fault. Putting his hand on Thomas's shoulder, he said, "I understand there are several varieties of butterflies in this area that we may not have studied at Harrington Grange. What do you say to finding out tomorrow?"

"I would like that!" The boy's grin returned.

"Good. Take yourself off to bed, then, and meet me at the wedding breakfast. I am sure that Milborough will excuse us from all the toasts while we explore his gardens."

Thomas sped off toward the stairs, nearly careening into a dowager who gave him a reproving scowl. Even that could not dampen his smile. He shouted his apology in his wake.

Justin took Angela's arm and steered her away from the dowager, who was looking for someone to blame for Thomas's behavior. When he saw an open door ahead of them, he drew her outside onto the brick terrace edged with flowering bushes he could not identify in the twilight that came so late at this time of year.

"Do you have something to say to me?" she asked as he sat her on a stone bench topped by plush cushions, an affectation he appreciated when he sat beside her.

"I find that words never are onerous between us."

She smiled, and he wondered if he had been witless to bring her out here because he could not read the warmth in her eyes. Or mayhap that had been the wisest thing he could have done. With a laugh, she asked, "So are you no longer vexed with me?"

"I would like to say yes, but I find that you endlessly challenge me to reconsider everything I have assumed to be true. And not just about Delicia."

"About the duke?"

"Not directly, but I have realized that only a fool would let his anger at a man he has no respect for get in the way of his delight with a woman he has the greatest admiration of."

"Oh."

He folded her hand between his, although he longed to enfold her to him. "That is not a very satisfactory answer."

"I find that things are not always satisfactory."

Hearing regret in her voice, he whispered, "What is wrong, Angela?"

"There are several answers I could give you." She swallowed so roughly he could hear it. "But the one that echoes through me with every heartbeat is why you reacted as you did when I suggested that you consider that school in France for Delicia."

"Overreacted, you mean."

Her smile sparkled even in the dim light. "Yes."

"And you are curious why?"

"Yes."

He knew he owed her the duty of the truth, but that meant opening too many doors in his memory that he had sealed, vowing never to unlock that vault again. The man he had been then was one he did not want to recall. The pain he had experienced then he was not sure he could face again. Better to leave it all in the past where it belonged. If that were so, then why was he, for the first time in more than five years, even considering opening those closed doors once more?

"France is so far from Harrington Grange," he said, despising himself for resorting to a banal answer. He feared she would despise him even more if he spoke the truth.

"And Delicia is such a little girl." She smiled. "I understand."

Self-loathing threatened to choke him when she touched his cheek as lightly as he had hers. By Jove, he was guaranteeing that she would be hurt if she ever learned the truth of the hell he had endured in France and the greater grief he had found when he returned.

And now . . . with a groan, he framed her face with his hands. She gazed up at him, and he did not dare to speak. A single word might destroy this moment he had waited for since the last time he had seen her. The moment he had thought of through the endless hours of the night when sleep refused to grant him release from his yearning for her. Even when he found a few moments of sleep, his dreams were all of holding her.

She whispered his name in a soft breath that stroked his lips as he found hers. He tugged her against his chest while his hands slid down the back of her silk gown that was not as smooth as her skin. When she quivered as his fingers cupped her nape, he wondered how long he could be satisfied with only this. His fantasies were far more sensual, for he wanted to explore all of her as his touch released each of the passions that she could no longer mask.

She drew back and leaned her head on his shoulder. Her fingers lingered on his chest, slipping beneath his waistcoat. "I have missed you," she whispered.

"And I have missed you." He laughed. "I have missed your stubborn determination to help everyone instead of thinking of yourself once in a while."

"I think of myself once in awhile." Raising her head, she whispered, "And I think of you far more."

Justin's answer was halted when another couple came through the door. Coming to his feet, he offered his arm. "Angela?" he asked when she did not move.

"Must we go so soon?"

Bending, he cupped her cheek. "I thought you were the tutor of all things proper for Leonia. What sort of example would you give your young charge if you were discovered here in my arms?"

"The wrong one for her," she replied. Putting her hand on his arm, she stood with a grace that suggested she was dancing. "However, I am not sure if it would be the wrong one for me."

A craving to hold her ricocheted through him, so he did not answer as he led her to a place where light from the ballroom spilled through yet another door onto the bricks. She regarded him with soft eyes that suggested she would have favored remaining in the shadows. Mayhap he had been a fool to bring her out into the light, but where else could he see her glorious smile? And, he had to own, he did not trust himself to be alone with her in a secluded corner any longer, for he wanted so much more than her captivating kisses.

When she slipped her hand into his, he went with her to a bench at the very edge of the arc of light escaping the ballroom. He sat beside her and smiled when she rested her head on his shoulder. It seemed to belong there, and he was suffused with a sense of wonder of why he had had to wait so long to discover that.

When she ran her fingers through the leaves on a bush beside the bench, he asked, "Are you looking for a fairy hiding in there?"

"No, not a fairy. I know they do not come out unless the moon is full."

He looked up at the curved sliver rising above the chimneys. "It will be a fortnight at least before you shall have the chance to catch one."

"I never have been able to." She tilted her head back and smiled up at him. "Mayhap I should look for butterflies instead."

"Even more fruitless." He chuckled. "You will not find them at this time of night, because butterflies seem to adore the sunshine."

"The moonlight would wash out the beautiful colors from their wings."

"Instead of glistening on them and turning them into flying rainbows." *As the sunlight does to your hair.* He ran his finger along one of her curls, which had become silver in the dim light.

"Did you ever wonder where butterflies sleep?"

He let the single curl twist around his finger like the tiny hand of a child. "When I was Delicia's age, I believed that butterflies must spend the nights deep within the flowers that closed up when the sun set." Leaning his cheek against her fragrant hair, he murmured, "I infuriated my mother that summer by peeling open all her blossoms so I could look inside to find a sleeping butterfly."

Laughing, she looped her arms around his, which was wrapped around her waist. "No wonder you and Thomas are such good friends. I can imagine him doing the very same thing." She nestled closer to him as she drew her feet up beneath her on the bench.

"And you were an angelic child?"

"Of course!"

"Pardon me if I find that difficult to believe."

She laughed, and he gathered the lilting sound around him so he could hear it again and again when she was no longer in his arms. When she began to tell him about one of her childish misadventures, he knew he must find a way to keep this night going on for as long as he could. He knew it was a stolen moment . . . and how unlikely it was that they would have another.

"Where have you been?"

At Leonia's testy tone, Angela's footsteps, which had seemed as bouncy as if she were walking through clouds, became quite earthbound. She walked across the antechamber of the suite of rooms to where Leonia sat hunched on a low settee by one of the windows.

"It is nearly dawn!" Leonia gasped, flinging out her hand toward the window.

"I know."

"Where have you been?"

"One of the things you must learn about the *ton* is that the hours they keep have little to do with the sun." She ran her fingers lightly over the back of the settee, remembering how Justin's hair had glided through them.

"But I looked for you! I went back to the ballroom when you did not come upstairs. You were not to be found."

"I had gone out on a terrace."

Angela thought that Leonia might demand an explanation of why Angela had left the ballroom, but Leonia said only, "You knew I was upset."

"I thought you might like some time to sort out your

thoughts before we talked." She yawned and smiled an apology.

"You do not care about my broken heart!"

Dropping to her knees beside the distraught young woman, Angela folded Leonia's hands between hers. "You know that is not so. I care deeply about you, but I know there is nothing I can say or do to alter your situation."

"I know." She sighed and blinked back tears, luminous in the first light of the dawn. "What can I do? I am sure I love him, but he thinks I am just a child."

"What you need to do now is get some sleep." Standing, she brought Leonia to her feet. "The younger children will be up soon."

"How can I sleep when I am so sad?"

"Mayhap in your dreams, you can find a solution to your sorrow." She raised one finger as she saw hope fill Leonia's eyes. "I am not talking about a wishful dream, but a dream that might reveal to you some truth you have overlooked."

Again, Leonia's shoulders drooped, but she went into the room she shared with Esther.

Angela opened her own door. Would she be able to follow her advice to Leonia? She could not conceive of sleeping when her heart was threatening to burst with joy. She never had guessed how splendid it would be to sit through the night and share reminiscences and kisses with a man who so often vexed her. Undressing and getting into her bed, she leaned back against the pillows and stared up at the wooden canopy above her. She slowly recreated Justin's face in her mind, relishing each strong line. As she closed her eyes as she had when his lips found hers, she let the waking dream dissolve into sleep where spending a lifetime of nights with him forever was not impossible.

Angela tried to keep from rubbing the sleep from her eyes and gave Leonia a sympathetic smile as Esther and Seth ran through the room, eagerly awaiting the chance to join the other guests at the wedding breakfast. The two hours of sleep she had gotten must be enough until she could return to the room for a nap in the afternoon. Thomas sat to one side, fingering the butterfly net that he must have put in the carriage's boot when no one was paying attention. He kept glancing at the clock.

"You will not be able to go looking for butterflies until after the wedding breakfast," Leonia said, her fatigued voice cranky.

"Mayhap I can go earlier."

"You cannot leave the wedding breakfast."

"I can if Justin does, too."

Leonia spun to face Angela. "Lord Harrington is here?"

"Yes," Angela replied. "He is also an old friend of Lord Milborough."

"You knew he was here?"

"I saw him last night."

Leonia's mouth became a perfect circle, but she asked no more questions. Instead she stood to one side while Angela calmed Esther and Seth enough so they could go down to the wedding breakfast.

The dining room where the guests were already serving themselves by the time Angela arrived with the children was bigger than the rooms they had upstairs. A trio of doors were opened to the gardens where roses bloomed. More flowers were set in huge bunches in vases on the long table and the various sideboards around the room. Servants wandered among the guests, offering drinks and assistance.

Thomas waved wildly, and Angela looked to her left to see Justin walking toward them through the press of guests who all seemed eager to be the first to sample the dishes that filled the room with tempting aromas. She had not thought he could appear more handsome this morning than he had last night, but she had been wrong. He wore a vest embroidered with vines as green as his coat. His smile held no hint that he had had as little sleep as she had.

"How long do we have to stay here?" Thomas asked with a grin.

"Can I, at least, say good morning to these three lovely

ladies?" Justin smiled and, bending toward Seth, added, "And to this good-looking young man."

Seth giggled along with Esther, and Angela was tempted to join them as her head was giddy with happiness when Justin stood and gave her his warm smile. She offered her hand, and he bowed over it before pressing his lips to it. He did not release it as he bowed over Leonia's hand, too.

"Good morning, Lord Harrington," she said coolly.

Justin arched a single brow at Angela, but she could not say anything without embarrassing Leonia.

She wished she had said something—anything—to end this conversation when she saw Leonia's eyes glow with delight at the same moment that Justin's became emerald slits. Turning, she saw the duke standing behind her.

His frown could not lessen the strange color of his face, which was far too ashen. "Harrington."

"Oslington." Justin's clipped tone matched the duke's.

"Children, I think you should come with me." The duke started to turn his back on Justin, but he did not have a chance to walk away before Lord Milborough pushed through the crowd of guests.

The groom was not tall or well-favored, but he had a kind smile. He put one arm around Justin's shoulders and the other over the duke's. "I am so glad that both of you came to Milborough Manor for my wedding." His jovial laugh suggested he had already enjoyed several servings of the wines being offered along with breakfast. "Just like it was when we were as young as these children here. The three of us looking for all sorts of trouble."

"Yes," the duke said, his jaw still taut.

"And now you are married, old chap," Justin added. He was not going to let Oslington's low spirits ruin his good time at this wedding.

"When are you two going to walk down to the altar yourselves?" Milborough asked. He jabbed Oslington with his elbow. "Now that you are home and have that grand title, it is time for you to find a pretty lass and put an end to speculation. Why not one of these young ladies?"

Justin did not expect the stab of anger that sliced into him as Oslington glanced at Angela. When the duke looked back at him, Oslington wore a superior smile on his oddly pasty face.

"Something to consider," Oslington said with a chuckle.

Angela colored prettily. She put her arm around Leonia's waist as she said, "I will remind you, gentlemen, that a lady's heart is not won by being stared at like a mare at market."

Milborough crowed with laughter before steering Oslington and Justin through the guests to meet his bride. Justin tried to avoid being dragged along by giving an excuse about needing to speak with Thomas, but Milborough refused to listen. Oslington looked daggers at him. Justin ignored him as he had so often in the past five years after his attempt at reconciliation was thrown back in his face.

More than a half-dozen times, as the wedding breakfast unfolded, Justin saw Thomas trying to get his attention. He motioned for the boy to have patience. Before he could leave with Thomas to scour the garden for interesting butterflies, he wanted to find out if Angela had any plans for the afternoon, because he could imagine nothing more delightful than spending it with her in some quiet bower deep in the gardens.

Every effort he made to speak with her was stymied by one of the guests. Because he had not been to Town in more than two years, many of them were curious about what he had been doing and any gossip he might have heard in the country. He kept his face from disclosing his growing aggravation when he was asked over and over if, as Oslington's neighbor, he knew about Miss Needham. The supposition was that she must be the duke's mistress, an arrangement given countenance by her so-called position as companion for his ward.

Finally, more than two hours later, he saw Angela by one of the doors to the gardens. He went to her and took her arm and led her, rather unceremoniously, out onto the terrace.

"Take care," she said.

"Did I hurt you?"

She shook her head, a phantom of a smile hovering on her lips. "You might damage your reputation, Justin, by being seen with your neighbor's convenient."

"You heard, too?"

"How could I help it?" She amazed him when she laughed.

"I am surprised you find this gossip amusing."

"I don't, and I sent Leonia upstairs, ostensibly to rest, so she does not hear it."

He rested his elbow on the stones of the house, but let his fingers linger along her arm. "Are you certain you don't want to use this as a lesson for her?"

"She will learn soon enough how poker-talk follows one, whether it is true or not." She paused as cheers came from inside.

Justin looked back through the door. Glasses were being raised in a toast to Milborough and his bride.

"Are you thinking of the day when you married Delicia's mother?" Angela asked.

He must have betrayed himself in some way, but he would not lie to her . . . about this. "I doubt anyone forgets one's wedding celebration."

"What was her name?"

"Elizabeth. Elizabeth White."

"You must have loved her very much."

"On the day I married her, I loved her with every ounce of my being." He faced her and took a slow breath. "I have not said that to anyone in a very long time."

"Does Delicia know?"

Justin recoiled at her question. "How would I know what she might be aware of?"

"Esther seems to understand Delicia very well. When we return to Oslington Court and I can arrange for the children to have a chance to play together again, you shall see."

He drew his arm from beneath her hand. "That is a matter I had hoped not to speak to you about today."

"Why not?"

"I did not wish to distress you."

Her eyes narrowed. "Distress me? How?"

How had the conversation taken this turn? It was too late to backtrack now. "I do not think that playing with the other children is a good idea."

"Why not? She has had a wonderful time when we were at your house."

"She has had a wonderful time, but she cannot truly be part of their play."

"You are quite wrong." Taking his hands, she looked up at him, her face lit well by the sunshine, her hair a golden aura around it.

He saw her dismay, and he forced his sorrow from his face. "I wish I could believe that, for I would gladly own to being wrong. I think I am correct."

"You are wrong, Justin. Esther tells me that she and Delicia have learned to understand each other."

"I don't understand how *you* can put so much faith into what must be just childish play."

"It is not childish play, but it is quite simple, Justin. Remember how I told you about the school that teaches deaf children to use their hands to speak? It seems that Delicia has already developed a language of her own, and she is teaching it to Esther."

He stared at her, amazement widening his eyes as he sought something to say.

"Justin, she is your daughter," she whispered as if she did not dare to speak more loudly. "She must have your intelligence."

"I had hoped so, but I could never know for certain if anything other than thoughts of her most basic needs were going on within her mind."

"That is because you have assumed she cannot be reached." Putting her fingers to his lips, she said, "When Delicia did this to me, you suggested it was just a game she played. It is not. She touches Esther's lips when she is trying to comprehend what Esther is talking about. Then she touches her own. She wants to speak as we do."

"I know she wishes to be like us, but I fear that is impossible."

"It will be impossible as long as you deny her the chance to learn what she can."

"I will not send her away to school." He turned away.

"Is that what you are arguing about? Not sending her to school? This has nothing to do with whether you send her to that school in France or another or none at all! You cannot deny that she is trying to communicate with us."

When she grasped his sleeve so tightly that he heard a thread snap, he looked back at her. "Angela, this is my problem. Mine alone."

Her eyes grew wide, and her bottom lip trembled. "I understand. I am sorry that I have meddled where I should not have."

"Angela!" he called as she stepped around him and walked away into the press of guests in the dining room.

She did not answer.

He took one step to follow her, then halted. What could he tell her if he gave chase? The truth? It was too late for that now, he suspected. Far too late.

Thirteen

Shouts rang from every corner of the house, Angela was sure, when she paused in the doorway of Oslington Court. Esther slipped her fingers into one of Angela's hands, and Seth did the same on the other side. Leonia wore an expression that suggested she wished Angela had saved a hand for her to hold, and even Thomas edged a half-step toward Angela. When he glanced toward the door, his thoughts of fleeing visible, she shook her head. He hunched into himself.

Only the duke walked farther into the foyer. His steps were slow and studied. Their trip from Milborough Manor had been interrupted often as it had been during their journey north. The duke had appeared somewhat hale at the wedding, his coloring better, but now Angela wondered if that was because he was seldom seen without a glass of something. He put his hand on the newel post at the foot of the stairs.

When she saw how his knuckles bleached, Angela suspected he was gripping the carved post because he was struggling again to keep himself on his feet. She was not so sure of that when she saw a woman coming down the stairs, a bevy of servants rushing before her like quail flushed from a thicket.

"Rodney!" called the woman, who was nearly as tall as he. Her gray hair curled perfectly around the face that brought the duke's instantly to mind. This must be his mother, for her clothes were as flawless as her hair. As she bustled to a stop on the lowest riser, her gown barely swirled around her ankles.

Mayhap it did not dare. Angela was glad no one else had heard that thought. Her mother had always spoken with the greatest respect about the Duchess of Oslington.

"Mother, this is an unexpected pleasure," the duke said.

Did anyone else notice how his emphasis had been heavier on "unexpected" than on "pleasure"? Angela remained silent as the duke gave his mother a proper kiss on the cheek.

"I thought," the duchess replied, "to see how you were doing now that you are settled in here at Oslington Court. I thought I should judge for myself how you are managing with Colonel Sutton's poor orphans."

Those "poor orphans" bristled on either side of Angela. A quick glance at each of them was enough to warn them to be silent, but nothing could diminish the fury in their eyes. What Angela had seen right from the beginning—that the Sutton children had not lost their pride—was something that the duchess must acknowledge straightaway, or there would be trouble. When she saw Esther and Thomas share a quick smile, she frowned. They were already plotting mischief. Somehow, she and the staff would have to block anything they devised without the duchess being aware.

"Children," the duke said, "this is my mother. Mother, Leonia, Thomas, Esther, and Seth Sutton." His voice suggested he was deeply tired.

The children did not move until Angela gave Leonia a shove with her elbow. Docilely, the other children followed as she went to greet the duchess. Making a good first impression was impossible because their clothing was stained and dusty from their long journey. She was pleased to see that their manners were the best she had ever witnessed. Mayhap they understood—at last—how important this encounter could be.

The duchess looked past the children, and Angela understood what no one had to say. Coming forward, she dipped her head to the duchess. "Good afternoon, Your Grace. I am Angela Needham."

"So you are Agatha's daughter."

"Yes, Your Grace."

The duchess stepped past the children. She eyed Angela up and down. "I see you favor your father's family. Any resemblance to your mother, other than your coloring, is slight."

"So I have been told, Your Grace."

"That is regrettable, because your mother was a very handsome woman." She gave Angela no chance to reply before turning again to the children, who had not been able to hide their expressions that *this* was not the homecoming they had imagined. She shook her head and made a "tsk-tsk" sound. "Rodney, I must say that Colonel Sutton asked too much of you to leave you the duty of saddling yourself with four children. You are a young man who should be thinking of other things than raising a dead man's off-spring."

Knowing that she was risking a rebuke, Angela edged toward the children again. They swarmed forward, the younger two again grasping her hands in a near death-grip. She winced as they crushed her fingers, but did not release their hands.

"If you will excuse me, Your Grace," she said, looking at the duke rather than his mother, "the children are fatigued from their sojourn in Scotland. I believe it would be best if they retired now."

"Yes," he began, "that might be—"

"Nonsense," the duchess said, tapping her foot. "Children do not like to take naps."

Angela lowered her eyes as she heard Seth murmur an agreement. Mayhap the duchess was not so cold-hearted as her words had made her appear.

"*You,* Rodney," the duchess continued, "look as if you could use several good nights' sleep. I assume you enjoyed yourself in Scotland."

"We attended Milborough's wedding." His answer

sounded as guilty and naughty as when Angela had caught Thomas with Justin.

"Go and rest. If you drank so much that you are still gray with a headache days later, you should rest in your rooms."

"Mother—"

"Do not fret about me, Rodney. I have been looking forward to returning to Oslington Court, and I can entertain myself quite well." Without a pause, she turned, jabbed a finger in the direction of the children, and said, "You."

Leonia pointed to herself. "Are you speaking to me, Your Grace?"

"Who else, girl? Step forward. Stop lurking in the shadows."

The duke cleared his throat. "Mother, Angela was correct. The children are tired after our long journey, as I am. I trust any questions you have for them can wait until later."

"I have urged you to go and rest, son," the duchess cooed, patting his cheek. "Angela, take the three younger children upstairs to where I am sure their governess is waiting for them." She put out her hand as Leonia turned to follow her grateful siblings. "I will speak with you now, Leonia."

The young woman gave Angela a desperate glance. Wishing she could help Leonia, Angela gave her the only answer she could—a bolstering smile.

For once, the children did not complain as Angela herded them up the stairs. Behind them, servants followed with the bags they had taken to Milborough Manor. Everyone, it seemed, was eager to avoid the notice of the duchess. Leaving the children with Mrs. Meyer, the governess, Angela went to Leonia's room to wait.

That was a mistake, she realized when she went to look out the windows. They gave her a remarkable view of Harrington Grange. Had Justin returned there? After their conversation on the terrace during the wedding breakfast, she had seen him only once—when he was riding away from Milborough Manor. She had not been sure if he was leaving for home or going somewhere else. What would she have said if she had had a chance to speak with him? That he could keep hiding from whatever he could not face in his past, but by doing so he was risking his daughter's future? She had said that . . . more than once, but she also knew that she had been honest when she said she should not have meddled.

Hadn't she learned that she could not make everything go as she wanted simply because she wished it to be so? She had tried all she could to help her mother. She had struggled to make herself useful at her brother's house. She had ignored her heart's yearning to be close to Justin, but she had failed at all of those. Mayhap she should learn her lesson and stop trying to persuade Justin to be sensible.

Hearing the door open behind her, Angela whirled. It was a maid bringing in clean linens for the bed. Giving the woman a tentative smile, Angela turned back to look out the window. She must try to be patient. Someone would know when Justin arrived home to Harrington Grange. Thomas surely would be looking for Justin as well, because their planned outing to find butterflies at Milborough Manor had been halted when the duke had insisted that Thomas join him for a ride.

This time when the door opened, Leonia rushed into the room. She halted and scanned the chamber. When she saw Angela, she ran toward her, then froze when another maid entered the room.

Angela took Leonia's hand and led her into the bedchamber. Asking the maid who was remaking the bed to leave, Angela closed the door and leaned back against it. She must wait for Leonia to speak first.

As she had feared, Leonia began to weep. "That woman is simply awful." Leonia threw herself on her bed. "By all that's blue—"

"You should not use such cant, Leonia."

Sitting, Leonia crossed her arms over her chest, then wiped away more tears. "I swear that I shall give voice to curses far more horrific than that mild oath, Angela, if I have to spend even a moment longer with that woman."

"The duchess is—" Angela was not certain if Leonia even

heard her as the young woman jumped down from her bed and prowled the room as if looking for an escape hatch. Trying again, she began, "Leonia, I believe that the duchess is—"

"Mad! She seems to think I must already know every detail of a complete litany of the lives of every member of the *ton*. By all that's . . ." Leonia flashed Angela a guilty glance. "Sweet heavens, Angela, I have not even met anyone yet. Even when we were in Scotland, I had to remain at the edges of the room, save when I danced with Rodney." More tears washed down her face.

Angela handed her a handkerchief and said, "I think it would be best if we dealt with one problem at a time."

"Rodney is not the problem. *She* is! You and I have chatted about how I should greet those who can welcome one into the Polite World or blackball one for being gauche, but even if you have tried to instill in me information about all their names and how they are related to each other, how can I possibly keep track of that?"

"I shall be glad to talk with her on your behalf." Angela quelled her shudder at the thought. Already she had failed to meet the duchess's expectations of being the mirror image of her late mother.

"She was furious that I did not know the name of the family that has the house next to hers on Berkeley Square. I know the house belongs to Lord Hillings, but I was so flustered I swear my brain was as empty as the day I was born."

"When I speak with her, I shall reassure her that you were unsettled."

Leonia grasped Angela's hands. "No! She will see that as a sign that I am not yet ready to be fired-off. Rodney promised me that we would go to London in the spring. I do not want to wait longer."

Picking up a hairbrush, Angela sat next to Leonia and began to brush the young woman's hair. The auburn strands were unfashionably long and straight, but a competent abigail could arrange it beautifully. "Do not fret," she said.

"Just be grateful that Rodney is your guardian instead of his mother."

"That is true!" Leonia gave her a watery smile. "I keep telling myself that she is wise in the way of the Polite World, and I should respect her opinion."

"That will help."

"She does seem eager to do what, as she said more than once, is the right thing for us." She took the brush from Angela and, rising, set it on the dressing table. "She believes Thomas and Esther should be sent away to school."

"That would be the customary course at their ages."

"That would make them miserable, and I think how sad the rest of us would be if they were sent to school."

"You must think of them—especially Thomas, who will soon be regarded as an adult, too. He should learn the skills an Englishman needs."

"What skills do you think he needs?"

Angela was lost for an answer. She had seen that Thomas rode with the ease of someone who has been in the saddle since his earliest memories. Leonia often mentioned one of her brother's *bon mots,* so Angela was assured that the young man had a keen wit which he could use in the quick conversation of Town. The truth was that he needed the same polishing his sister required.

But it was true, too, that these children needed each other now as they struggled to remake their lives without their beloved father. To be separated from the duke now might do irreparable damage. She must help the duchess to understand that.

Glancing toward the window and its view of Harrington Grange, she wondered how she could expect the duchess—or Justin—to change when she could not change herself and her determination to help those she loved.

"But Rodney did not say we could not continue to call at Harrington Grange on Thursday afternoons," argued Thomas as he climbed the stairs with Angela.

"The duchess has insisted that you complete your history class and that Leonia study her music this afternoon."

"Rodney did not say we could not go."

"I know, but I have seen nothing of him since we returned from Scotland. Until he countermands his mother's orders, you are obligated, as his ward, to obey her. You need to study with Mr. Weare now."

Thomas grumbled something under his breath.

Angela knew she would be jobbernowl to ask him to repeat it. It would be just as silly to own that she was as frustrated. Every day, she had to soothe Leonia's tears and ease Esther's outrage that Wallah was not welcome anywhere beyond the nursery. Seth hid behind Angela whenever the duchess came near him, although Angela had to confess that Her Grace had been kind to the little boy.

Although she might be ruining her tenuous friendship with Thomas, Angela escorted him to the upper floor and the nursery to leave him under Mrs. Meyer's supervision until Mr. Weare finished his midday meal. The rotund governess seemed perturbed by the fact that Angela had come with him. Looking from the sullen boy to Angela, she shook her head in dismay.

Mrs. Meyer said, when Thomas had stamped away, slamming the door to his bedchamber resoundingly, "Thomas is my responsibility, not yours. I would thank you not to distress him more."

"I am not distressing him, but he has to recognize that he needs to acquiesce to the duchess's commands."

Mrs. Meyer adjusted the small glasses that perched on the very end of her nose, clearly amazed that Angela agreed with her. "Forgive me, Miss Needham. I fear the children have had little in the way of decent upbringing in that wild land where they were born. Such a savage place it is."

"Nonsense! They have excellent manners . . . usually." She walked through the nursery's main chamber. Peering into the room beyond where Esther slept, she saw Esther and her younger brother playing with a stack of blocks. The scene could have been of any family in any English country house—save for the monkey chewing on a red block. Angela turned back to the governess. "They have been taught pretty manners. They simply—like any children who think they can escape the canons of propriety—choose to ignore them when it is convenient or when they are frustrated from doing what they truly wish."

"Have you had much association with children, Miss Needham?"

"No."

Mrs. Meyer raised her chin, revealing another pair of chins beneath. "*I* have spent the past three decades tending to children. I started first as a nursery maid and now am a governess. Let me tell you that I never have seen children who act like these. They can set one all on end before the morning is half passed." She shivered. "And to think that Thomas gave the duchess back talk . . ."

As if on cue, Seth let out a shriek and aimed a block at his sister's head. Esther ducked as the block sailed past her to strike the fireplace mantel.

Not waiting to see if the governess would scold them or simply suffer a *crise de nerfs,* Angela took Esther by the hand and said, "Come with me."

"*He* threw the block!" Esther protested.

"And that is why *he* shall not get to go for a walk in the garden."

With a superior smile, the little girl scooped up her monkey and walked out of the room. Seth's lower lip quivered.

Angela bent to whisper to him, "I shall take you for a walk tomorrow morning when the dew is heavy. Then we might find a fairy beneath a leaf."

His eyes brightened. "I would rather find a frog."

"Why?"

"Esther is afraid of frogs."

She laughed. She could not halt herself.

When she went out into the hall and away from Mrs. Meyer's frown, Angela was astounded when Esther insisted on bringing the perambulator. The little girl put her monkey into it and tucked a doll's blanket around the creature. Wallah glowered at her, but subsided when Esther gave him a piece of dried fruit to nibble on.

"You must be certain that Her Grace does not chance upon you taking Wallah out of the nursery," Angela said with a smile. She did not add that she would not have agreed for Wallah to come along, except that she guessed the monkey needed fresh air as much as Esther did.

"Can Leonia come with us?"

Angela lifted the perambulator and carried it down the stairs. The monkey chattered at her, clearly nervous, until Esther peeked into it. Then it subsided and ate its fruit. Setting the perambulator on the foyer floor, Angela replied, "Leonia is practicing her singing. Hush! Mayhap you can hear her."

"I do not want to."

"What a horrible thing to say!"

"But true."

Angela chuckled. Leonia had no musical gift. Her torturing of the scales had set every nerve on edge when Angela had passed the music room door earlier. "That is why I thought you might enjoy walking in the garden and enjoying the pretty flowers."

"What is in the garden that *I* would want to see?" Esther scowled. "I like the flowers in the conservatory better. They are more like the ones we had at home."

"At home?" Seeing the child's morose expression, Angela put her hand on Esther's shoulder. "Do you mean in India?"

"That is where I was born. I hate England! And I hate everything and everyone here!"

Angela stared after her as Esther raced away, pushing the perambulator at a pace which was sure to upset the monkey. The situation was just getting worse. Angela glanced toward the duchess's rooms. The duke's mother was doing what she deemed in the best interests of the children, but it was going to undo all that Angela and the rest of the staff had worked to achieve.

A quick search of the garden told Angela that Esther

would not be found. The little girl would come back to the house when she finished her sulk.

With a sigh, Angela went back into the house. She would apologize to the little girl later. Now, Leonia should be almost done with her lesson, and she was certain to need a chance to talk with someone about every slight—real or imagined—from the duchess.

Climbing the stairs, Angela paused on the landing. She could see the tip of the chimneys at Harrington Grange from here. If she hurried, she might be able to reach the house and return before Leonia finished her lesson. But on what excuse?

"Mayhap 'tis time for the truth," she said to herself as she continued up the stairs. But even that had been useless when last they spoke.

The corridor was dreary. She had seen clouds gathering on the horizon. The walk in the garden would have been short even if she had not sent Esther up into the boughs. As she loosened the ribbons of her bonnet, she smiled wryly. The weather was as bilious as her mood.

Angela gasped when a form appeared out of the shadows that were gathering near every door. Heat clamped on her cheeks when she looked up into the duke's startled face. He wiped the emotion from his features before she could react to the unexpected sight. All that was left was the unhealthy tinge that had clung to him for days.

"Miss Needham," he said as he snapped closed a book he was carrying, "you should not linger in the shadows."

"Yes, Your Grace." When he regarded her steadily, she felt obligated to add, "I was about to take Esther for a walk in the gardens, but—"

"Esther? Odd, after my mother's comments about Leonia's unreadiness for the *ton,* I would have thought you might spend this afternoon working with Leonia."

Angela fought to keep her smile. How he had changed since his mother's arrival! He had been coolly polite before, but now he was coolly rude, treating her as if she were the lowest servant in the house. Raising her chin, she said, "I was on my way to talk to Leonia just now, Your Grace."

"I urge you to hurry to that meeting. My mother was speaking of taking her on a call tomorrow afternoon. If you deem it necessary for Leonia to have further instruction, that must take precedence over any other activity."

She nodded, recognizing his attempt to protect Leonia from another scold by his mother. Nodding toward him, she realized he had already returned his attention to his book. She continued along the corridor. It was going to be a very long afternoon.

No, she would not succumb to brooding like everyone around her. Nor would she allow the children to sink into melancholy.

After an hour of reading in her room while she waited for Leonia, she went to the nursery and collected the children, who were sitting in the classroom with Mr. Weare. The tutor did not hide his relief that she was willing to entertain them so he could enjoy his usual reading in the afternoon.

Taking the children to Leonia's room, Angela offered Esther a gentle smile. The little girl's eyes flooded with tears, and Angela put her arm around her narrow shoulders. She could not give Esther a scold simply because the little girl was nostalgic for the only other home she had ever known.

Thomas and Seth perched on the bottom of the chaise longue while Esther toyed with the fringe on the drapes as the storm went past. They all looked up in dismay as Leonia came into the room, the now-familiar tears on her face.

Handing her a handkerchief, as she did each day after Leonia's lessons with the duchess, Angela said, "I believe it is, as Thomas reminded me, Thursday."

"Yes, it is." Leonia dabbed at her eyes. Abruptly she looked up. "Do you mean . . . ?"

"It is Thursday," Angela said, smiling at each of the children. "By taking the air now, we shall be gone from Oslington Court for exactly the two hours until tea."

Seth jumped to his feet. He started to cheer, then glanced at his brother and sisters and sat, nodding as they did.

Angela sighed. The duchess's arrival had done the very thing the duke had asked her to avoid. The cheerful spirit within these children had been doused, leaving them wraiths. Mayhap that was how the duchess expected children to act, but Angela missed the mischievously shared looks and the smiles that signaled trouble yet to be discovered.

The children acted as if they were skulking through enemy territory as she led them down the back stairs, through the garden, and into the field between Oslington Court and Harrington Grange. As soon as they were out in the grass, Thomas let out a cheer. Seth and Esther danced about, ignoring the heavy air that warned that the storm would eventually reach them.

"We did it! We escaped!" crowed Leonia.

Angela knew she should chide Leonia for speaking so, but how could she when she agreed? Her heart was singing with the anticipation of seeing Justin again. The evening at Lord Milborough's wedding had been magical until the argument began, and she was eager to see if they could resolve their differences. Then mayhap they could discover if the magic had followed them back here.

When Leonia began to sing, Thomas grimaced, then joined in. Angela swung Seth and Esther's hands as they strolled through the field. Keeping an eye on the dark clouds, she was glad to see that they were not growing thicker. The storm might linger to the west. She sighed. A storm would mean that they could remain longer at Harrington Grange.

Esther raced up to the door and knocked. Bouncing from one foot to the other, she grinned at Angela. How Angela wished she could act just the same! Her heart was cavorting at the prospect of seeing Justin again.

The door opened, and Mrs. Graves peered out. Her smile was strained. "I am sorry, Miss Needham. Lord Harrington and Delicia are not within. I do expect them back for tea. If you and the children would like to wait . . ."

Angela swallowed another of the sighs that had come too often since the duchess's arrival at Oslington Court. She saw the children's shoulders sag with regret. Unwilling to add to their dejection, she asked, "Do you know where they went?"

"I believe they were going to look for berries. With the storm coming, they should be here soon. If you do not want to wait, Miss Needham, you should hurry back to Oslington Court. The storm is not far off."

"Thank you. Will you let Lord Harrington know that we called?" As the door closed, Angela added, "Do you know where they might be, Thomas?"

"No." He dug his toe into the dirt between the stones in the path. "We never have gone berrying."

Looking both ways along the road, Angela saw no one. She held out her hands. No one spoke as the younger children slipped their hands into them. Walking back along the road toward Oslington Court, she waited for one of them to speak. The only sounds were their footsteps and the distant sound of thunder.

She should say something—something about next week and the opportunity to visit with Justin and Delicia then. What could she say that would not be hypocritical? She did not want to wait another week to see Justin. Tears clogged the back of her throat, searing and threatening to overflow.

Abruptly Seth jerked his hand out of hers. With a shriek, he raced along the road toward where the walls of Oslington Court shadowed the road in the fading sunlight. She stared after him in amazement. When she saw two people walking toward them, she had to fight her feet that wanted to run with him to Justin and Delicia. Instead, she froze, unable to move, even when Esther tugged on her hand.

The distance between her and Justin melted away as she stared at him. He was dressed as he had been the first day she met him, including the butterfly net balanced on his shoulder. But then he had been a stranger. Now he was a part of each thought.

As Esther took Delicia to one side and began to prattle as if she had forgotten Delicia could not hear a single word, Justin paused before Angela. His hand rose to cup her cheek.

"Good afternoon, Justin," she said, knowing that she sounded silly to be so prosaic when she longed to spill out the hopes within her heart.

"We are well met."

"Yes."

"Where are you bound?"

"It is Thursday."

His forehead furrowed. "You are right. I was thinking it was already Friday, because this week has been endless." He looked down when Seth tugged on his coat. "Yes, Mr. Sutton?"

"You were supposed to be home when we came to call," Seth said.

"I shall remember that." He looked back at Angela. "I owe you an apology, Angela."

"And I owe you one."

"No, you don't. Caring about Delicia so much that you speak your mind is not a crime."

Taking his arm, she turned him toward Esther and Delicia, who were deep in their private form of conversation. Their whole bodies seemed to be part of it as they paid no mind to the fitful wind that tugged at their hair. Esther talked endlessly, but pointed here and there and up and down. Delicia seemed to understand because she kept nodding and pointing as well.

"Unbelievable," Justin said in awe.

Angela slipped her arm through his. "Think about the school I told you about, Justin. I will be glad to bring you the newspaper article again."

"You saved it?"

"Yes."

He cocked a brow at her. "If you will return it to me, I will promise to read it this time."

"But?"

"I promise I will read it. That has to be enough for you now."

She touched his lips. "That is not enough for me now."

His mouth lowered toward hers, and she closed her eyes,

eager to lose herself in the pleasure. When he lifted her hand and kissed it, she stared up at him in astonishment. He looked past her, and she recalled how many witnesses there were to this conversation.

With a chuckle, he slapped Thomas companionably on the back. "I am sorry, too, old chap, that we did not get the chance to study the butterflies at Milborough Manor. Mayhap next week, Delicia and I can show you the butterflies we discovered not far from the stream."

"You are teaching *her* about butterflies, too?" Thomas's wide eyes were filled with apprehension. And jealousy, Angela realized when he stammered, "I—I thought that was something you and I—I mean, that we . . ."

"Thomas, you know I could not be teaching her anything without your wonderful drawings. I hope you will join us on our next sojourn across the moor. I would appreciate your skill at catching butterflies in your net. It surpasses even mine now."

The boy's grin returned. "I would be happy to, Justin."

"Excellent."

"Can we go by ourselves sometimes?"

Justin laughed. "Of course. I suspect Delicia is far more interested in your sister than in butterflies, so we can leave them playing at Harrington Grange while we pursue our prey." Thunder crackled. "Blast! That storm is coming fast."

Rain splattered around them before Angela could reply. Taking his hand, she said, "Come with us."

"Where?"

"To Oslington Court, of course."

He shook his head. "Oslington told me to stay away."

"You are too far from Harrington Grange." She shuddered as lightning flickered across the sky. "Do not let your pride cause you to risk Delicia." Raising her voice, she called, "Run as fast as you can for the house!"

Angela gathered up Seth as Thomas picked up Delicia and ran toward the gate. Leonia chased after him. When Justin, muttering an oath, scooped up Esther, who squealed with excitement, and rushed past her, Angela followed him through the gate. She cringed as lightning flashed and thunder followed so quickly she knew that the storm was almost overhead. Wind buffeted her, and the trees at the edge of the road whipped about as if being stirred in a giant pot. She tried to run faster. Pain burned under her ribs, but she did not slow.

The door was thrown open, and her arm was grasped as she hurried up the steps. Seth was taken from her, and she leaned against the wall. She gasped when a fierce crack was followed by branches crashing to the road where she had been running just moments ago.

Strong arms surrounded her, and she leaned her cheek against Justin's chest. His heart was beating as rapidly as hers. When she tilted her head back and saw the longing in his eyes, she did not care who might be watching. She drew his mouth down to hers. The tempest surging through her as his kiss deepened was more powerful than the one beyond the walls. Her arms curved up his back, delighting in the flow of muscles she had been afraid she would not be able to touch again. There was so much that needed to be said between them, but now she wanted only to exult in his caresses.

"Thank heavens!" came a shout. "You are back!"

Pulling away from Justin, Angela was astounded to see Hervey coming down the stairs at a speed for which he usually chided one of the children. She gasped when the butler grabbed her hands and pulled her toward the stairs. She looked back and saw the children and Justin were as bewildered as she was.

"Hervey, is something amiss?" she asked.

" 'Tis His Grace. He is deathly ill."

Fourteen

Leonia pushed past her siblings and ran to Hervey. "Is it both a fever and chills?"

"Yes! That is what his valet said." The butler wrung his hands. "Culver sought me out when His Grace swooned in his book-room. We just got him to his room."

Angela turned to Leonia. "His Grace has suffered from something similar before?"

"It is a condition he got in India from the bad airs there."

"Malaria," Justin said softly.

Leonia faced him. "May I impose on you to go for Dr. Young, Lord Harrington? Hervey can call for a carriage to be brought for you to fetch the doctor."

"I shall go immediately." He looked past her to meet Angela's eyes. "Do you need anything else?"

"Just the doctor." Angela motioned for the children to go with Mrs. Meyer, who was coming down the stairs. She was glad that Esther still held Delicia's hand and led her after Seth and Thomas. Lowering her voice, she asked, "Hervey, where is Her Grace?"

"With her son." As quietly, he added, "She is not one who is good in a sickroom, I fear."

Wanting to say that was no surprise, Angela held her tongue. She put her arm around Leonia as they went up the stairs toward the duke's apartment. The door closed loudly on the ground floor, and she knew that Justin was on his way to get the doctor. Thunder crashed overhead, and she shivered.

"Do not fret, Angela," Leonia said. "He shall be fine."

"Justin or His Grace?"

"I hope both of them." Leonia adding nothing else as they went to the double doors that opened into the grandest private rooms in the house.

Angela did not take time to admire the elegant furniture or the ceiling painted with a sylvan scene like the one on the ballroom ceiling at Milborough Manor. She skirted maple tables covered with books and passed through one of a trio of doors set opposite a huge bay that reached nearly twenty feet to the ceiling.

"Where have you been?" the duchess asked, coming forward to meet them. "Rodney is so ill. How could you disappear at a time like this? Where is the doctor?" The last question was aimed at the butler.

"We have sent for him," Hervey replied, bowing his head.

"Who did you send? Not that dolt in the stable, I hope."

Leonia's nails bit into Angela's arm, but Angela removed her bonnet as she said, "We sent Lord Harrington for the doctor."

"Lord Harrington?" The duchess's eyes grew round. "Are you mad? He was *here?*"

"He sought shelter from the storm for both himself and his daughter. Would you send a little girl out into the midst of the thunderstorm?" Angela did not give anyone a chance to answer. "As I said, he is on his way to get the doctor."

Leonia piped up, "I wish to see Rodney."

"Impossible!" The duchess folded her arms in front of her. "You are a young girl. You have no place in a man's sickroom."

"It would not be the first time." Leonia's chin rose to jut at the duchess, amazing Angela. "I know what should be done."

"I will not have improper behavior under this roof."

"The most improper thing would be to let him die!"

When the duchess puffed up, appearing about to explode,

Angela intruded with, "Your Grace, if Leonia can give instructions to His Grace's manservant, certainly there can be nothing wrong with that."

The duchess glared at Leonia. "She is just a chit. She has no idea how to handle herself in polite society."

"We are not talking about an assembly, Your Grace," Angela argued. "We are talking about your son's life."

Slowly the duchess faced Angela. Her face was almost as colorless as the duke's had been when Angela last saw him in the hallway. Taking the duchess's arm, Angela helped her sit on a comfortable chair. She motioned, and Hervey brought a stool so the duchess could prop her feet. Ordering the butler to bring some tea for the duchess, Angela motioned to Leonia to do what she must.

She was not astonished when Leonia took her arm and gave her a grateful smile. She went with the young woman to the half-opened door. As Leonia pushed it aside, a short, white-haired man that Angela knew was the duke's valet sprang out of the room and nearly embraced Leonia.

"Thank the heavens you are here, Miss Sutton!" he exclaimed in a loud whisper. "I do not know what else to do. I put His Grace to bed. First, he is too hot. The next minute, he is too cold. I fear if something is not done, he is going to die."

"Nonsense," said Leonia with the same serenity that she had shown in the foyer. Pulling off her bonnet, she pushed it into the man's trembling hands. "Have Dr. Young brought up as soon as he arrives. Meanwhile, have a fire set on His Grace's hearth. Send for more blankets."

"But, right now, he is sweating with a fever!"

Angela said quietly, "Do as she says, Culver. She knows more about these Eastern diseases than any of us."

"Eastern?" He shuffled his feet, looking as young as Thomas. "You are right. I know nothing of them. I was not with His Grace in India, Miss Needham. I have been at Oslington Court for all the years I have been in service."

She patted his arm. "You need not apologize when you are already doing your best. Just do as Miss Sutton asks."

Relief eased the deep lines on his face. "That I can do."

Angela looked past him to where Leonia stood by the grand bed with its red-and-gold bedcurtains. The young woman seemed to have gained years of maturity, for her face was tranquil as she placed a damp cloth on the duke's forehead. If there had ever been any doubt in Angela's mind about Leonia's feelings for her guardian, they would have been banished now.

When Hervey poked his head past the door, Angela went to him. "How is Her Grace?" she asked.

"I put some sleeping powder in her tea, so she will rest." His lips quirked. "And so she will not interfere with Miss Sutton."

"Thank you." She looked past him as a short, stout man entered the outer chamber. A quizzing glass dropped from a chain over his sedate waistcoat, and his hair was the same dark gray as his coat. She knew he was the doctor when she saw Justin in the hallway beyond the door. Wanting to go to him, she said instead, "This way, Dr. Young."

"You are?" he asked in a thin voice.

"Miss Needham, companion to the duke's ward." She stepped back to allow him into the room. "This way, sir."

He bustled into the room. When she looked past him, she saw the duchess asleep on a settee. The hallway was empty. Although she wanted to ask if Justin had gone to get Delicia and was going back to Harrington Grange or if he planned to wait somewhere else, she could not take the time.

Following him to the bed, Angela watched the doctor greet Leonia. She smiled to herself when Leonia began to pepper the doctor with questions that it quickly became clear he had no answers for. She suspected Dr. Young had no more knowledge of diseases from India than the valet did.

At a groan, Angela saw the duke's eyes were partially open. She put another cool cloth on his forehead because Leonia was still deep in conversation with the doctor.

"Miss Needham?" the duke asked, his voice a thready whisper.

"Rest," she murmured. "The doctor is here."

He mumbled, but she could not understand a single word. His eyes closed again, and she guessed he was lost once more in his fever.

The doctor examined the duke far more swiftly than Angela had expected, not even asking her or Leonia to leave. There was no need, because he did no more than check the duke's eyes and put his hand on his forehead.

When he turned from the bed, Leonia began to ask him another question. He paid her no mind. He walked away from the bed and gestured to Angela. She went with him to the door.

Reaching into his bag, he pulled out a small container. "Give her this powder, Miss Needham, or I fear she shall make herself quite ill with worry."

"Her? Her Grace?"

"No, Miss Sutton."

"Leonia is fine."

"She is acting quite unlike herself. She is making endless suggestions."

Angela smiled. "I know, but it is because she knows best how to help His Grace."

Grumbling, Dr. Young put the packet on the duke's writing table. "If she needs it . . ."

"What about His Grace?"

"I believe what you are doing is the best thing one can do."

Not sure how to respond when the doctor was offering no help, Angela stepped aside again as he brushed past her to take his leave. Her dismay must have been visible, because Leonia left her post by the bed and came over to her.

"Do not worry, Angela," she said. "This spell is not as bad as the one he had on the ship from India. I know how to care for him."

"Mayhap because you care for him so much." She squeezed Leonia's hand.

"Tell the others that Rodney will be fine. He needs to rest, but as long as he is kept warm, he will be fine."

Angela nodded. "Culver and Hervey are here to help you. Her Grace is asleep."

"That will help as well." She ran back to the bed as the duke groaned. "Go," she added. "We will take care of him."

Slipping out the door, Angela was glad to see Culver go into the bedroom. There would be no impropriety when the duke was so sick or even when he was hale, but there must be no hint of it.

The Sutton children were waiting anxiously in the nursery, and she was delighted to share Leonia's prognosis with them. Looking about, she did not see Delicia before Hervey knocked on the door and motioned for her to come with him.

Angela followed the butler down the stairs to the first floor, answering his questions as best as she could. More than once, she had to reply, "You must ask Miss Sutton about that. She knows so much more about this condition than I do."

When he opened the door to the duke's book-room, she saw a silhouette in front of one of the rain-swept windows. She rushed across the room. "Justin! I had hoped you would wait here."

"I did not wish to take Delicia out in the rain."

"Delicia? Is she here?"

He shook his head, his dark hair falling forward over his forehead and teasing her fingers to brush it back. "She is asleep up in the nursery."

"That is why I did not see her when I went to speak with the children."

Weaving his fingers through hers, he led her to the closest settee. He sat her there, then went and closed the door to the hallway. Sitting beside her, he asked, "How does Oslington do?"

"Leonia has assured me that the fever and the sweating are normal parts of the progression of the disease."

"What about the doctor?"

"He was useless. I fear he is no more familiar with maladies of the Orient than I."

He chuckled without humor. "He is an excellent doctor

for setting broken legs or offering laudanum to ease sleeplessness. Otherwise, you are right. He is useless."

"Was he the doctor when your wife died?"

"Yes."

Putting her hand over his, she combed that defiant strand back from his eyes. "I am so sorry."

"And so worried."

"Of course. His Grace is too young to be laid low by this debilitating illness."

"Anyone who is want-witted enough to seek a career in India must be willing to suffer."

Angela stood, unable to believe her ears. "Can't you relinquish your hatred of him long enough to have sympathy for him?"

"I am no saint," he replied, setting himself on his feet. "You may be asking more than I can give."

"Can or will give?"

Walking to a sideboard, he poured a glass of wine and handed it to her. "You look as if you could use this."

Her fingers quivered as they closed around it. She tried to halt them. For the children, for the household, for herself, she must appear strong. "Thank you," she said as she took a sip of the sweet Madeira. She put the glass on the table beside her. "But it is not what I need."

With a moan, he pulled her into his arms. She wound her fingers through his hair as his mouth found hers with the hunger of the days they had been separated. His kiss said what he had not in the midst of their angry words. These longings mixed with exasperation could so easily tear them apart. She needed him to strengthen her, and she sensed that he wanted her strength as well. But it was more than that. In his arms, she could give herself wholly to this ecstasy. Nothing existed but his lips on hers, his tongue caressing the inner secrets of her mouth, and her breasts soft against his hard chest.

His lips coursed along her neck, and she trembled with the craving that had no name. It simply was. It was part of him and part of her and part of what drew them together, no matter how many other things tried to drive them away from each other.

He whispered against her ear, "You are so delicious." His tongue traced the edge of her ear, and she tightened her hold on his coat. She did not want to be thrust away by the power of this longing.

Steering his mouth back to hers, for her lips were lonely for his, she slipped her arms beneath his coat. The cool length of his back waited for her exploration, and she did not hesitate. Against her legs, his strong ones pressed, urging her back one step, then another toward the settee. With one arm around her waist, he drew her other hand to his lapel in an invitation to ease his coat aside. She started to draw it over his shoulder as he brought her down to sit, his eager mouth pressed to hers.

Suddenly Justin seized her hands, pulling them away from him. Angela gasped in astonishment. "What is wrong? Are you out of your mind?"

"I would ask the same of you, Miss Needham," came the duchess's furious voice from behind her.

Angela looked over her shoulder and jumped to her feet at the same time. The duchess rested one hand on the doorframe. Behind her, Hervey was holding out his arms, warning that he expected her to collapse at any moment.

"Your Grace," Angela said, "I thought you were sleeping."

"Is that your excuse for allowing *that* man to paw you like a common strumpet in my son's house?" The duchess lurched into the room. Waving aside Hervey, who begged her to sit, she did not pause.

Angela moved out of the way, suspecting the duchess would walk right over her. The duchess paused in front of Justin, who had come to his feet and was adjusting his coat.

"Your Grace," he said with the slightest bow of his head.

"You know you are not welcome here. Not after what you did!" The duchess pointed to the door. "I trust I will not need to call for someone to have you removed."

"No, Your Grace. I will take my leave as soon as I retrieve my daughter from the nursery."

Angela stared from one furious face to the other. "Please explain to me why there is so much hostility between these two families."

"Be silent!" ordered the duchess.

"Your Grace," Justin said, his calm voice not hiding his rage, "you need not speak so to Angela. Her only mistake is offering a haven to Delicia and me during a vicious thunderstorm."

"Her only mistake?" The duchess flicked a lock of Angela's hair which had fallen to her shoulders. "It seems she has made another error in judgment by allowing you to attempt to seduce her. If you will take your leave, Lord Harrington, I shall deal with this problem in my household as I believe is appropriate."

Angela knew she would infuriate the duchess more, but she put her hand on Justin's arm to forestall his back-answer. When he looked at her, she said, "Mayhap it would be for the best if you took Delicia home now, Justin."

"As *you* wish," he replied, glaring at the duchess. "I shall take my leave, so I am not an additional burden on you while you oversee the duke's recovery. I know—once he is well enough to have a rational thought in his head—Oslington shall also demand an explanation of why I was allowed to step foot in his house." He smiled coldly. "Good day, Your Grace."

Angela bit her lip as he took her hand and bowed over it with the perfect manners he could exhibit whenever he chose. When he stood straighter, she wished to say so many things to him, but she could not when the duchess might overhear. In his eyes, she saw an apology for focusing the duchess's anger on her. She wished to tell him that she could endure anything after her sister-in-law's tempers. She said nothing.

"Angela, please keep me informed of Oslington's condition." He reached for the butterfly net that she had not noticed leaning against a bookcase.

"Yes . . . yes, Justin," she said, glancing at the duchess, who bristled at the use of his name.

When he turned and walked out of the room, Angela yearned to follow. Instead, she faced the duchess, who signaled to the butler.

"Hervey, we will be disturbed only if my son needs me," the duchess said in her imperious tone.

"Yes, Your Grace." He backed out of the room, closing the door in his wake.

The duchess sat, but did not grant Angela leave to do so. Appraising her candidly, the duchess sniffed. "You are a sight!"

"The storm winds—"

"Do not fill my head with out-and-outers, young woman!" She tapped the wooden arm of the chair. "Your behavior with *that* man is intolerable."

"*That* man," Angela fired back, knowing she should keep her mouth closed, but unable to, "went for the doctor to help your son. Justin went out in the middle of that horrible storm, risking his own life, to bring Dr. Young."

"I suspect he did so only to gall Rodney."

"What?"

"Did you ever consider, Angela, that the only reason he volunteered was so that he could gloat at forcing an obligation upon Rodney when my son had no other choice?"

"That is ludicrous!"

Angela knew she had spoken out of turn when the duchess erupted to her feet. For the next half hour, she was treated to a listing of all her shortcomings and foolish behavior. The duchess showed no signs of being the worse for the sleeping powder, save that she had to sit halfway through the scold.

"And," the duchess finished, "I would turn you out of Oslington Court without a recommendation if not for the long-standing respect I had for your mother. However, if there is another mistake, you will be gone. Do you understand?"

"Yes."

"Do you?"

"Yes."

"Do you really?" the duchess persisted. "Let me reassure myself that you do. You will have nothing more to do with Lord Harrington while you reside beneath this roof."

"But, Your Grace, I am obligated to escort the children to play with Delicia Harrington each Thursday afternoon."

"Who agreed to such an addled arrangement?"

"The duke."

"Why?"

"Thomas has been studying butterflies with—"

"Bah! Butterflies! If Lord Harrington wishes to waste his life, that is one thing. I shall not have anyone in this house do so."

"But Esther and Delicia have become friends. They look forward to their times together."

The duchess strode toward the door, her steps still uneven. Gripping the door, she said, "I shall hear no more of this balderdash! Everyone knows that his child is witless, and she shall not be inflicted on any of these children. Her madness might spread to them."

"Madness? She is not mad. She cannot hear!"

"So who knows what is going on in her head? No, I shall not have the children playing with her. You will inform them that these visits are curtailed."

"I will tell them, but . . ." Angela took a pair of steps toward the door, then stopped when the duchess's eyes narrowed. "Delicia's friendship with Esther has been good for both little girls."

"Do not argue with me! The Sutton children are Rodney's responsibility, and it is his duty to make sure they are not infected as that child has been."

"Infected?"

"With the sins of the father." Her mouth worked. "And the mother. You will go to your room, Angela, and stay there while you consider that." She strode away, leaving Angela to stare after her in disbelief.

Fifteen

Angela lowered her needle as a knock sounded on her door. Rising, she put the bonnet on her table. Another few stitches and the flowers would be secure again. She wished Wallah had not taken such a like to her bonnet, but was sure that Esther was sincere when she promised to watch her pet more closely. Scolding the little girl was the last thing she had wanted to do when the children already were so upset about being forbidden to call at Harrington Grange.

Foolish Thomas had tried to sneak away from Oslington Court when the duchess had overseen one of Leonia's music lessons. He had realized how determined the duchess was to prevent any more visits. Now the lad was banned from leaving the house without a footman in tow. Between his anger and Esther's tears and Leonia's tears, for nothing she did seemed to find favor with the duchess, and Seth's pouts because he was upset that his siblings were upset, the whole house was in an uproar.

Did the duchess have no idea how much her son had appreciated the quiet he had found in these walls before her arrival? He needed that peace now more than ever before as he struggled to get better.

All in all, Angela had been so busy that she should not have had a second to think of Justin. In truth, he had been constantly on her mind. How many times had she wandered into Leonia's room simply to gaze out the window at Harrington Grange? She had considered slipping out to call there, but she guessed the duchess was having her watched as closely as Thomas.

Another sharp knock came at her door, and Angela hurried to open it. She was startled to see the duke's valet on the other side. "Culver, is something amiss?"

"Quite to the contrary." The white-haired man was smiling broadly. "Miss Needham, I would like to extend an invitation from His Grace for you to give him a look-in now."

"He is himself again?" Once the crisis had passed, and the duke was sleeping with the powders that Leonia had ordered, Angela had spent hours by the duke's bedside when Leonia had needed to rest. She had bathed his forehead with cool cloths and followed the instructions that Leonia had given her.

"Yes."

"Then I should not . . . I mean . . ."

In Culver's eyes, she saw a twinkle for the shortest second. "You will be happy to know, Miss Needham, that His Grace is well enough to enjoy the sunshine on his small balcony off his sitting room."

"Did Leonia give him permission to—" Angela interrupted herself with a laugh. As headstrong as any of the children, the duke would not remain in bed if he believed himself fit enough to walk a few steps.

Going with the valet toward the wing where the duke's rooms were situated, Angela heard her name called. She turned and waved to Leonia.

"Are you coming to the duke's chambers, too?" Angela asked.

"No." Leonia glanced over her shoulder like a felon being followed by the watch. "Her Grace expected me for tea nearly five minutes ago." Holding out her hands, which were filled with a half-dozen books, she asked, "Would you take these to him? When I saw him yesterday, he was restive, and I thought they might persuade him to sit quietly."

"Yesterday? I thought you were checking on him much more frequently than that."

"The duchess has been gracious enough to spend a majority of her waking hours working with me to have me ready for my entrance into the Polite World." Her frown suggested she was not as grateful as her words sounded.

Taking the books, Angela said, "As soon as I can find a way, I shall remind Her Grace that I was brought here to perform that task."

"No!" Leonia grasped Angela's arm. "Do not! She is always in a pelter whenever your name is mentioned. I fear that, if you challenge her now, she will turn you out. Then I shall have no one to confide in."

Angela nodded, knowing how lonely it could be to live in a house where nobody seemed to care about the needs of her heart. She had escaped from her brother's house, but Leonia would only escape from the duchess when she married. With a sigh, Angela knew she must not do anything that would persuade the duchess to banish her and leave Leonia without a confidante.

But that meant turning her back on Justin. Her hands tightened on the books. Could she protect Leonia at the cost of heartbreak? She had no answer, so she forced a smile and said, "Leonia, I have no intention of leaving as long as the duke wishes me to remain."

"Rodney appreciates what you do! I wish he was himself again! Then he would set his mother to rights."

"I hope your guardian knows how much you have done for him." She could not agree with Leonia, for the duke had complied with his mother's wishes since her arrival. Or had that been because he was too ill to begin a brangle?

"I hope so, too." Leonia rushed away along the hall as a clock somewhere chimed the half hour.

Angela followed Culver in the opposite direction. The valet had been wisely silent. Glancing back, Angela promised herself that she would find a way to spend more time with Leonia now that His Grace was on the mend. And if the chance arose to mention this problem to him today, she would do so.

Tilting the books Leonia had given her, she read the titles.

Notes of a Journey in India. Egypt and Its Many Lost Treasures. The Indian Ocean and the Subcontinent. She smiled, delighted that the duke had such books in his library. She must ask him if she could read them as well, for she loved the idea of traveling beyond England's shores. How she had dreamed of wandering far from England! When the children spoke of their long journey from India and the wonders they had seen in that distant land, she had hidden her envy.

Culver opened the duke's door, and Angela entered to see that a set of drapes that had always been closed were now pushed aside. A pair of glass doors were thrown open to let fresh air into the room. Sitting on a chair on the small balcony, the duke was bundled in blankets as if the day were as chilly as midwinter.

"Miss Needham, Your Grace," the valet said with a bow.

"Thank you, Culver." The duke's voice was weak, and his hand quivered as he gestured to another chair. "Do sit, Miss Needham."

"Shall I bring tea?" Culver asked.

The duke glanced toward the sky. "Ah, I see it is already time for that. Yes, bring some tea and some of Cook's excellent chocolate cake if she has any."

"I shall find out, Your Grace." With a glance that seemed to warn Angela to treat the fragile man with all gentleness, the valet went back into the house.

"The day goes quickly when one naps most of it away," the duke said as Angela crossed the balcony.

She set the books on a low table beside the stone railing. "Leonia thought these might entertain you during your convalescence."

"She is a dear child."

"She is not a child any longer, Your Grace." She sat and faced him. His coloring was still pale, but he looked better than he had any time since they had returned from Scotland. "Leonia taught Dr. Young and Culver what they needed to know to tend to you."

He tapped his fingers on the arm of his chair, and she

stiffened, for the motion brought his mother to mind. "I should have brought Mohun with me."

"Mohun?"

"My servant in India. He wished to stay in his native land. He would have served me better than that kindly old man that my father bequeathed me along with his title." He raised his hand. "Do not think that I am belittling Culver's skills, for he is an excellent valet. It is that he does not understand this condition I suffer from."

"None of us did, save for Leonia." She smiled. "And what matters is that you are recovering nicely. I daresay you soon shall be riding about the countryside."

"Thanks in large part to you, Miss Needham." He took her hand, shocking her. "There were so many times when I was half-awake, and I could hear you giving orders to see to my comfort and well-being."

"I was glad to help, but I was only there when—"

"Angela!" Seth raced out onto the balcony. He did not seem to notice his guardian as he grabbed her hands. His large, blue eyes were filled with trepidation. "Angela, Esther needs your help. Wallah is climbing to the very top of the curtains in the nursery, and Mrs. Meyers is threatening vapors, and—"

"She does not wish the duke to be disturbed," interrupted the duke.

The child blushed as he turned to face his guardian. "Rodney, I thought you were in bed!"

"I was, but now I am speaking with Miss Needham and telling her how grateful I am for her care." He smiled at the little boy who was standing as straight as a tin soldier. "Will you be so kind, Seth, to inform your sister that Miss Needham is busy speaking with me?"

"Esther will not like that."

"I did not think she would." He smiled, a sight that always astonished Angela because it changed his whole demeanor. "Ask Mrs. Meyer to take herself to her room. I fear Mrs. Burkhardt is far too busy to burn feathers to rouse a swooning governess. Have your brother fetch Wallah down from the ceiling, and tell Esther to keep him on his leash."

"Thomas is not here." He clapped his hands over his mouth and looked guiltily at Angela.

"Where is he?" asked the duke.

Angela stood and went to look past the trees edging the balcony. As she had hoped, she could see the roof of Harrington Grange from here. "It is Thursday," she said without emotion. "I suspect he chose not to obey Her Grace's edict that the children stay away from Harrington Grange."

"I told them that they could continue to call there on Thursdays."

"True."

"My mother countermanded that order?"

"Yes." She bent and gave Seth a shove toward the door. "Go and tell your sister what the duke has asked you to tell her. Mr. Weare should be able to fetch Wallah down from the curtains."

"All right, Angela," he said, his eyes wide as he looked at his guardian, who was now scowling.

"It appears, Miss Needham," the duke added as soon as the hallway door closed behind the little boy, "that there have been some changes since I took ill."

She did not want to speak against his mother. When she stumbled over a noncommittal answer, he said, "Do not fill my ears with useless comments. You need only answer one question: Why have you allowed Thomas to pay a call at Harrington Grange without you?"

"I find it impossible to be in two places at the same time."

"Do you?" He arched a brow, and a hint of a smile returned to his lips. "I have to own that, as proficient as you have proven in altering my household, Miss Needham, I am astounded you cannot perform so minor a miracle."

"If you wish me to retrieve him at Harrington Grange—"

Her hope that she finally had the excuse she needed to call on Justin vanished when the duke said, "No!"

She stared at him, shocked by his sharp retort.

"Forgive me." He laughed shortly. "You cannot guess

how it nettles me to see all of you going *ventre-à-terre* to that blasted place. Pray do not glower at me, Miss Needham. I know I agreed to these weekly calls. However, on this matter, I may have to agree with my mother, something that I do not do often. I would like the children to see less of Harrington." He rested his chin on his fist. "I believe he has been using them to further his own goals."

"His own goals? I do not understand, Your Grace."

His brows arched again. "No? Think, if you would, Miss Needham, why I asked you to come to Oslington Court. Although you have taught Leonia some of your charming graces, your foremost concern should be assuring that she does nothing beyond the canons of propriety."

In spite of herself, heat scorched Angela's cheeks. These words she comprehended all too well, for they were equally insulting to her and to Justin. She guessed the duchess had come to the duke after dressing Angela down for letting Justin embrace her.

"Your Grace, I assure you that nothing I have done—"

"You?" He shook his head, then put his hand to his forehead. "Miss Needham, I have no quarrel with your actions. I worry instead about Harrington's. Leonia is an impressionable young girl."

"Leonia?" Angela almost laughed. Apparently the duchess had not regaled him with how Angela had been discovered in Justin's arms. "You need have no worry in that quarter, Your Grace. The viscount treats Leonia just as he does the other children."

"Good, for I have no wish to hear of an announcement from that quarter." He sighed and leaned back in his chair. "You need not look as if I have put you to the stare, Miss Needham. As Leonia's guardian, *my* obligation is to be certain that she makes a match that will be both pleasing and proper for her."

"She will be pleased to know that." There must be a way for Angela to tell him that Leonia's heart already was aching to be given to a man she loved. Again the temptation to laugh taunted her. The duke believed that Leonia might fall for Justin when Leonia loved her guardian. At the same time, Angela could not find an excuse to go to Harrington Court to ask Justin to be honest with her . . . as she would be when she told him that she was in love with him. Knowing she must add something else, she said, "I can assure you that Leonia will be well prepared to be fired-off when the next Season begins."

"I have no idea where Leonia or any of us shall be by the time the Season starts anew. Burn it! England is boring."

"Your Grace?"

His gaze focused on her. In the sharpest tone she had ever heard him use, he snapped, "You need not act so dashedly polite every minute of every day. Don't you get tired of being prettily mannered and having to do the same blasted things every day until you are sure you will go quite mad with *ennui?*" When he put his hands on his chair to push himself to his feet, she stepped forward to make certain he did not collapse. "Stay back, Miss Needham. I am not ready to cock up my toes yet."

"As you wish."

"As I wish? What do you wish?" He set himself on his feet, but was prudent enough to keep his hand on the back of the chair. "Is *this* the life you dream of? A tranquil house in the country where you can hear the walls moldering around you?"

"No."

"Neither do I!" He was steadier on his feet than Angela had dared to hope as he walked the few steps to the edge of the balcony. Leaning on the thick wall, he said, "I have had a lot of time to think about this while I was bed-bound. Now I know that I have made a mistake, and I intend to rectify it as soon as possible. But, first, I need you to do something for me."

"Your Grace?"

"Miss Needham, take the pony cart and retrieve Thomas and his sketches from Harrington Grange posthaste."

"But you said—"

"I made a mistake there as well." He did not face her, so

she could not read his expression as he said, "Do not think me mad, Miss Needham. Mayhap this bout with the malaria was a blessing in disguise, for it has shown me that I am a fool not to do as I wish."

"Yes, Your Grace." She had no idea what else to say.

"And right now, I wish for Thomas and his sketches to be retrieved. Tell Thomas to bid his farewells to Harrington, because he has made his last call there."

Angela was glad the duke could not see her expression, which was certain to reveal her despair when she whispered, "Yes, Your Grace."

"Posthaste, Miss Needham."

Going into the house, she narrowly missed bumping into Culver. She mumbled an apology to him as she went out into the hallway. Numb, she went along the hallway. The duke was planning something. She was not sure what. The only thing she was certain of was that this could very well be her final call at Harrington Grange.

Sixteen

Angela held her head high as she knocked on the door at Harrington Grange. Otherwise, she feared tears would leak from her eyes, and she would reveal the sorry state of her heart.

When the door opened, Mrs. Graves had barely a chance to greet her before a small, pale-pink whirlwind rushed out to throw her arms around Angela. "She has been waiting anxiously," Mrs. Graves said.

Squatting, Angela smiled at Delicia. "Good afternoon, Delicia." She put Delicia's fingers to her mouth and repeated herself.

The little girl grinned, her lips moving in a copy of what Angela had said, although no sound emerged. Then she waved both hands in the air at about shoulder level.

"I don't understand," Angela said.

Tapping Angela's arm, Delicia made the motion again, this time with impatience.

"I am sorry, Delicia. I do not understand."

"She is asking," Justin said as he walked toward them, "where Esther is. That is the motion she makes when she greets Esther."

Angela came to her feet slowly. Her eyes feasted on the sight of him. His collar was missing, and his waistcoat was unbuttoned to reveal the easy ripple of muscles with each step. His feet were bare beneath his breeches, and she was sure she had never seen him look more beguiling. His tousled hair teased her fingers to sift through it, and she could not keep from staring at his sensuous lips.

A tug on her skirt pulled her from her dream of being in his arms. Looking down at Delicia, who was making the motion again, Angela shook her head. "Esther is not here."

Delicia's face fell.

"Mrs. Graves?" asked Justin.

"Yes, my lord." Putting her hands on Delicia's head, she turned the little girl's head toward the kitchen. "Come, lamb, and let us make your favorite cake."

Delicia broke away and ran to her father. Once more, she made the motions. He shook his head. Her shoulders sagged, and tears glistened in her eyes when she took Mrs. Graves's hand and walked out of the entry hall.

"She has been making that motion since our midday meal was served," Justin said, not coming closer to her.

"I did not think that you put much value into the signals she makes with her hands."

"I have changed my mind."

"So has the duke."

His face became grim. "I was afraid of that when your usual time to call came and went without any hint of anyone but Thomas."

"What did he tell you?"

Stepping forward, he cupped her elbow and said, "I think it would be for the best if we spoke where no one else can overhear."

"Yes." She put her fingers over his on her arm, unable to keep from touching him.

He glanced at her and then quickly away. As she sat on the small settee by the hearth, he took the chair where he had been reading the first time she called here.

Sorrow washed over her like an icy wave slapping her to the sand. This was not the way she had imagined her final visit to Harrington Grange would be. *Final!* She did not want to believe that, but finding a way to persuade the duke to see the good sense of allowing the children to play together might be impossible now.

"I suppose," Justin said, picking up a glass of brandy that had been on the table beside him, "I should inquire first about Oslington."

"He is better. He regained his senses a few days ago, and now he has managed to leave his bed for short periods of time to take the air."

"I assumed he was awake. Otherwise, he could not have given the order that keeps the Sutton children imprisoned in Oslington Court."

She nodded, biting her lower lip.

"And he has sent you to bring Thomas back with orders not to come here again, I assume as well."

"Yes, Justin."

"What of you?"

She clasped her hands in her lap. "It has been made very clear to me that continued calls here would mean the termination of my employment at Oslington Court."

"Good."

"Good?" She sat straighter. "How can you say that? If I am banished from here, I would have to return to London and live on the scant generosity of my brother and sister-in-law, who have begrudged me every morsel I ate and every inch I took up when I was under their roof."

His hard expression eased, and he set the glass back on the table. Leaning forward, he grasped her hands. "Angela, I had no idea."

"Do you think I would have endured the duchess's scolds the day the duke took ill if I had had any choice?"

"I have to own that I gave it no thought." His smile was crooked. "I was so angry at Her Grace's lack of appreciation for what you had done that I could think of nothing else."

"And her lack of appreciation for what you did for her son."

"I had you defending me on that matter." Lifting her hands to his lips, he kissed one and then the other. "You are quite the virago when you fly up to the boughs, Angela. That is a fact I would be wise to keep in mind for the future."

She extracted her hands from his. Rising, she said, "I thought you had understood that I cannot call again, either."

"You are a resourceful woman." He set himself on his feet and chuckled. "I trust that you will find a way to give me another look-in."

"You *trust?*" She blinked rapidly because her eyes were heavy with tears. "That is the whole of it, Justin. Leonia *trusts* me to teach her what is right. How can I do that if I skulk here as Thomas does?"

"Oslington's edict is wrong."

"I agree, but that changes nothing."

His brows rose before dropping in a fierce frown. "Do not cause me to think that you are no different from him, that you cannot see past rules and regulations."

"There are rules, Justin. Rules of the *ton,* and rules of that household. I am obligated to follow all of them while I live at Oslington Court." She reached for the bellpull and tugged.

"What are you doing?" Justin asked.

"I was given the task of bringing Thomas back to Oslington Court, and that is what I should do."

Mrs. Graves appeared in the door. "My lord?"

"Bring Thomas," Justin said, but he continued to stare at Angela. Could he have been so mistaken when he had believed she was a way to bring fresh air to the musty halls of Oslington's estate?

"Yes, my lord." His housekeeper rushed away, an unsettled frown on her face.

"Satisfied?" he asked.

Angela clasped her hands before her like a disobedient child. "Why are you being so rude?"

"Because I had hoped that you would be sensible."

"Me? I *am* being sensible. Thomas must obey the rules set forth by his guardian."

"More rules!"

"That is how the world runs, Justin."

He shook his head. "Not mine. Not any longer. I will not be constrained by other people's expectations or their assumptions that I will act in a certain way simply because someone decreed some rule so many years ago that no one remembers why any longer."

"So you will just collect your butterflies and care not a tuppence what anyone else thinks?"

"Yes, I will do that." He seized her shoulders and pulled her up against him. Ignoring the amazement in her eyes, he stared at her soft mouth. "And I will do this."

Enveloping her with his arms, he savored her softness against him as he slanted his lips across hers. Her bonnet fell back when he deepened the kiss, wanting to hold her ever closer. When her breath pulsed, uneven and undeniable, into his mouth, he threaded his fingers through her tawny hair. This was almost everything he wanted—this woman in his arms, her mouth on his and her soft curves offering the very invitation that plagued him through sleepless nights. Everything that he wanted would include her beside him during those starlit hours when she would glow next to him more brightly than the moon.

"What is it, Justin?" Thomas's gulp of astonishment was like a crash of thunder through the room, nearly drowning out the fevered pulse of Justin's heartbeat.

She started to pull away; Justin refused to release her until he saw the unmistakable dismay in her volatile eyes that still burned with the passion he yearned to unleash. Slowly he let his hands fall back, his fingers aching to touch her again. As she drew on her bonnet, trying to tuck her hair beneath it, he noticed how her hands quivered. He did not need to ask if she yearned to be back in his arms again. Her kiss had told him that truth.

Angela gave up with her hair that refused to be restrained under her bonnet. As she braided it down her back, she said, "Thomas, go and gather your sketches together."

"But—" He swallowed with difficulty, revealing his embarrassment at interrupting.

What would he say—what would *Justin* say—if she whispered that she was grateful that Thomas had intruded when he did? A moment longer . . . she was unsure if she could resist Justin's masterful seduction that enticed her to toss aside all good sense and surrender to the passion they shared.

"Please, Thomas! Please do as I ask."

Again he looked to Justin. Some signal she could not comprehend must have passed between them, because the boy nodded and, head down, went out of the room.

"It will take him some time to gather his sketches together," Justin said. "Do you wish to sit or are you proscribed from doing that?"

"Do not be hateful, too."

"Too?" Justin swore as she turned away. "Forgive me, Angela. I know what you must be enduring in that great block of a house. As overbearing as Rodney Abernathy can be, his mother is worse. I heard that she dared to speak back to the king when she was younger."

"She probably instructed him in the proper way to behave."

"I do not like to hear bitterness in your voice."

She faced him, wishing she could revel in that smile she saw in the moment before he kissed her. "What else do you expect to hear? Joy? I cannot call here again, and you are prohibited from entering Oslington Court. The duchess is even more unwilling to compromise than the duke."

He laughed shortly. "Like mother, like son. None of the Oslingtons will ever forgive or forget when they believe they have been wronged."

"Wronged?" Her knees folded, and she sat again. "What happened between you and the duke?"

"Something that happened almost a decade ago."

"A decade? You have been enemies for a decade, but you were friends before that."

"Yes."

"What happened? Why won't you tell me?"

He picked up his brandy and downed it in a single gulp. "I do not speak of it."

"Why not?"

"Because the pain remains too fresh."

"After so many years?"

His mouth twisted into an ironic smile. "It has not been that many years. As I told you, during the years we were growing up, Oslington and I were friends. Even when he went away to serve in India, he often gave me a look-in during his leaves here in England." He went to a cupboard and opened it. Pulling out a bottle, he started to put more brandy into his glass.

She came to her feet and put her hand on his arm to halt him. "Drinking yourself into oblivion will not help anything."

"It will help me forget how much I want you, Angela."

A quiver raced through her, but she suppressed it. She could not let him change the subject, even when she longed to speak of her desire for his kisses. "Please do not shut me out on this."

"It might be better that you do not know." He glanced toward the window. "If you are living under Oslington's roof, you should be blissfully ignorant of the darkness in that man's soul." He grimaced. "If he even has one left."

"That is an appalling thing to say."

"But 'tis the truth." He ran his fingers along her cheek. "He vowed that he would trade his very soul to Old Nick in exchange for the chance to have Elizabeth for his own."

Angela edged away again and stared at him. "Elizabeth? Your wife Elizabeth?"

"My late wife." He put down the bottle and the glass, then closed the cupboard door. "He professed to love her, too."

Sinking to his chair, she whispered, "You were best friends who fell in love with the same woman?"

"I tried not to. Oslington was my friend. I did not want to stand between him and happiness, but then Elizabeth revealed that she had a *tendre* for me, too. When I offered to tell Oslington, she warned me to take care. I was a fool. I thought our friendship was strong enough to survive, but

Oslington did not agree. He was furious, and he cursed both me and Elizabeth."

She stroked his arm. "It must have been horrible."

"It was." He shrugged. "But it was not as if there were a choice between my friendship with Oslington and my affection for Elizabeth. She told me that she did not love him, so I married her."

"For which Oslington never forgave you?"

"Neither he nor Elizabeth."

"What?" She was certain she must have heard him wrong. "But you said that she professed to love you."

He picked up his pipe and lit it. The fragrant smoke oozed from its bowl as he took her hand and drew her to her feet and to the settee where he sat beside her. "You have a gentle heart, Angela. You are guileless in so many ways, for you see everyone as honest as you are."

"Quite to the contrary. I learned that some smiles can hide alarming thoughts."

"Did you learn that from your brother's wife?"

She nodded.

"It was a lesson you could have learned from my wife as well."

"But you never have spoken of her with anything but the greatest affection."

"Which has been honest." He puffed on the pipe, then lowered it. "Mine for her, although hers was not so sincere toward me once she learned that Oslington was going to be the heir."

"He had an older brother?"

"Who was killed in France."

She frowned. "France? Does that have anything to do with why you don't want to take Delicia there?"

Before he could answer, Thomas returned, his arms filled with rolled papers and stacked canvases and a butterfly net stuck under one arm. "I have everything. Just as you requested, Angela." He was scowling.

Justin replied, "Take your sketches out to the pony cart and wait there."

"Angela?" asked the puzzled lad.

"I will be with you in just a moment." She watched as he backed out of the room, balancing his artwork with care. Looking back at Justin, she said, "He will not wait for long."

"So you want the quick version of a long story?"

"I want the truth."

"The truth is that Elizabeth missed the pursuit of two men once she was wed to one of them." He sighed. "I believe she had affection for me, but she quickly came to miss the thrill of the hunt. Then Oslington was named a hero."

"For saving Colonel Sutton's life?"

He did not try to hide his astonishment. "How did you know that?"

" 'Tis an obvious guess, for that would explain why the colonel chose the duke as guardian for his children. A man who knows he can trust another man with his life will know he can trust that man with his children." Leaning toward him, she put her hand on his arm. "Justin, what did this have to do with you and your wife?"

"She could not hide that she was having second thoughts about her choice. I thought she might regret marrying a man instead of the hero she could have had in Oslington, so I obtained a commission of my own."

"Justin! How could you do something so foolish!"

"Because I was a fool. I can see that so readily now when I look back at the errors of the past." He looked out of the room toward where his daughter was working with Mrs. Graves in the kitchen. "In my zeal to become a hero, I was sent to fight against Napoleon."

"In France!"

"Now you understand."

Folding his hand in hers, she whispered, "Why didn't you tell me this when I spoke about the school for Delicia? I would have known why you reacted with such vehemence. No one wants to return to a place where they have been part of a battle."

"That is not all of it." He withdrew his hand. Leaning back, as if he wished to put as much space possible between them, he said, "I came home to discover I had come home too late. I had not known when I left that Elizabeth had conceived. Apparently she was unhappy with the restrictions that kept her from enjoying the Polite World, and she railed against them. She decided to go to London."

"When she was in a delicate condition?"

"I did not have a monopoly on being foolish." His words were jesting, but his voice was taut. "There was a message that she was in a difficult way, but I was on a mission, and I never received it. If I had, I might have been able to get home in time to get another doctor for Elizabeth and for Delicia."

"Instead of Dr. Young?"

"He is an inept quacksalver." He sighed. "He did manage to save Delicia, but not Elizabeth. Nearly a year later, we discovered Delicia could not hear." Coming to his feet again, he turned his back on her, as if he could not bear to let her see his expression when he said, "I have asked myself over and over if things might have been different if I had not rushed off in a caper-witted quest for glory."

Angela tried to keep her tears in her eyes. It was impossible. She put her hands to her face and sobbed. He had been right when he warned her that the grief was too fresh for him, even years later.

Her hands were drawn down, and she met Justin's sorrowful eyes. "Angela, I did not mean to make you cry. This pain is not one I intended to inflict on you."

"How could I not be moved by what you have endured?" She raised her hand to edge along his cheek as he had done to her so often. "I love you, Justin."

All color raced from his face. He released her hands and stood. "Are you mad?"

"No, I am being honest." She reached up for his hands, but he held them away from her. A sickness burst from her heart to fall through her like a stone through water. "Why are you acting like this?"

"Because I had hoped that you would not be as foolish as I have been."

Slowly she stood. "Are you saying that you love me, too? Or are you saying . . . ?" She choked on the words she could not speak.

"I thought you realized why I told you the truth."

"Because you wanted to be honest with me." She grasped his sleeves as she stepped around him so she could see his face. "And I am being honest with you. For some reason that I cannot explain or some fate that has been determined to complicate my stay at Oslington Court, I have fallen in love with you, Justin."

He plucked her hands off his sleeves. "I never thought you would be so foolish."

"Foolish? You think falling in love with you is foolish?"

"Yes." Again he walked away from her.

"Mayhap you are right, but I cannot halt my heart from wanting to be yours." She went to him and put her fingertips on his back. "Will you take it?"

"No."

"No?" She recoiled as if he had struck her.

"No. I was a fool for love once. I shall not be one again."

Her eyes widened, and she grasped his sleeve. When he did not face her, she stepped around him so he could not evade her. "So that is it?"

"It must be."

"Then I suspect there is nothing more to say," she whispered.

"You probably are right."

"Save that a heart that refuses to risk itself again is already dead."

This time, he winced, but he only repeated, "You probably are right."

Angela waited for him to add something else. Anything that would suggest this wraith was not the vibrant man she had fallen in love with. That man loved life and all its experiences while he filled her dreams with laughter and the luscious memory of his embrace.

He said nothing.

She walked out of the parlor and then out of the house.

Thomas was waiting with impatience by the pony cart, which was stacked high with rolled papers and the butterfly net.

"I was wondering if you were going to make me wait all day," he grumbled.

"Completing my conversation with Lord Harrington took longer than I had expected." That was a lie. She had hoped that the conversation would go on and on as they spoke of a love they shared.

"You should have considered that before you banished me prematurely from Harrington Grange."

"Do not get into a pelter with me! 'Tis your guardian who has insisted that you do not call here again."

"And you are determined not to do anything to fall out of favor with him, aren't you?" His lip twisted in a sneer. "Guardian's angel!"

She looked away from his anger, not wanting him to discover how that name hurt today when he had not used it in so long. Her heart was too fragile now to argue with him. She motioned for him to get into the cart, then climbed in herself. Picking up the reins, she did not look back as they drove away from Harrington Grange for the last time.

Seventeen

"Bow first, then turn," Angela said as she clapped her hands to mark the rhythm of the quadrille. "Otherwise, you will run into another lady in the pattern."

Leonia nodded. "It looks so much easier than it is to do it myself."

"You will learn."

Running to where Angela sat on a low bench in the parlor, Leonia took her hands. "What is amiss, Angela? I swear that I have not seen you smile in more than a week."

"How can I smile when you are not working on your dance steps? Her Grace will be irritated at us."

"She is always irritated at one or another of us. Mayhap we should give her cause to be for once instead of her just deciding on what we have failed at today."

"That is cynical."

"Why are you decrying me as cynical when you have been utterly dejected?"

Angela drew her hands from Leonia's. She owed the young woman an explanation, and she would give Leonia one once she had devised it. To speak the truth now was too painful. She could not talk of how she had dared to offer her heart to a man who did not want it.

It would be a good lesson for Leonia to know that she is not the only one whose love is not reciprocated.

She paid that small, taunting voice no mind. Raising her

hands, she said, "Let's continue, Leonia. I would like to have you have one set perfect before Her Grace comes to see your progress."

"I do not care a rap what Her Grace thinks of my ability to cavort about a ballroom."

"By all that's blue, Leonia! You should not speak so."

"Me?" Leonia's eyes were in danger of popping clear out of her head. "I thought you said such cant was not appropriate for a lady."

Angela nodded. "You are correct, for I was correct. I fear I have quite forgotten myself."

"Why?" Again Leonia seized Angela's hand. "You are trembling. Either you are frightened, or you are suffering from some great emotion you do not wish to share. As I have seen that you are less daunted by Her Grace than the rest of us, I can only deduce that it must be the latter."

"Leonia, please leave well enough alone."

"But you are my friend, Angela! I do not want you to be upset."

"I am your *companion,* here to teach you the niceties of the Polite World. I must not disappoint my employer, or I shall find myself without a roof over my head."

Lowering her eyes, Leonia said, "You do not disappoint Rodney. He has told me so himself not more than a day ago. He said you had proven yourself to be far more adept in teaching me than he had imagined when his mother arranged for you to come here." Puzzlement filled her voice. "That I comprehended, for I share his opinion on that. However, I do not know why he continued by saying that he suspected you would prove your value to this household to an even greater measure soon."

Angela was not sure how to answer. That the duke was pleased with her work and intended to keep her on at Oslington Court should be a great relief, for she would not have to crawl back to London to beg her brother's charity. Yet, she longed to leave so she did not find herself, far too frequently, gazing out a window like an abandoned child toward Harrington Grange. Justin had made his opinion clear, and, now that she had made certain he had the information he needed to help Delicia, she should banish him from her mind and her heart.

"You are," Angela said in her sternest voice, "spending too much time in prattling that could be better spent with you learning this quadrille."

For a moment, she thought that Leonia would balk, but the young woman nodded and went back to the center of the room. Angela began again to call out the steps while she clapped her hands to match the rhythm of the dance.

Leonia was halfway through the set of steps when slow footfalls paused by the doorway. When Leonia whirled, and her eyes filled with joy, Angela knew the duke must be entering the room.

Coming to her feet, Angela forced a smile. The duke was looking much better than he had a week before. His healthy color was returning, and his gait was much steadier. Dressed in prime twig, as if he were about to embark on calls in Town, he gave Leonia a pat on the cheek as he passed her to go to where Angela stood.

"Good morning, Miss Needham," he said. "I see Leonia's lessons are going well."

"Very well, Your Grace." She glanced at Leonia, who was now quite crestfallen, but trying to keep a brave façade in front of her beloved guardian. "She is mastering these steps with a skill that many would envy."

"I am pleased to hear that." Without looking at Leonia, he said, "Go to the nursery and collect your siblings. Please take them into the garden for some fresh air, Leonia, before the rain in those gathering clouds on the horizon starts falling."

Dismay filled the young woman's eyes, and she gave Angela a pleading look.

Knowing it was useless, Angela began, "Your Grace—"

He held up his hand. "One moment, Miss Needham. Is there something you wish to say before you take your leave, Leonia?"

"Yes . . . I mean . . ." She clenched her hands at her sides, then said, "I shall see you for luncheon, Rodney."

"Mayhap." He seemed to take note of her despair, for he added, "You and the other children will be joining Mother and me for dinner this evening, because I have something I wish to tell you."

"About what?" Leonia gazed up at him with adoration.

He either did not see it or acted as if he had not. "Be patient, Leonia. Now go and retrieve your siblings from the nursery."

Her "Yes, Rodney" was barely audible.

Angela tried to stifle the pulse of anger that swept through her. How she would like to dress down both Justin and the duke! They might deride one another for leather-heads, but, if the truth be owned, they were much alike. Too much alike, because they could not see the truth on the faces—and in the hearts—of those around them.

Knowing that she would be wise to keep her tongue between her teeth, Angela said quietly, "Your Grace, Leonia is no longer a child."

He arched an eyebrow. "She is barely out of the schoolroom. You have said yourself that she still has many lessons to learn before she can enjoy her coming-out."

"But she is older by several years than the other children, and she yearns to be separated from them. Not by distance, for she loves them dearly. But she aches to be welcomed into the adult world."

"That time will come when it is right."

"You may be surprised how close that time is, Your Grace." Again she knew she was overstepping herself, but she wanted to ease Leonia's distress. "Are you still planning to fire her off during the next Season?"

Instead of answering, he gestured, "Please sit down, Miss Needham. I would like to speak to you of a sensitive matter."

Angela stiffened. Mayhap Leonia had been mistaken when she heard the duke speak of keeping Angela here at Oslington Court. As she sat where she had been watching Leonia practice her steps, she fought her yearning to rush to the window and peer out at the roof of Harrington Grange. How much more want-witted could she be? She should be thinking of a way to avoid returning to London rather than lamenting about not seeing Justin again.

But it was futile. Her heart sent a flood of tears to her eyes. Even worse than being beneath her sister-in-law's thumb, required to listen to a litany of her complaints about Angela, would be to know that there was no hope of chancing upon Justin during a walk or at an assembly. She could live with a broken heart. That she had learned during the past week. Living without hope was something she was unsure if she could endure.

The duke proved once again that he was oblivious to anyone else's emotions when he was focused on his own goals. She let her sigh sift soundlessly through her teeth. Faulting the duke for something that was part of his nature would gain her nothing but more misery.

Reaching for a piece of folded paper, he opened it on his lap. His fingers tapped the page as he said, "I own that I have given firing-off Leonia some thought, but I have made no decision."

"Because you still see her as a child, I am afraid."

"Not exactly a child, Miss Needham, even though I have known her since she was very young." He continued to drum on the paper. "I realize she is nearly grown, but I also acknowledge my obligations to her father. The colonel would not be pleased if I abandoned even one of my duties as Leonia's guardian."

"I did not mean to suggest that."

"I know." A rare smile barely tipped his lips. "Forgive me, Miss Needham. It is an effort for me not to take my duties *too* seriously."

She smiled. "I understand that."

"Yes, I am certain you do, for you have taken your duties here very seriously." Again that ghost of a grin appeared. "Even when Mother has made every effort to get in your way. She will be leaving to return to London by the week's end."

Angela was not sure how to reply. She must never give any hint of her relief at the thought of Her Grace being far from Oslington Court, and she must caution the children to be as circumspect. Was that possible? She almost laughed aloud at the idea of Esther or Seth keeping the truth to themselves.

"I trust she has enjoyed her visit," Angela said, knowing she must not remain silent.

"She is leaving, not because she does not enjoy Oslington Court, but because the rest of us are leaving, too."

"Leaving?" A heaviness dropped deep through her stomach. If the duke was planning to depart from Oslington Court, he might have no further need of her services . . . and she would have no choice but to return to London far from Justin.

"It is clear that the children are not happy here."

"They have been adjusting."

He waved aside her words as if she had said nothing of import. Holding up the page, he said, "I have arranged passage on a ship from Dover to take the children to Europe and Africa and eventually back to India."

"India?"

"They are homesick for the world they knew."

"Mayhap the younger ones, but I know that Leonia is anxious for her Season."

"She will have it, but later. Another year or two should make no difference." He glanced out a window toward the east, and she knew that the one who had the greatest nostalgia for the East was the duke. Her evaluation was confirmed when he added, "I was mistaken to bring them here in the first place."

"What if the children do not wish to go?"

"Why would they not wish to return home?"

Angela wanted to have sympathy for him, because it was clear that the one who had been unhappiest in Oslington Court was the duke. She must not feel sorry for him when his decision was sure to demolish Leonia's dream of a Season in London. "Your Grace, I believe they are beginning to see England as home. They were so pleased to come home to Oslington Court after the wedding."

"So they could play with Harrington's deaf child."

"Her name is Delicia."

Again he waved the page at her. "I was speaking of my plans to take the children on a journey."

"Yes, Your Grace."

"Leonia has told me that you have a yearning to travel."

"I have had." She lowered her eyes, so he could not read the truth in them. Once she had craved the opportunity to see horizons far beyond England's. That dream remained, but the timing was not right. For now, she wanted to stay here so she could discover if there was a way she could bridge the chasm that had opened between her and Justin.

"There is little enthusiasm in your voice." He leaned forward, startling her. When she looked up at him, he said, "I hope you will have more enthusiasm when I speak of what I must next."

"I will endeavor to."

"No, do not endeavor to. I wish your *honest* reaction to the question I am about to ask."

"I promise I will be honest."

"And do you always keep your promises?" He stood and sat next to her, so close that she could smell the pungent aroma of his favorite snuff. "I own that I cannot imagine you breaking a promise."

"I am sure I have." She smiled uneasily. He was acting so oddly. His gaze kept catching hers, then skittering away like Esther when she knew she had misbehaved. "What is it that you wish to ask me, Your Grace?"

"I would ask you to become my wife."

Angela stared at him in disbelief. *His* wife? Her dreams had been filled with hearing Justin speak these words, but she had never imagined the duke saying them.

"Do you have no answer, Miss Needham?" That whisper of a smile returned. "Or I should say: Do you have no answer, Angela?"

"Your Grace—"

"It would not be inappropriate for you to address me at this moment as Rodney."

She nodded and forced her lips to shape his name. "Rodney, you overmaster me with your proposal."

"I do not understand why. It is a sensible solution. I cannot handle the children alone during our journey. When we traveled from India, several servants came with us. They have since returned there, because they had no fondness for England's cool weather." He took her hands in his.

She was stunned by his smooth skin, for she had expected a soldier to be hardened by his life. Quickly she reminded herself that the voyage from distant India had been a long one. Mayhap it had been long enough to allow his palms to soften to the texture of Leonia's. He had not ridden at Oslington Court. Here, he had sequestered himself away from everything in his book-room where he could lose himself in books about the East.

He stroked her fingers, but with no more passion than he would have shown one of the children. "You should not be surprised. You know how dependent this family has become upon you."

"Dependent?"

"You look displeased. I meant only to compliment your gentleness and your skills which have brought a serenity to Oslington Court that I had not been aware of until Mother's arrival. Even in the midst of her visit, you have kept the house tranquil. After all, it has been nearly a week since Esther loosed her monkey in the conservatory, and I have not had to chide Leonia once for her mooniness." He stood, bringing her to her feet. Gently, he tugged on her hands to draw her closer. "Do consider this proposal."

In spite of herself, her voice squeaked when she gasped, "Your—"

"Rodney," he corrected. "I await your answer, Angela."

"I fear I shall embarrass myself if I speak my thoughts."

"Never fear, Angela, to speak the truth to me."

"I have no idea what the truth might be at this time." She

tried to keep heat from climbing her cheeks as rapidly as Wallah scaled the nursery curtains.

"The truth is that I am asking you to be my wife. I have seen that you love these children."

"Yes," she said cautiously, tensing for the question that she suspected would come next.

"And I know that you love the idea of traveling, for I have heard you often asking the children about their journey here. In addition, I saw how pleased you were with our journey to Scotland."

"Yes." She did not add that a great part of her pleasure had been the thought of coming back here and the chance to see Justin again. How much more she would have anticipated the sojourn if she had guessed she would be able to spend a glorious evening with him, his lips on hers!

"Then why not come with me?"

Angela lowered her eyes again. She could give him one reason. It came from the depths of her heart. She did not have a *tendre* for him. She was in love with a man he despised . . . a man who had thrown her out of his life.

"I need time to think," she whispered, wondering if even an eternity could make her more certain about this unexpected proposal. The duke—Rodney—was correct. It made sense for her to stay with the children, especially during this trip across Europe. Yet she did not need to be a duchess to accompany them. Her position as Leonia's companion would lend respectability to the arrangement.

"We leave the day after tomorrow for Dover. I will need an answer by then."

"But that would make it impossible for us to marry, and I could not possibly travel with you as your *fiancée*." Her qualms were incredibly soothed by this excuse that would not offend him.

"Do not be so parochial. You think only in terms of England. The laws are quite different beyond these shores. We need only set sail, and the captain of our ship can speak the wedding ceremony before we reach Calais."

When she took a step away from him, he released her

without comment. She wished she could hear her thoughts over the rapid pounding of her heart. *This* she had not guessed was on his mind.

She began, "This is a great honor—"

"You sound as if you are about to make a speech in the House of Lords. Speak plainly."

Angela gnawed on her lower lip, then said, "I am not sure what to say."

"Angela, the answer is simple. Say that you will marry me."

"I will—"

At a gasp from the other side of the room, Angela spun to see Leonia and the children. The younger ones were wide-eyed with astonishment, but Leonia's eyes were swimming with tears. They fell along her cheeks as she whirled and ran out of the room.

Angela stared after them in dismay as she realized her request to have more time to think about his offer had been misunderstood. Leonia's gasp had interrupted at the very worst moment. She must speak to Leonia.

"Angela?" The duke took her hand and drew her a step closer.

In dismay, she stared at him. Her heart thumped against her breastbone. As he bent toward her, she stiffened. Was he planning to kiss her? She could not kiss a man she did not love, especially when she longed to be in the arms of the man she did love. When the duke gave her a taut smile, she feared he had perceived the course of her thoughts.

"I must go and talk to Leonia," she whispered.

"She—"

"Please let me talk with her now."

He nodded, although his expression revealed his confusion.

Angela ran after Leonia and reached the young woman just as Leonia was going into her room with her face awash with tears.

Leonia turned to face her. "Why are you following me? Don't you have any decency?"

"I want to talk with you. I think you have misunder-stood."

"Misunderstood what? Rodney asked you to marry him and you told him yes."

"No, I did not tell him yes. I was about to tell him I needed some time to think about his offer."

Leonia shook her head. "I trusted you, Angela! I trusted you with the truth of my hopes and dreams. And then you—you do *this.*"

"I have not agreed to marry the duke."

"But if you tell him no, he will just ask someone else." Her voice broke as she whispered, "Whether it is you or someone else, it does not matter."

"You love him so much?"

"Yes! I thought you knew! I thought you would be the one person who would understand." She grasped the door. "I should have listened to Thomas when he chided you as my guardian's angel. Now you will be Rodney's Angela. I hope you will be very happy knowing you have broken my heart. I thought you would understand!"

The door slammed.

Angela knocked on it and called Leonia's name. She heard only the sound of desperate tears. With a sigh, she sat in a chair in the corridor. She *did* understand. All too well, she understood having a broken heart.

Eighteen

"I hope you are satisfied."

At Mrs. Graves's unusually sharp tone, Justin looked up from the article that had been delivered in just the past hour from Oslington Court by a very nervous footman. Angela must have been determined that he would not toss aside the idea of sending Delicia to the school for deaf children near Paris. The information in the newspaper article was cursory, but it had, as Angela must have known it would, piqued his curiosity. Dozens of questions bounced through his head.

Not one was focused on the school. Instead, his mind taunted him endlessly with the scene of Angela leaving Harrington Grange. She had not left in anger, but hurt by his words that had guaranteed she now would easily come under Oslington's thumb and stay far from Harrington Grange. The pain that he had vowed to avoid had been shunted over onto her, and he had not escaped it himself. He had made a muddle of the whole of it.

"I can assure you, Mrs. Graves," he replied, "that I am far less than satisfied."

Her brows rose at his tone that was as uncommonly sharp as hers. She started to speak, then stepped aside, with a slight smile, as Delicia rushed into the parlor.

Justin held out his arms, and his daughter clambered into his lap. As Delicia cuddled close, he sighed. He adored these moments when his daughter curled up against him as she had when just a baby. Yet his arms ached for a more mature love . . . the very love that Angela had offered him, the very love that he had denounced.

"So you have heard?" asked Mrs. Graves.

"Heard what?" He looked over Delicia's head to the housekeeper who continued to wear a frown that lengthened her thin face.

"The tidings from Oslington Court."

"I have heard that Oslington is taking his household away for an extended trip."

"Back to India, it is being said."

"That should please all of them, save for Her Grace. I cannot imagine her traveling farther from England's shores than Europe."

"She is not going anywhere but London."

"That is no surprise. Her idea of primitive conditions is living in a house with less than a dozen servants." He smiled at Delicia. "I must own that I shall be glad to hear that she has departed for London. That woman delights in creating an uproar wherever she goes."

Mrs. Graves's face took on an expression that might have been the very source of her name. " 'Tis as I suspected. You have *not* heard."

"There is more?"

"Yes." That single word seemed reluctant.

Justin frowned. It was not like Mrs. Graves to be so circumspect. Her forthrightness had made her service in Harrington Grange even more valuable. "If you were to enlighten me, Mrs. Graves, then I can tell you if I am already aware of the gossip or not." He glanced down again as Delicia tugged on his arm to get his attention.

Delicia's hands floated about her shoulders with an urgency he could not ignore. Did Delicia possess some sense that compensated for her hearing loss? He recognized what she was trying to communicate with her hands. She was asking about Esther at the very moment he was discussing the residents of Oslington Court with Mrs. Graves. Delicia put her fingers to his lips, then made the motion again.

He shook his head, and her face fell into grief. Regret pierced him like a long thorn. He never would have guessed that the echoes of a friendship that had been disintegrated before his daughter was born would still resonate to wreck her camaraderie with Esther Sutton. This was all wrong. What had happened when he married Elizabeth should have been forgiven and forgotten . . . by both him and Oslington.

"You really should listen to this," said Mrs. Graves.

Justin nodded, glad to escape the tangled mesh of his own recriminations. "I am listening, Mrs. Graves."

"The messenger who came from Oslington Court told me that there soon will be a wedding ceremony there."

"So Oslington is getting married, is he? To whom?"

Mrs. Graves cleared her throat. "My lord, it is said he is marrying Miss Needham."

"Angela?" He stood and set Delicia on her feet. "You must be mistaken, Mrs. Graves."

"I asked several times for the lad to confirm to me that his information was authentic and accurate."

"And he did?"

Mrs. Graves tried to speak, but seemed incapable of it. She nodded as her shoulders hunched.

Justin stared at her, then turned to go to the window that gave him a view with Oslington Court in its center. By Jove, he should have seen this coming. How like Oslington to take advantage of Justin's most foolish mistake!

When Delicia threw her arms around his legs, he bent and smoothed her hair back from her face. "Not again," he said. "I shall not make the same mistake again." Standing, he led Delicia toward where Mrs. Graves was standing. "Mrs. Graves, please get Delicia's bonnet."

"Where are you going, my lord?" Her voice dropped to a whisper as her eyes grew round.

"Where else? To Oslington Court."

"But you are not welcome there."

"Please get Delicia's bonnet." He reached for his coat and shrugged it on. When he realized Mrs. Graves had not moved, he added, "Mrs. Graves, Delicia's bonnet please."

" 'Tis not right for you to take that dear child to witness what I fear is going to happen."

He put his hand on her shoulder and gave her a bolstering smile. "Trust me, Mrs. Graves. Delicia shall see nothing untoward. I promise you that."

The housekeeper nodded, although he could see that she was unsure if she should believe him. He hoped that by day's end, he would not have to break that promise.

Angela stood with her hands clasped behind her back in the small parlor that opened into the garden. The duke sat in a pool of lamplight in the far corner, totally engrossed by whatever he was reading. In front of her, the duchess sat and continued to outline all the details of the wedding that Angela wanted to say she had not agreed to yet. The duchess did not give her the opportunity to speak.

Another hope dashed, for Angela had reassured herself with the thought that the duchess would not give countenance to her son marrying his ward's companion. Instead of lambasting her son, the duchess had stated where anyone within earshot—and that would be many because she stated it quite loudly—would know that she had selected Angela to come to Oslington Court as Leonia's companion simply for the purpose of allowing her son to do the wise thing and make her his wife to oversee his colonel's children. A most convenient arrangement for everyone involved, save that no one thought to ask if Angela truly wished to marry him.

Angela's second attempt to talk to Leonia had failed as miserably as her first. The young woman had locked herself in her rooms, allowing only her abigail in and out. Shelby had been as disinclined to speak to Angela as her mistress was.

"And furthermore," the duchess went on, barely pausing to take a breath after outlining the seating arrangements in the chapel, "you must . . ."

The door crashed open, and storm winds sent rain scudding across the stone floor.

"Oslington, I want to speak with you now!" Justin's words reverberated like thunder through the room. Beside him, Delicia was scanning the room, obviously searching for Esther.

The duchess came to her feet. "Lord Harrington, I have tried to be polite—"

"No, you have not," he returned, shaking water from his hair. "You have taken advantage of every opportunity to be rude to me because you believe I caused injury to your dear, dear son."

"Justin!" Angela gasped. "This is not the way to cure old wounds."

The duchess bristled. "You should not react to the words of a cur, Angela. As a duchess, you must learn to ignore the words of those who should know better."

"Is that how you have raised your son?" Justin asked with a terse chuckle. "To ignore the counsel of those who are wiser than he is so he will depend on your advice in every facet of his life?"

The duke stood. "Now see here, Harrington! That is no way to speak to my mother."

"Then I shall speak that way to your betrothed!"

Angela tried to convince her heart to beat more slowly, but it was impossible when Justin crossed the room to her, Delicia's hand in his. He stepped around the duchess, who tried to block his way, and paid no attention to how Her Grace tugged on the bellpull even as she shouted for Hervey.

"Will you heed the words of one who should have known better?" Justin asked as he stopped directly in front of her, so close that half a step would bring her up against him.

"I wish I could," she whispered, "but my heart will not believe that your heart denies me a place within it."

He ran his fingers along her cheek, then turned to the duke, who was scowling. "Oslington, if you sought to offer marriage to Angela to repay me for winning Elizabeth's hand, you are about to ruin your life as well as hers, for you never will be able to give her what she needs." He looked back again at Angela. "As I nearly destroyed mine by trying to give Elizabeth all I believed she needed, whether she did or not. It was impossible, because she did not want me." He held up the hand that was not holding Delicia's to halt the duke from speaking. "Nor did she want you, Oslington. She wanted both of us, or mayhap not even that. She wanted a great hero who would also never leave her side where he would sing courtly praises of love to her. That is neither you nor me."

"You have been asked to leave," the duke said. "Do so, or I shall be forced to—"

"To what? Demand satisfaction from me at grass before breakfast?" He smiled coolly. "If you do, I shall ask Angela to be my second."

"What?" she cried. "Justin, have you lost your mind?"

"No, only my heart." He released Delicia's fingers and caught Angela's arms in his. Cupping her elbows, he brought her to him. "I love you, Angela. I was a fool to try to pretend otherwise. I know I am an air-dreamer, but, Angela, will you tell Oslington that you cannot wed him because you are going to marry me?"

When she drew one arm away from him, she saw the pain burning in his eyes. She raised her hand to brush that thread of dark hair out of his eyes before stroking his rough cheek. "I am not going to marry him, Justin."

"You are not going to—?" He cursed, then demanded, "Why didn't you tell me instead of letting me make a complete chucklehead of myself?"

"You were giving such a fine performance, I could not bring myself to halt you . . . even if you had given me the chance."

His smile returned as he enfolded her against him. Caring nothing for the others watching, he captured her lips with the fervor she had sensed in his touch. He wanted no polite buss, she discovered to her delight, but demanded she cede her heart completely to him. Eagerly she gave him the answer he yearned for, because it was the same one she had dreamed of. She gasped when he tugged her more tightly to him, and she became entangled in the enchantment of his mouth against hers.

"Now see here," said the duke as he strode toward them. Seeing Delicia smiling beside her father, he paused. "Harrington, you have gone too far this time. You stole one woman from me. I shall not allow you to do so again."

When Justin opened his mouth to retort, Angela put her hand on his arm. She looked at the duke. "Your Grace, whether I marry Justin or not has no bearing on whether I marry you. You do not love me, and, although I have great admiration for you taking your duty to your colonel's children so seriously, I do not love you."

"You don't wish to marry me?"

His astonishment gave his face a childish dismay that brought Seth to mind. Fighting her reaction to comfort him as she did the little boy, she asked, "Do you love me, Rodney?"

"Love?" He seemed even more taken aback by her question than her refusal of his suit. "I have a great deal of admiration for you."

Angela drew her fingers out of his. "Admiration for a well-serving servant or the *tendre* you should offer your wife?"

"You said you—"

"I said I needed time to think about your offer." She put her other hand on his sleeve. "I am deeply honored that you would consider me for your bride, but you deserve someone who loves you, not someone who marries you simply because it is convenient or part of her duty."

The duchess puffed up with rage, her face reddening. "I will not listen to this a minute longer."

"Then you need not linger, Mother." The duke put down the book he still held and faced his startled mother. "I thank you for your counsel, but you must see as well as I do that Angela—Miss Needham has no inclination to marry me."

Before the duchess could reply, a soft voice asked from the hallway door, "May I join you?"

Angela turned. Hearing the duke's sharp intake of breath, she understood his amazement. She stared at Leonia, astounded by her rapid transformation from a child to a lady.

Her dress was the color of champagne—the perfect complement to her russet hair. When Esther rushed into the room to throw her arms around Delicia, no one looked away from the vision in the doorway.

Leonia held out her hand to her guardian with a grace that made his eyes widen. Like a man mesmerized, he reached for her slender fingers.

"Leonia?" he whispered as if he could not believe his own eyes. "I never realized . . . that is—"

Her laugh held a hint of coquetry, but there was no doubting the adoration in her eyes. "I know, Rodney."

When he pressed her hand to his lips in a fervent kiss, Angela motioned to Justin, who was grinning so broadly, one would have guessed he had orchestrated this. He turned and bowed to the duchess, offering his arm.

With a sniff, the duchess pushed past him and out of the room.

Angela took Delicia by one hand and Esther by the other. Leading them out into the hall, she left the door open so there would be no suggestion of impropriety. Esther began to prattle, but Angela hushed her. Looking back, she doubted if either the duke or Leonia, who continued to smile at one another, had heard Esther. They were lost in the delight of discovering a new relationship blossoming unexpectedly from an old one—at least for the duke.

"You taught her well," Justin said when Angela went with him into another small room across the hall. She left that door open as well, for, although she suspected there soon would be an announcement forthcoming about a real wedding at Oslington Court, there must be no whispers of indecorous behavior.

"Did I?"

"Yes, for Leonia made her entrance with the skill of a courtesan."

"I believe that Leonia, having almost lost the one she dreamed of once this week, will be determined not to be so careless again."

"A lesson she learned more quickly than I did."

Paying no attention to Esther and Delicia, who were standing in front of a rain-swept window, Angela laced her fingers through Justin's. "If you came here only to save me from the duke—"

"If you believe that, then I must show you how wrong you are." His mouth on hers sent a song of jubilation racing through her. Raising his lips from hers, he framed her face with his broad hands. "Just as I was wrong."

"You were wrong?"

He grimaced at her teasing tone. "I suspect you will never let me forget that I was wrong about letting you go as well as being wrong about taking Delicia to that school in Paris."

"You are going to take her there?"

"No, *we* are going to take her there. Shall we take our honeymoon in Paris, my angel?"

"But I thought you never wanted to return to France."

"It is time to return and put the demons of my past to rest and to find out more about that country now that it and England are no longer enemies." His smile promised delights she could only just imagine . . . now. "There are so many things I wish to explore with you."

"I—"

A screech filled the room.

Angela looked past him to see Esther and Delicia and Seth and Thomas, who clearly had entered unnoticed, trying to get a naughty Wallah down from the top of the drapes. She started to go to help, but Justin's hand on her arm halted her.

"Thomas," he ordered with a chuckle, "go and get that butterfly net that you took with you from Harrington Grange." He winked at Angela as the lad raced out of the room.

"Do you think he can get the monkey down with just that net?" She smiled, sure her heart was going to burst with this joy.

He said, in the moment before he kissed her again, "The boy is skilled with it. After all, he caught you in it long enough for you to capture my heart."

Author's Note

I hope you enjoyed reading *A Guardian's Angel*. The school for deaf children near Paris that Angela speaks of really existed. The teaching of sign language there was brought to the United States by Thomas Gallaudet, who established a school for the deaf in Hartford, Connecticut, in 1817.

My next Zebra Regency will be *His Unexpected Bride,* available in May 2002. When Tess Masterson awakens to find Cameron Hawksmoor in her bed, she does not want to believe that her father agreed to have her married by proxy to this handsome but vexing man. There must be a reason why. The only way to find that out may mean trusting the one person she has no reason to trust . . . her husband, Cameron.

I like hearing from my readers. You can contact me by e-mail at: jaferg@erols.com, or by mail at: Jo Ann Ferguson, P.O. Box 575, Rehoboth, MA 02769. Check out my web site at: www.joannferguson.com.

Happy reading!

More Zebra Regency Romances

BOOK YOUR PLACE ON OUR WEBSITE
AND MAKE THE
READING CONNECTION!

We've created a customized website just for our very special readers, where you can get the inside scoop on everything that's going on with Zebra, Pinnacle and Kensington books.

When you come online, you'll have the exciting opportunity to:

- View covers of upcoming books
- Read sample chapters
- Learn about our future publishing schedule (listed by publication month *and author*)
- Find out when your favorite authors will be visiting a city near you
- Search for and order backlist books from our online catalog
- Check out author bios and background information
- Send e-mail to your favorite authors
- Meet the Kensington staff online
- Join us in weekly chats with authors, readers and other guests
- Get writing guidelines
- AND MUCH MORE!

**Visit our website at
http://www.kensingtonbooks.com**